My Little Pony

Friends Forever

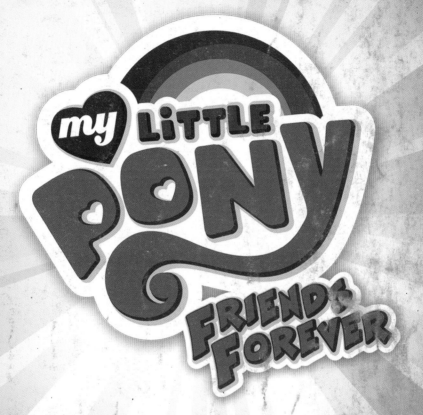

my LITTLE PONY
FRIENDS FOREVER

Zecora & Spike

Written by
Ted Anderson

Art by
Agnes Garbowska

Color Assist by
Lauren Perry

Princess Celestia & Pinkie Pie

Written by
Christina Rice

Art by
Jay Fosgitt

Colors by
Heather Breckel

Special thanks to Eliza Hart, Meghan McCarthy, Ed Lane, and Michael Kelly for their invaluable assistance.

For international rights, please contact licensing@idwpublishing.com

ISBN: 978-1-63140-596-9

19 18 17 16   1 2 3 4

IDW
Licensed By: Hasbro
www.IDWPUBLISHING.com

Ted Adams, CEO & Publisher
Greg Goldstein, President & COO
Robbie Robbins, EVP/Sr. Graphic Artist
Chris Ryall, Chief Creative Officer/Editor-in-Chief
Matthew Ruzicka, CPA, Chief Financial Officer
Dirk Wood, VP of Marketing
Lorelei Bunjes, VP of Digital Services
Jeff Webber, VP of Licensing, Digital and Subsidiary Rights
Jerry Bennington, VP of New Product Development

Facebook: **facebook.com/idwpublishing**
Twitter: **@idwpublishing**
YouTube: **youtube.com/idwpublishing**
Tumblr: **tumblr.idwpublishing.com**
Instagram: **instagram.com/idwpublishing**

FLUTTERSHY & APPLEJACK

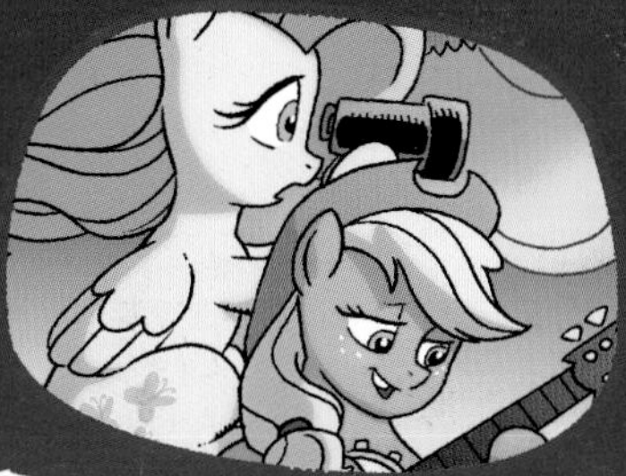

Written by
Ted Anderson
Art by
Tony Fleecs
Colors by
Heather Breckel

RARITY & GILDA

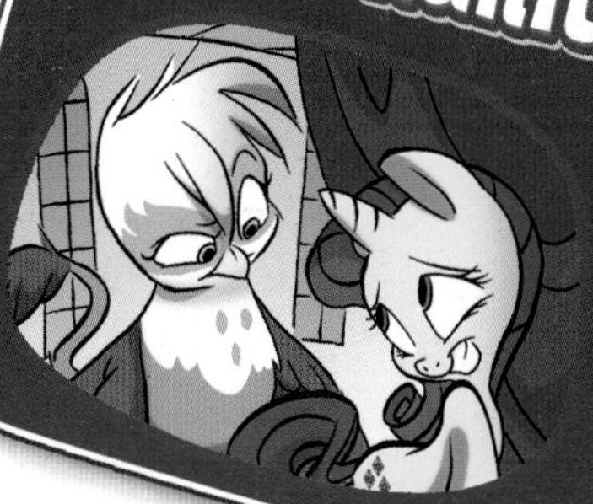

Written by
Georgia Ball
Art by
Jay Fosgitt
Colors by
Heather Breckel

Letters by
Neil Uyetake

Cover by
Amy Mebberson

Series Edits by
Bobby Curnow

Collection Edits by
Justin Eisinger & Alonzo Simon

Published by
Ted Adams

Collection Design by
Claudia Chong

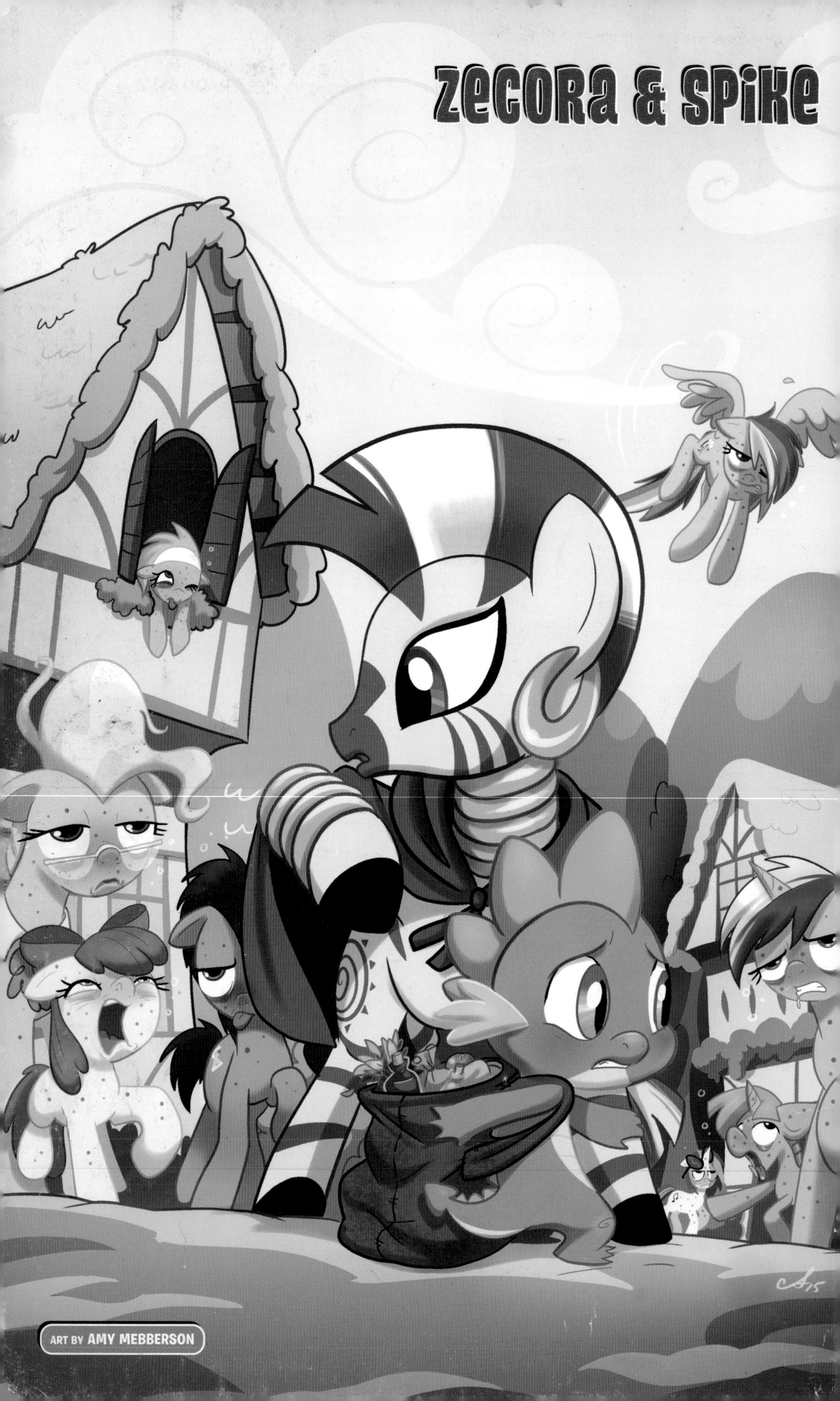
ZECORA & SPIKE
ART BY AMY MEBBERSON

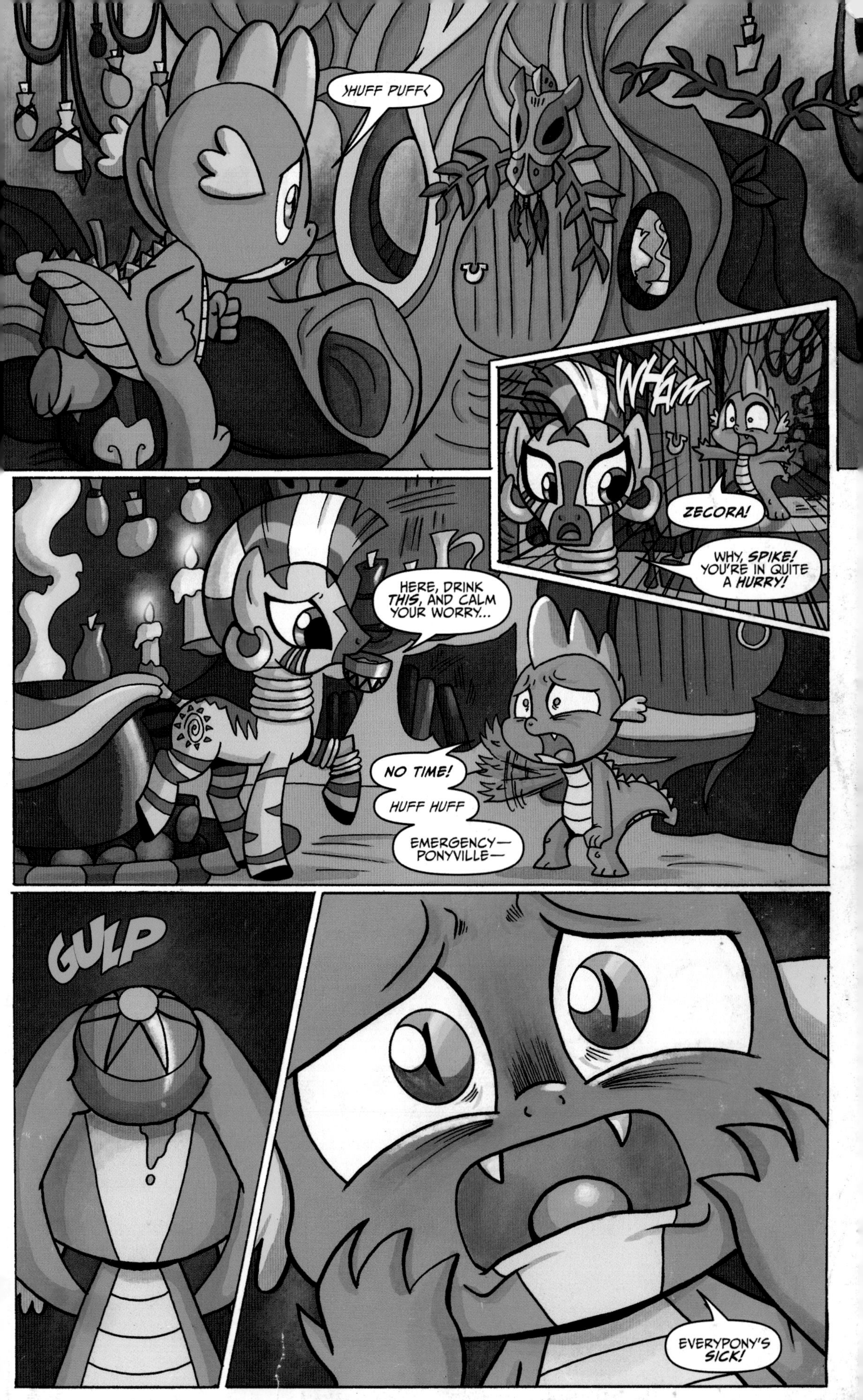

›HUFF PUFF‹
WHAM
ZECORA!
WHY, SPIKE! YOU'RE IN QUITE A HURRY!
HERE, DRINK THIS, AND CALM YOUR WORRY...
NO TIME!
HUFF HUFF
EMERGENCY— PONYVILLE—
GULP
EVERYPONY'S SICK!

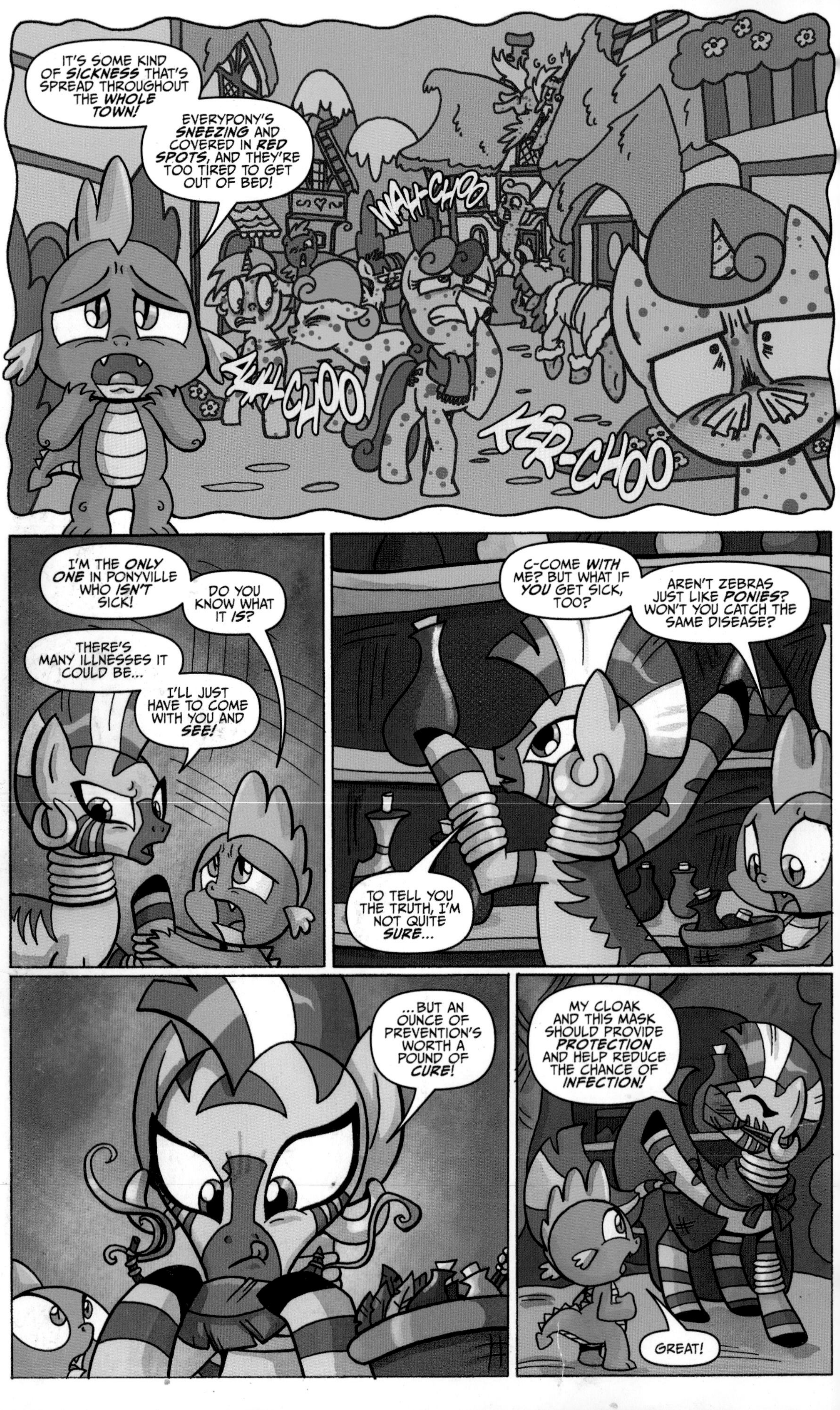
IT'S SOME KIND OF SICKNESS THAT'S SPREAD THROUGHOUT THE WHOLE TOWN!
EVERYPONY'S SNEEZING AND COVERED IN RED SPOTS, AND THEY'RE TOO TIRED TO GET OUT OF BED!
WAH-CHOO
AH-CHOO
KER-CHOO
I'M THE ONLY ONE IN PONYVILLE WHO ISN'T SICK!
DO YOU KNOW WHAT IT IS?
THERE'S MANY ILLNESSES IT COULD BE...
I'LL JUST HAVE TO COME WITH YOU AND SEE!
C-COME WITH ME? BUT WHAT IF YOU GET SICK, TOO?
AREN'T ZEBRAS JUST LIKE PONIES? WON'T YOU CATCH THE SAME DISEASE?
TO TELL YOU THE TRUTH, I'M NOT QUITE SURE...
...BUT AN OUNCE OF PREVENTION'S WORTH A POUND OF CURE!
MY CLOAK AND THIS MASK SHOULD PROVIDE PROTECTION AND HELP REDUCE THE CHANCE OF INFECTION!
GREAT!

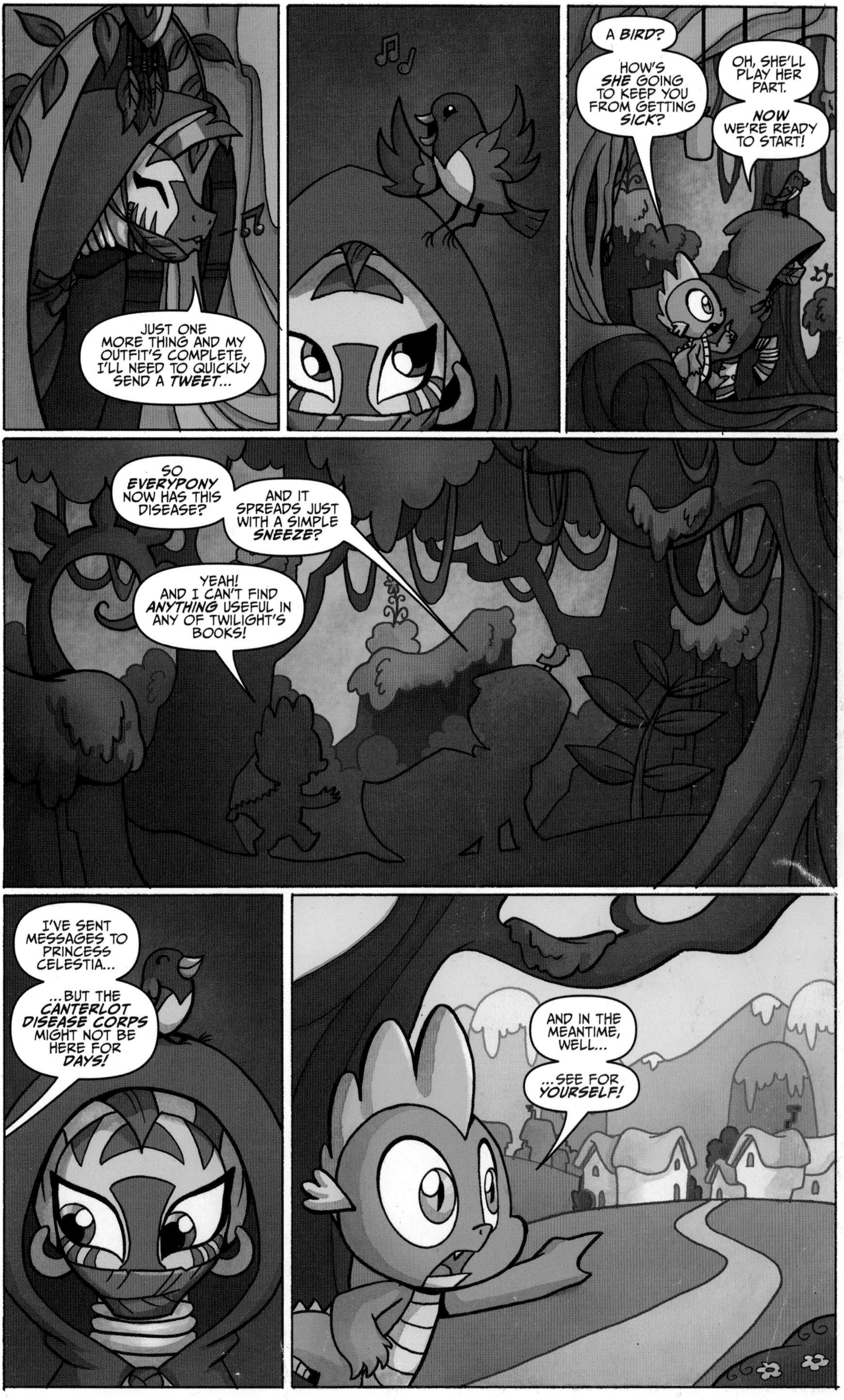
JUST ONE MORE THING AND MY OUTFIT'S COMPLETE, I'LL NEED TO QUICKLY SEND A *TWEET*...
A *BIRD*?
HOW'S *SHE* GOING TO KEEP YOU FROM GETTING *SICK*?
OH, SHE'LL PLAY HER PART.
NOW WE'RE READY TO START!
SO *EVERYPONY* NOW HAS THIS DISEASE?
AND IT SPREADS JUST WITH A SIMPLE *SNEEZE*?
YEAH! AND I CAN'T FIND *ANYTHING* USEFUL IN ANY OF TWILIGHT'S BOOKS!
I'VE SENT MESSAGES TO PRINCESS CELESTIA...
...BUT THE *CANTERLOT DISEASE CORPS* MIGHT NOT BE HERE FOR *DAYS!*
AND IN THE MEANTIME, WELL...
...SEE FOR *YOURSELF!*

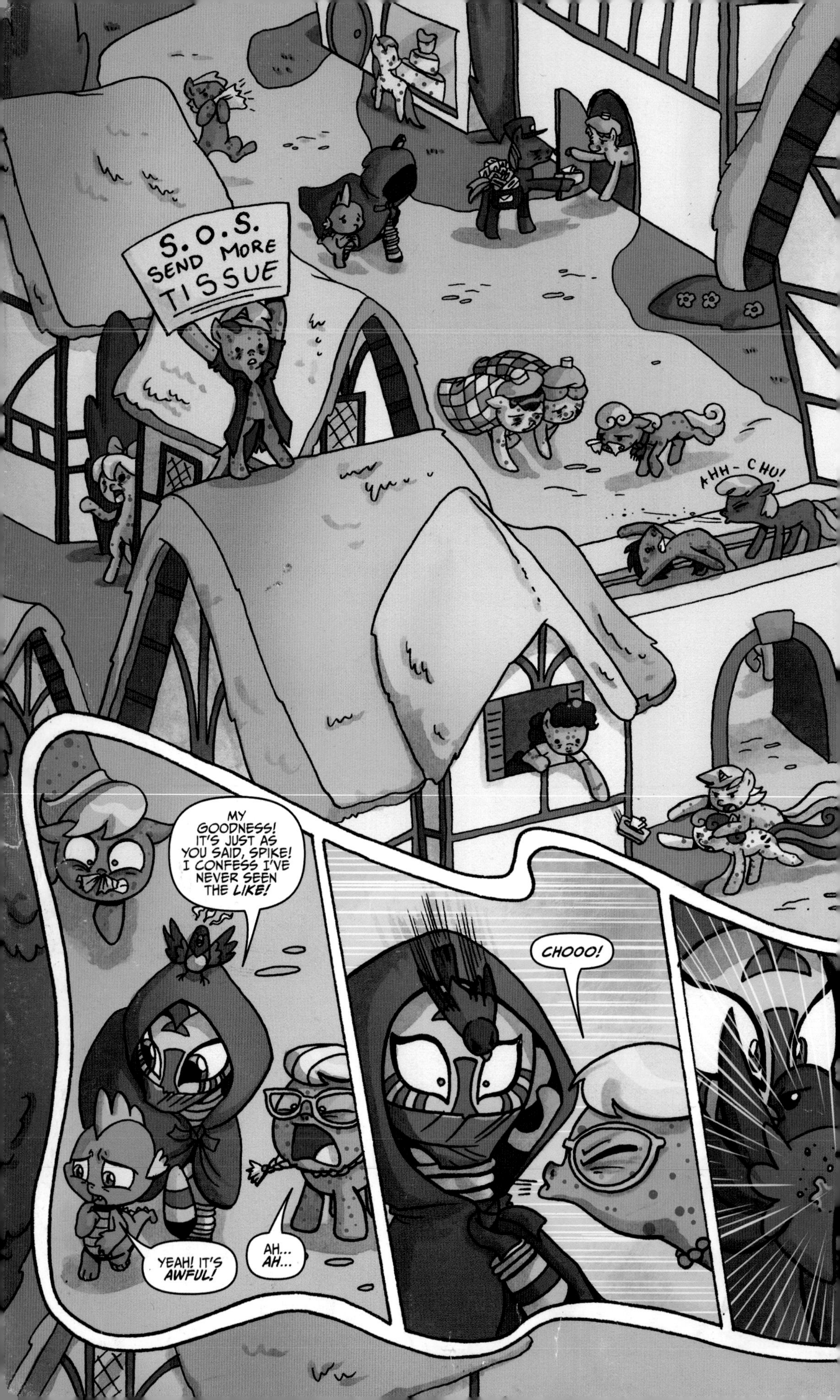

S.O.S. SEND MORE TISSUE
AHH-CHU!
MY GOODNESS! IT'S JUST AS YOU SAID, SPIKE! I CONFESS I'VE NEVER SEEN THE *LIKE*!
YEAH! IT'S *AWFUL!*
AH... *AH...*
CHOOO!

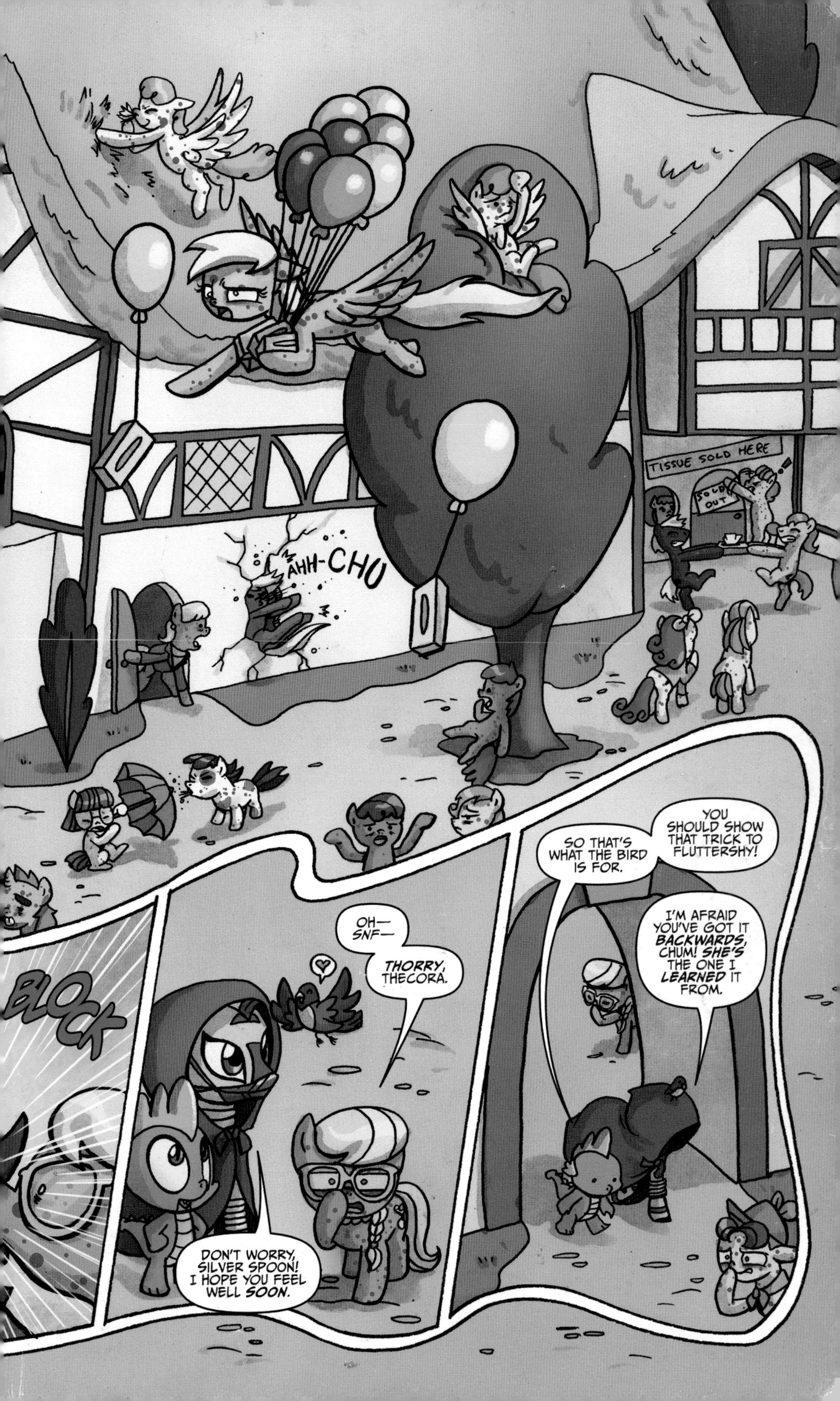
TISSUE SOLD HERE
SOLD OUT
AHH-CHU
BLOCK
OH— SNF—
THORRY, THECORA.
DON'T WORRY, SILVER SPOON! I HOPE YOU FEEL WELL SOON.
SO THAT'S WHAT THE BIRD IS FOR.
YOU SHOULD SHOW THAT TRICK TO FLUTTERSHY!
I'M AFRAID YOU'VE GOT IT BACKWARDS, CHUM! SHE'S THE ONE I LEARNED IT FROM.

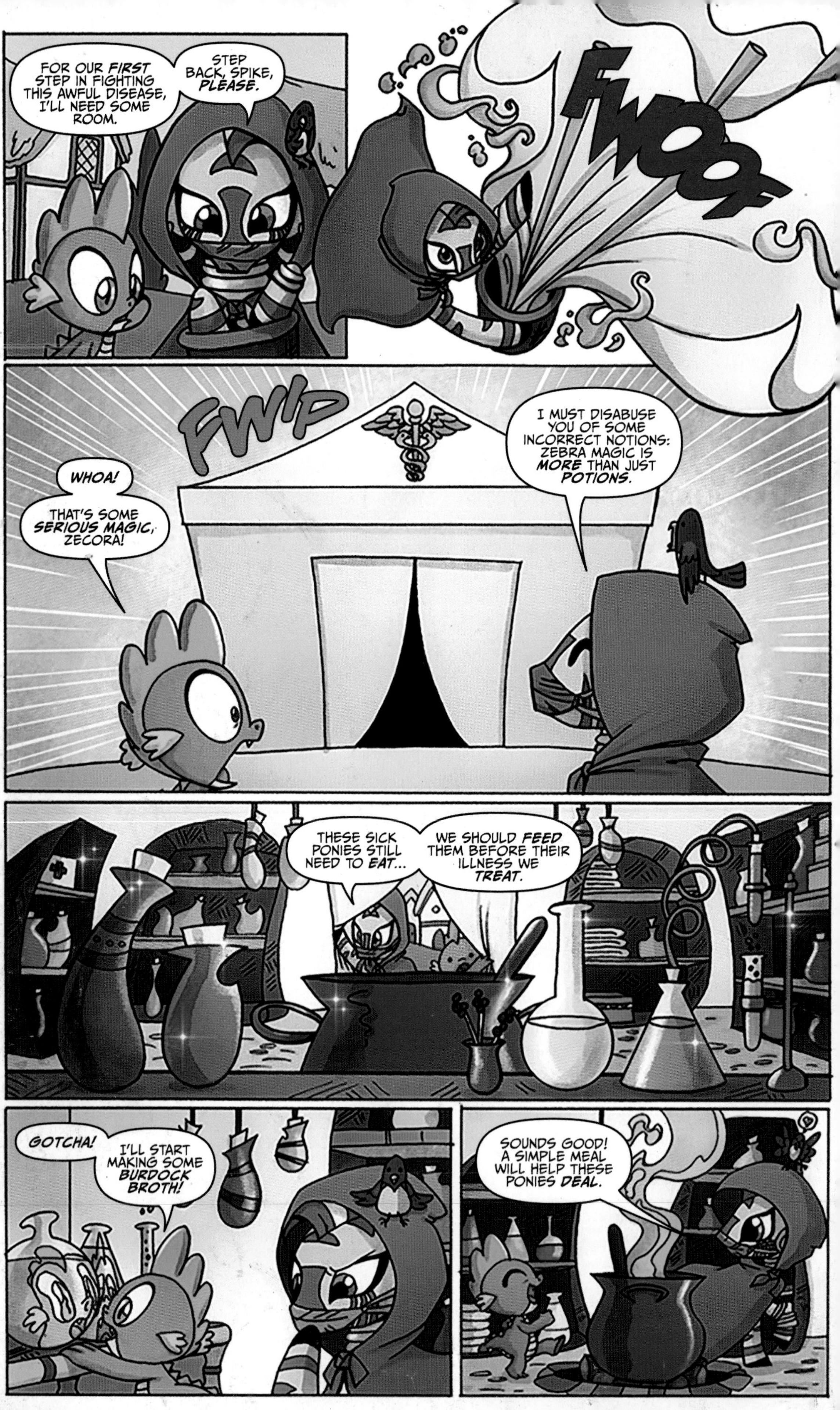

FOR OUR FIRST STEP IN FIGHTING THIS AWFUL DISEASE, I'LL NEED SOME ROOM.
STEP BACK, SPIKE, PLEASE.
FWOOF
FWIP
WHOA!
THAT'S SOME SERIOUS MAGIC, ZECORA!
I MUST DISABUSE YOU OF SOME INCORRECT NOTIONS: ZEBRA MAGIC IS MORE THAN JUST POTIONS.
THESE SICK PONIES STILL NEED TO EAT...
WE SHOULD FEED THEM BEFORE THEIR ILLNESS WE TREAT.
GOTCHA!
I'LL START MAKING SOME BURDOCK BROTH!
SOUNDS GOOD! A SIMPLE MEAL WILL HELP THESE PONIES DEAL.

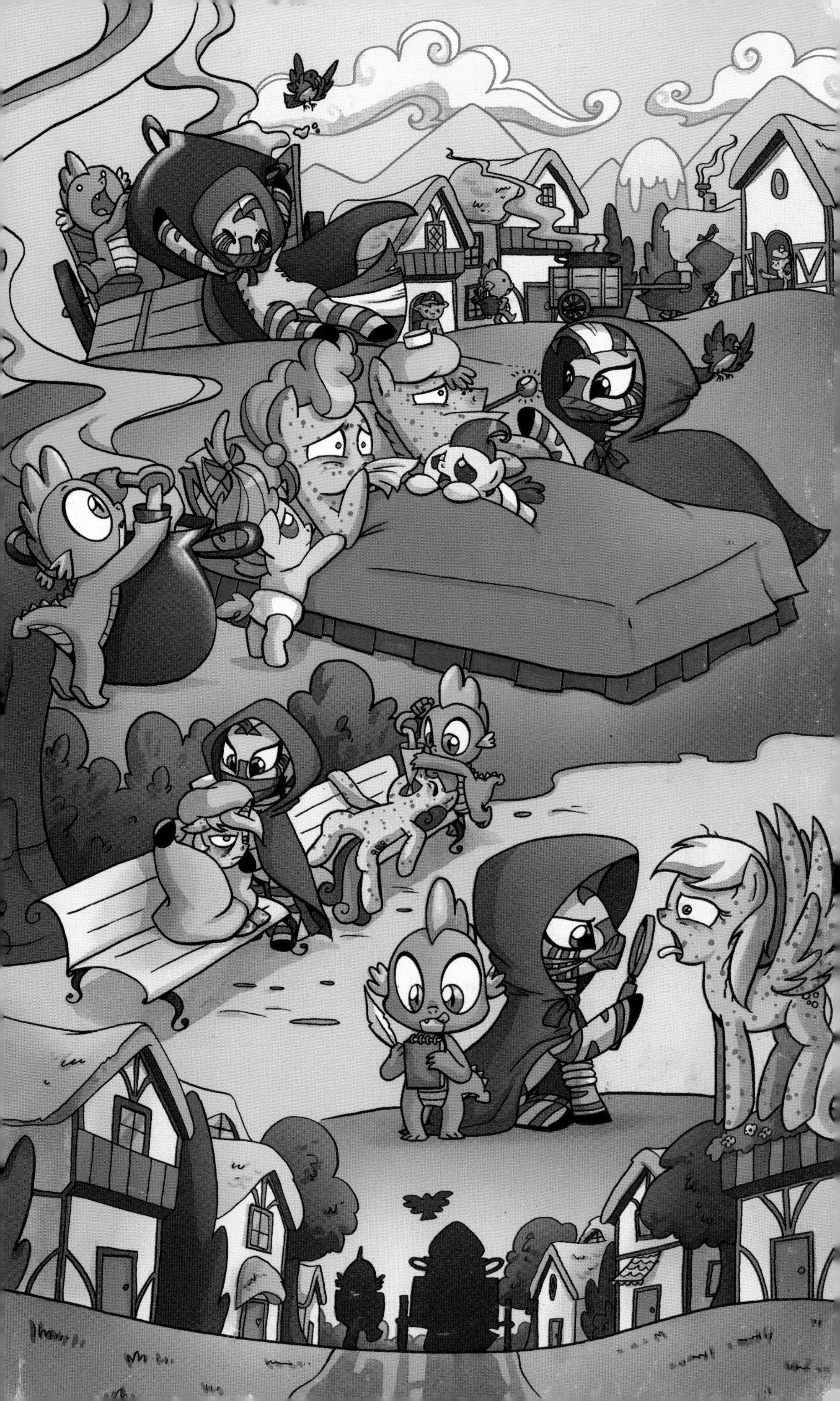

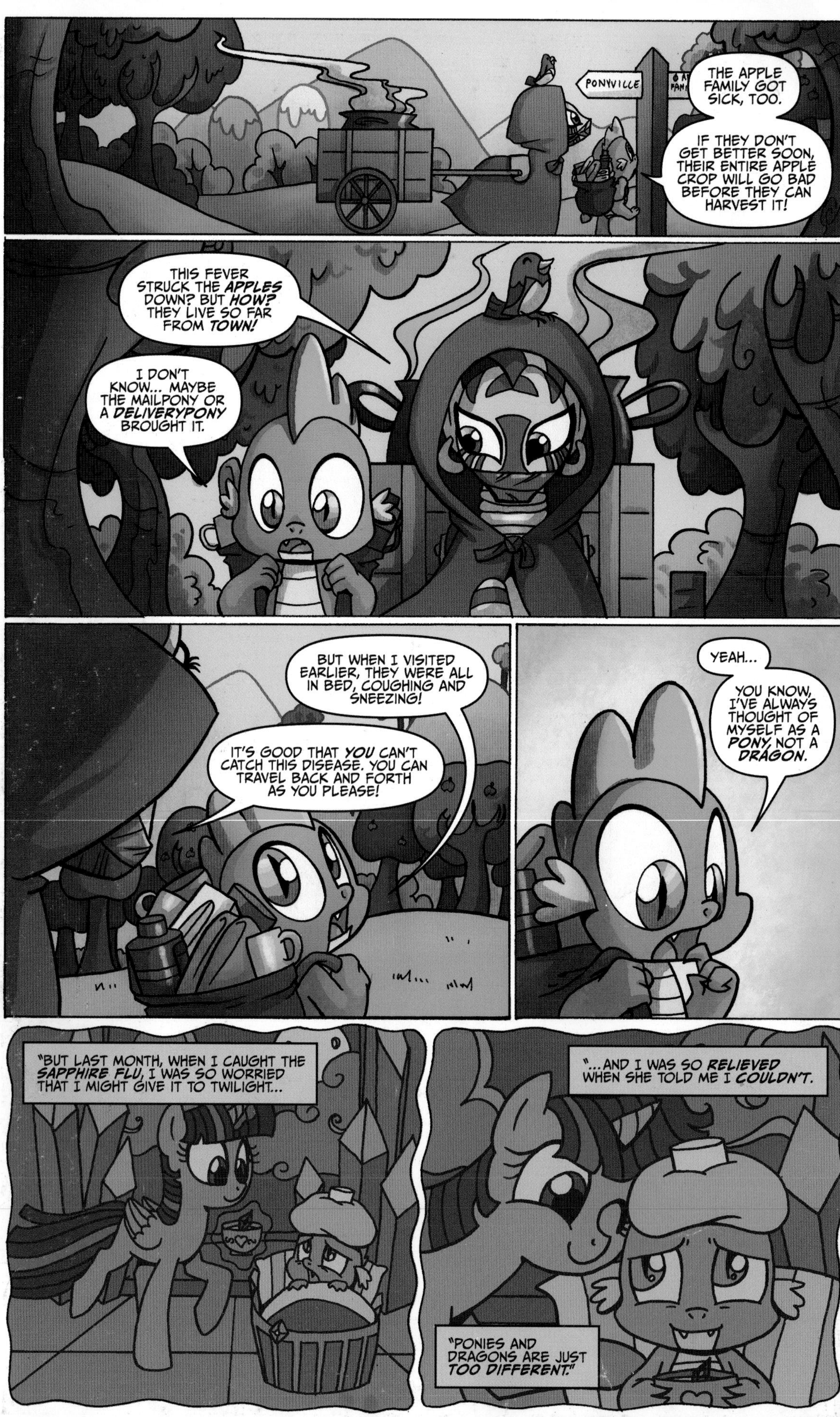
PONYVILLE
THE APPLE FAMILY GOT SICK, TOO.
IF THEY DON'T GET BETTER SOON, THEIR ENTIRE APPLE CROP WILL GO BAD BEFORE THEY CAN HARVEST IT!
THIS FEVER STRUCK THE APPLES DOWN? BUT HOW? THEY LIVE SO FAR FROM TOWN!
I DON'T KNOW... MAYBE THE MAILPONY OR A DELIVERYPONY BROUGHT IT.
BUT WHEN I VISITED EARLIER, THEY WERE ALL IN BED, COUGHING AND SNEEZING!
IT'S GOOD THAT YOU CAN'T CATCH THIS DISEASE. YOU CAN TRAVEL BACK AND FORTH AS YOU PLEASE!
YEAH...
YOU KNOW, I'VE ALWAYS THOUGHT OF MYSELF AS A PONY, NOT A DRAGON.
"BUT LAST MONTH, WHEN I CAUGHT THE SAPPHIRE FLU, I WAS SO WORRIED THAT I MIGHT GIVE IT TO TWILIGHT...
"...AND I WAS SO RELIEVED WHEN SHE TOLD ME I COULDN'T.
"PONIES AND DRAGONS ARE JUST TOO DIFFERENT."

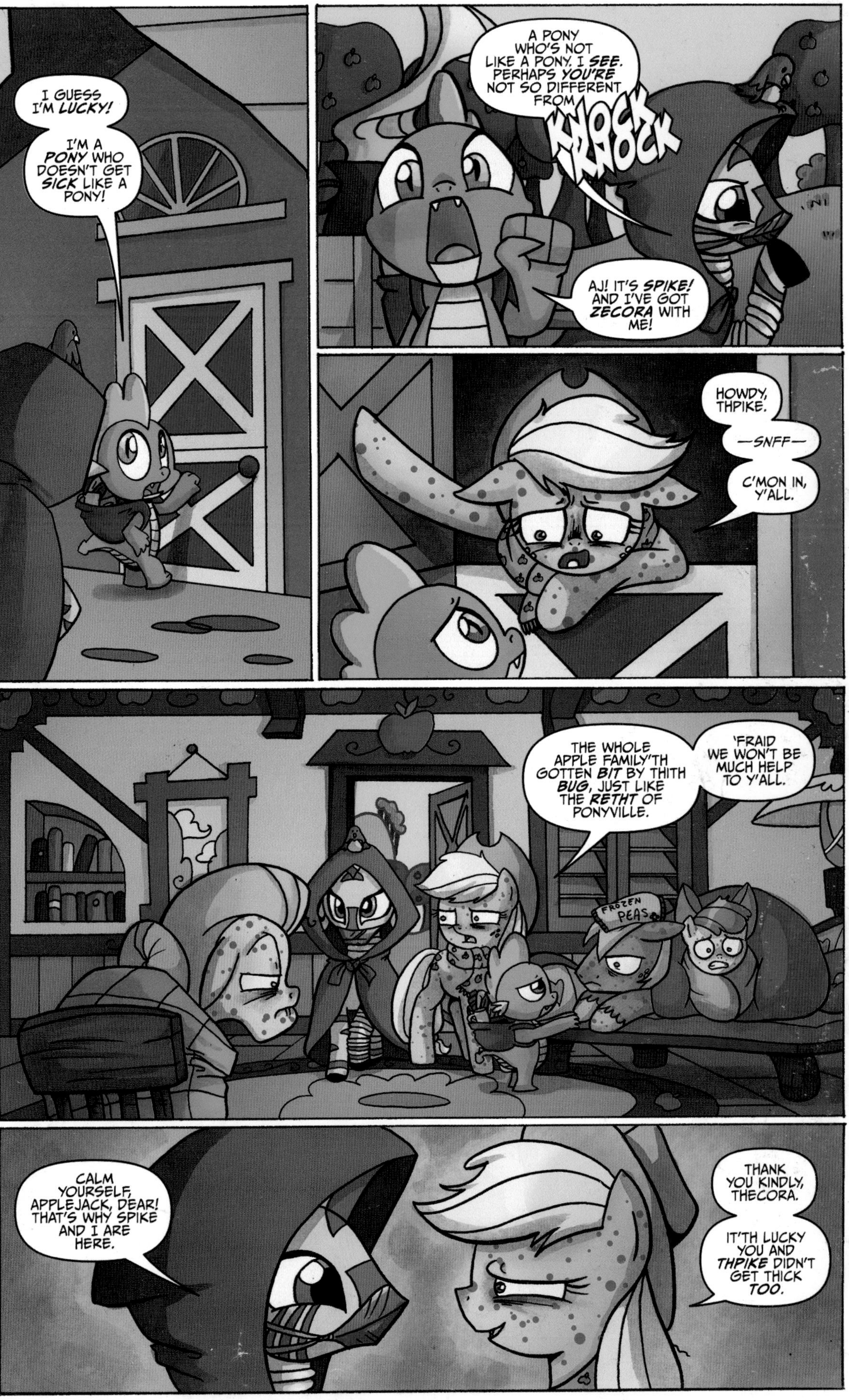
I GUESS I'M *LUCKY!*
I'M A *PONY* WHO DOESN'T GET *SICK* LIKE A PONY!
A PONY WHO'S NOT LIKE A PONY. I *SEE*. PERHAPS *YOU'RE* NOT SO DIFFERENT FROM
KNOCK KNOCK
AJ! IT'S *SPIKE!* AND I'VE GOT *ZECORA* WITH ME!
HOWDY, THPIKE.
—SNFF—
C'MON IN, Y'ALL.
THE WHOLE APPLE FAMILY'TH GOTTEN *BIT* BY THITH *BUG*, JUST LIKE THE *RETHT* OF PONYVILLE.
'FRAID WE WON'T BE MUCH HELP TO Y'ALL.
FROZEN PEAS
CALM YOURSELF, APPLEJACK, DEAR! THAT'S WHY SPIKE AND I ARE HERE.
THANK YOU KINDLY, THECORA.
IT'TH LUCKY YOU AND *THPIKE* DIDN'T GET THICK *TOO*.

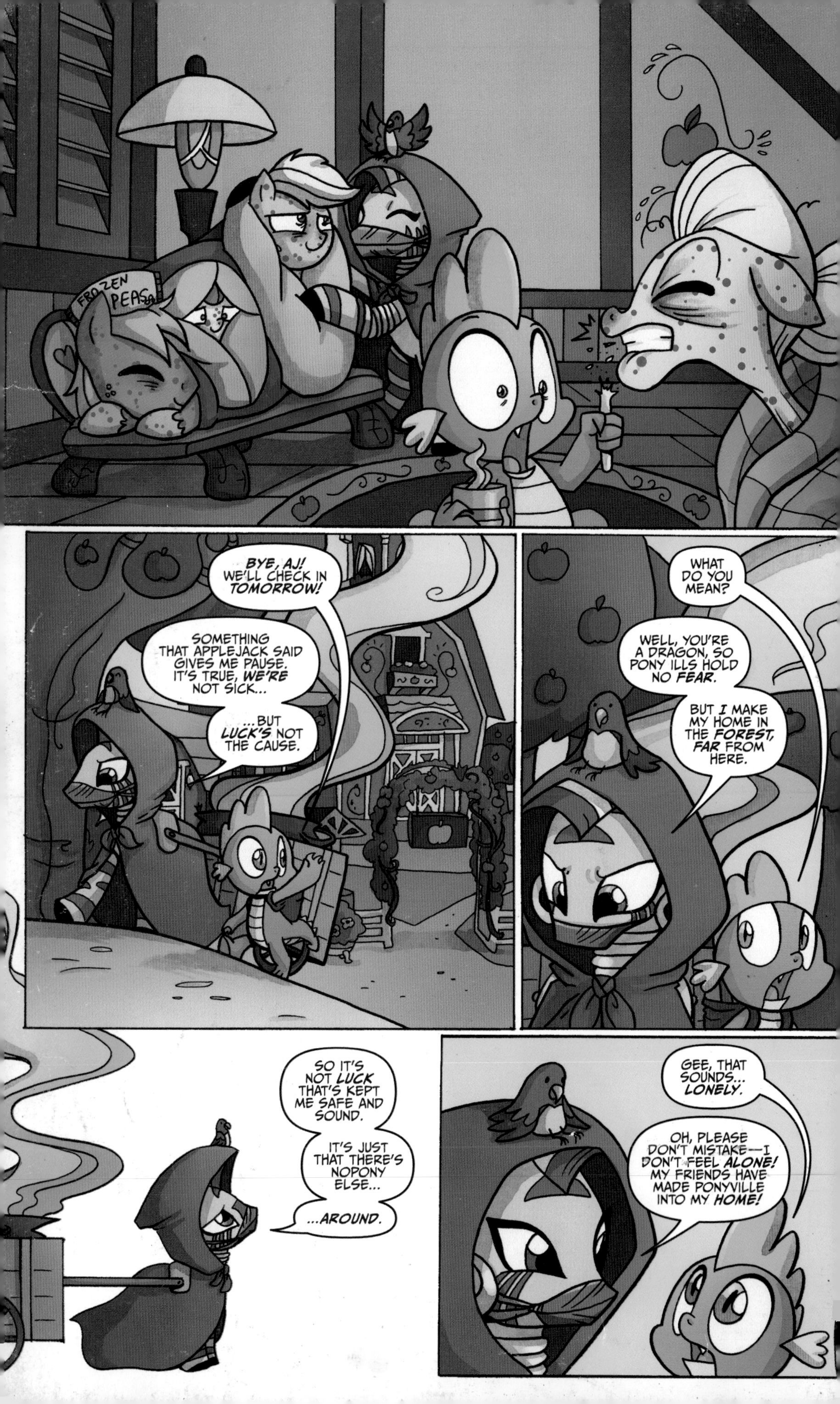
FROZEN PEAS
BYE, AJ! WE'LL CHECK IN TOMORROW!
SOMETHING THAT APPLEJACK SAID GIVES ME PAUSE. IT'S TRUE, WE'RE NOT SICK...
...BUT LUCK'S NOT THE CAUSE.
WHAT DO YOU MEAN?
WELL, YOU'RE A DRAGON, SO PONY ILLS HOLD NO FEAR.
BUT I MAKE MY HOME IN THE FOREST, FAR FROM HERE.
SO IT'S NOT LUCK THAT'S KEPT ME SAFE AND SOUND.
IT'S JUST THAT THERE'S NOPONY ELSE...
...AROUND.
GEE, THAT SOUNDS... LONELY.
OH, PLEASE DON'T MISTAKE—I DON'T FEEL ALONE! MY FRIENDS HAVE MADE PONYVILLE INTO MY HOME!

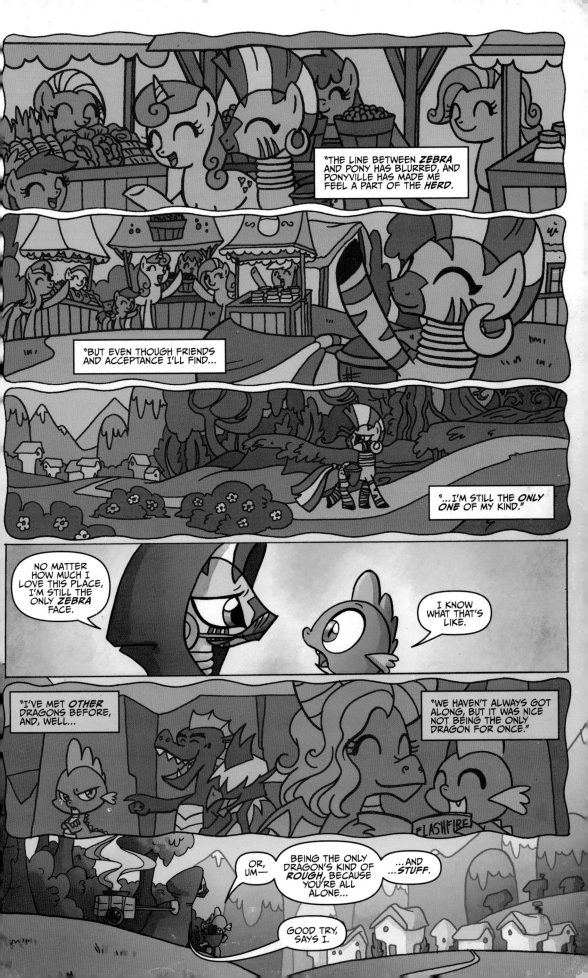

"THE LINE BETWEEN *ZEBRA* AND PONY HAS BLURRED, AND PONYVILLE HAS MADE ME FEEL A PART OF THE *HERD*."

"BUT EVEN THOUGH FRIENDS AND ACCEPTANCE I'LL FIND..."

"...I'M STILL THE *ONLY ONE* OF MY KIND."

NO MATTER HOW MUCH I LOVE THIS PLACE, I'M STILL THE ONLY *ZEBRA* FACE.

I KNOW WHAT THAT'S LIKE.

"I'VE MET *OTHER* DRAGONS BEFORE, AND, WELL..."

"WE HAVEN'T ALWAYS GOT ALONG, BUT IT WAS NICE NOT BEING THE ONLY DRAGON FOR ONCE."

OR, UM—

BEING THE ONLY DRAGON'S KIND OF *ROUGH*, BECAUSE YOU'RE ALL ALONE...

...AND ...*STUFF*.

GOOD TRY, SAYS I.

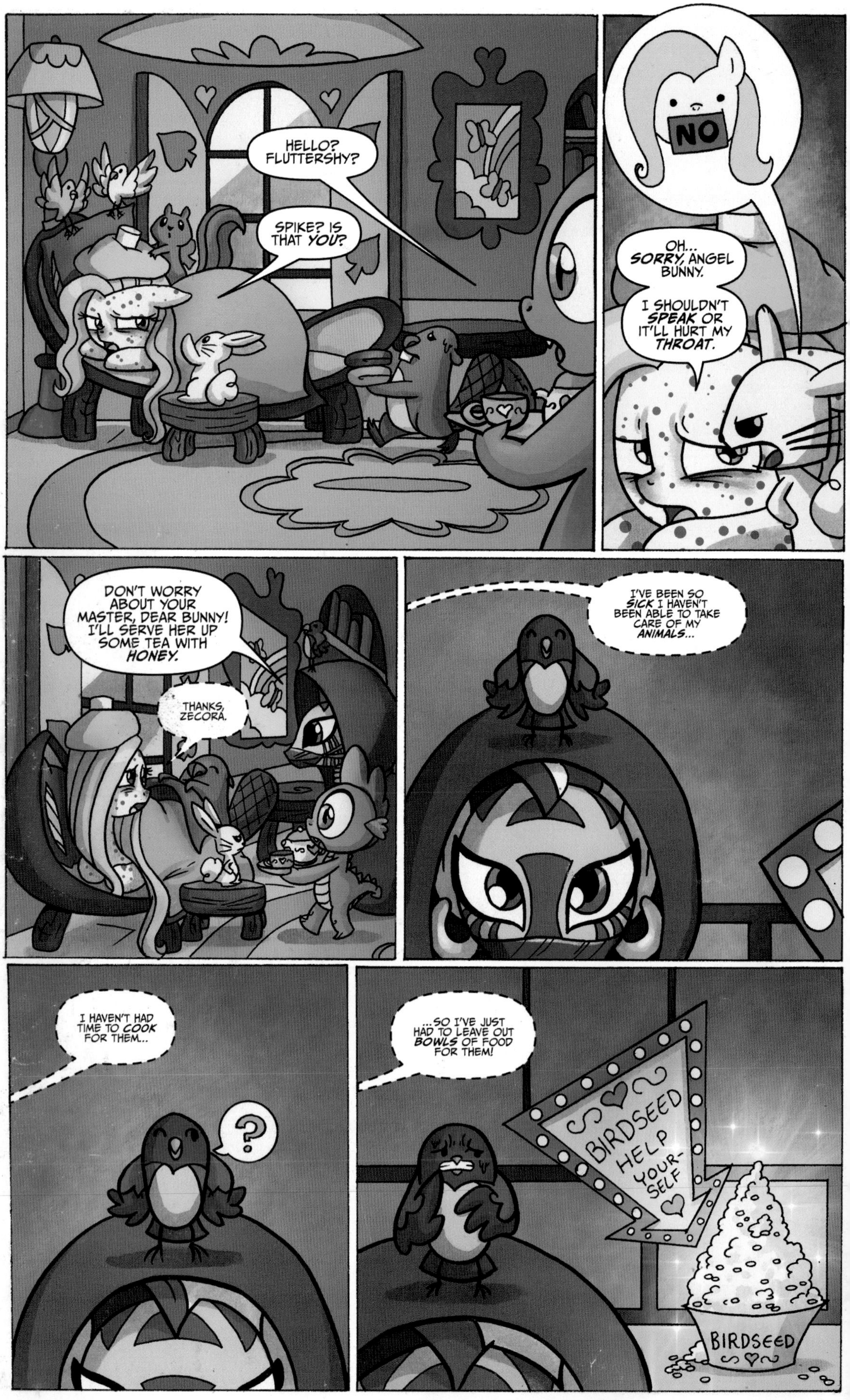
HELLO? FLUTTERSHY?
SPIKE? IS THAT *YOU*?
NO
OH... *SORRY,* ANGEL BUNNY.
I SHOULDN'T *SPEAK* OR IT'LL HURT MY *THROAT*.
DON'T WORRY ABOUT YOUR MASTER, DEAR BUNNY! I'LL SERVE HER UP SOME TEA WITH *HONEY.*
THANKS, ZECORA.
I'VE BEEN SO *SICK* I HAVEN'T BEEN ABLE TO TAKE CARE OF MY *ANIMALS*...
I HAVEN'T HAD TIME TO *COOK* FOR THEM...
?
...SO I'VE JUST HAD TO LEAVE OUT *BOWLS* OF FOOD FOR THEM!
BIRDSEED HELP YOUR-SELF
BIRDSEED

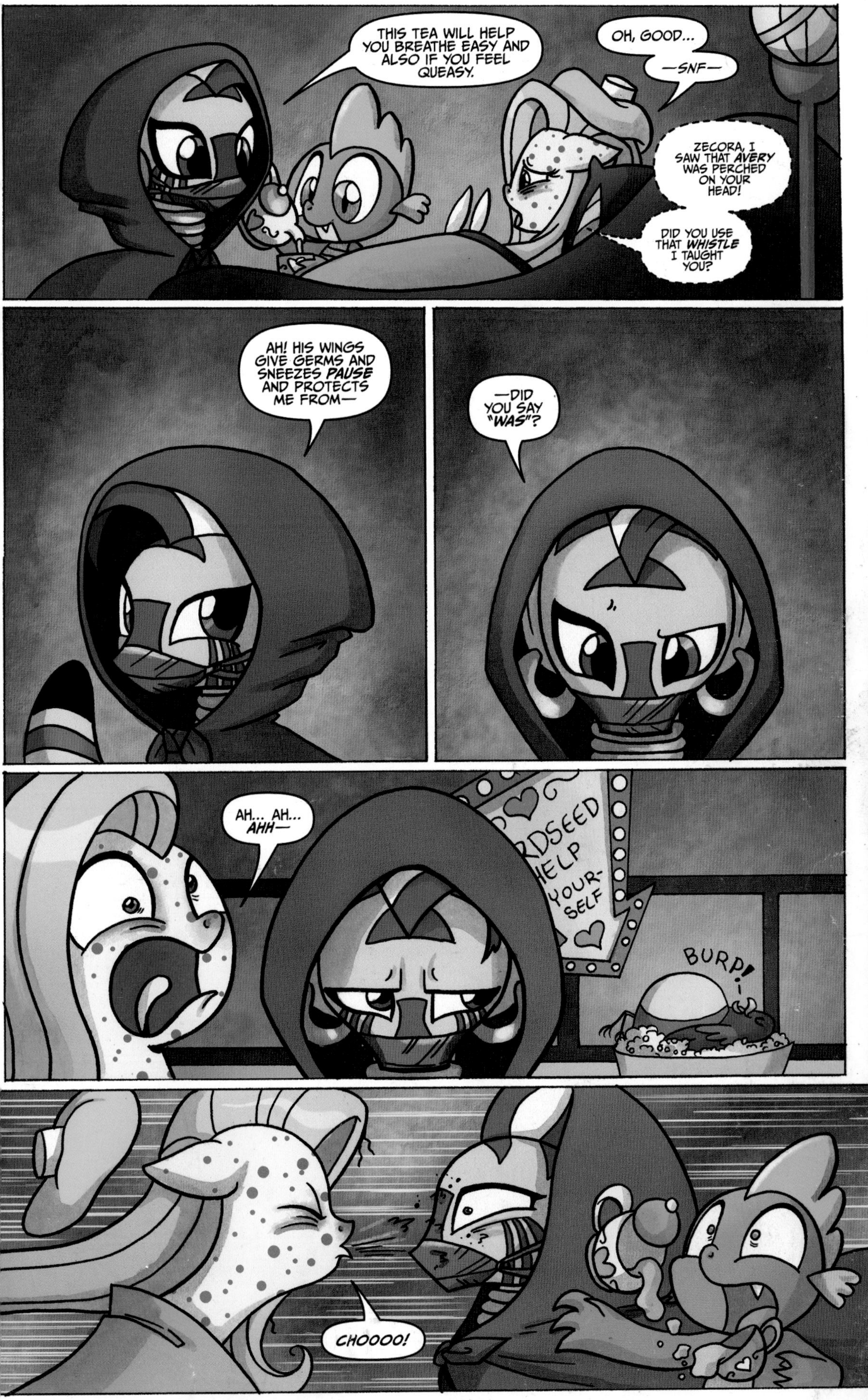
THIS TEA WILL HELP YOU BREATHE EASY AND ALSO IF YOU FEEL QUEASY.
OH, GOOD...
—SNF—
ZECORA, I SAW THAT *AVERY* WAS PERCHED ON YOUR HEAD!
DID YOU USE THAT *WHISTLE* I TAUGHT YOU?
AH! HIS WINGS GIVE GERMS AND SNEEZES *PAUSE* AND PROTECTS ME FROM—
—DID YOU SAY *"WAS"*?
AH... AH... *AHH*—
RDSEED HELP YOUR-SELF
BURP!
CHOOOO!

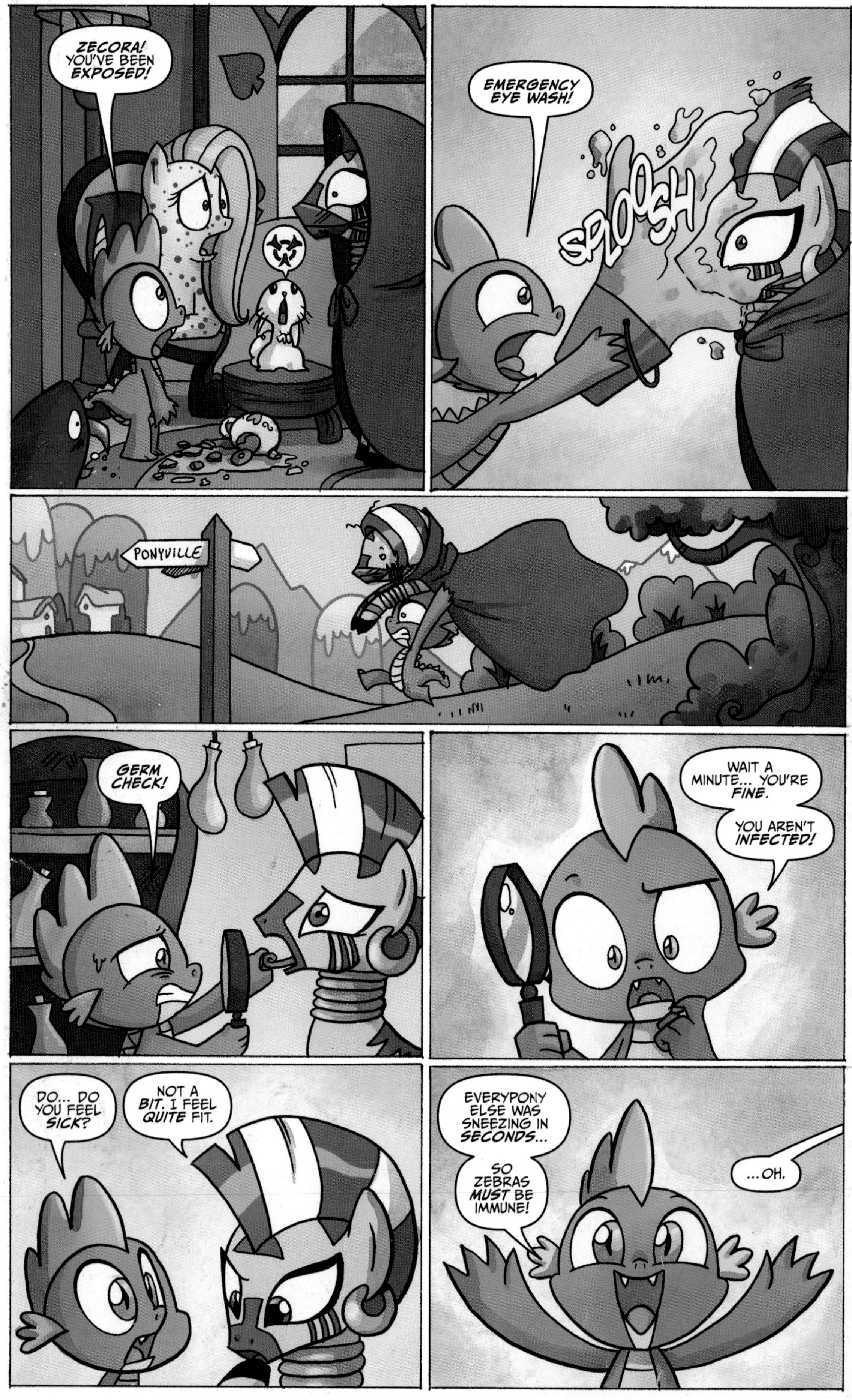
ZECORA! YOU'VE BEEN EXPOSED!
EMERGENCY EYE WASH!
SPLOOSH
PONYVILLE
GERM CHECK!
WAIT A MINUTE... YOU'RE FINE.
YOU AREN'T INFECTED!
DO... DO YOU FEEL SICK?
NOT A BIT. I FEEL QUITE FIT.
EVERYPONY ELSE WAS SNEEZING IN SECONDS...
SO ZEBRAS MUST BE IMMUNE!
...OH.

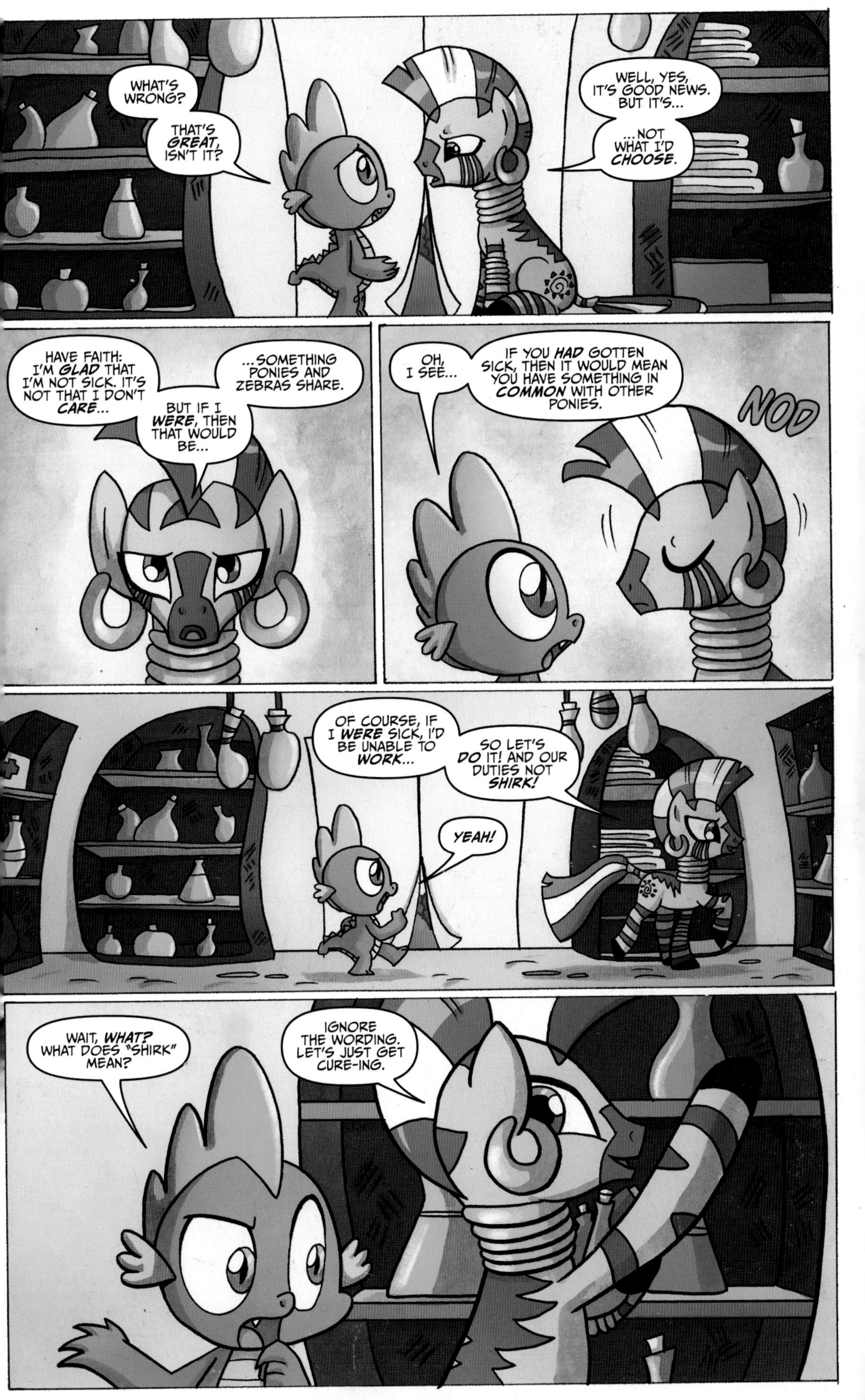
WHAT'S WRONG?
THAT'S GREAT, ISN'T IT?
WELL, YES, IT'S GOOD NEWS. BUT IT'S...
...NOT WHAT I'D CHOOSE.
HAVE FAITH: I'M GLAD THAT I'M NOT SICK. IT'S NOT THAT I DON'T CARE...
BUT IF I WERE, THEN THAT WOULD BE...
...SOMETHING PONIES AND ZEBRAS SHARE.
OH, I SEE...
IF YOU HAD GOTTEN SICK, THEN IT WOULD MEAN YOU HAVE SOMETHING IN COMMON WITH OTHER PONIES.
NOD
OF COURSE, IF I WERE SICK, I'D BE UNABLE TO WORK...
SO LET'S DO IT! AND OUR DUTIES NOT SHIRK!
YEAH!
WAIT, WHAT? WHAT DOES "SHIRK" MEAN?
IGNORE THE WORDING. LET'S JUST GET CURE-ING.

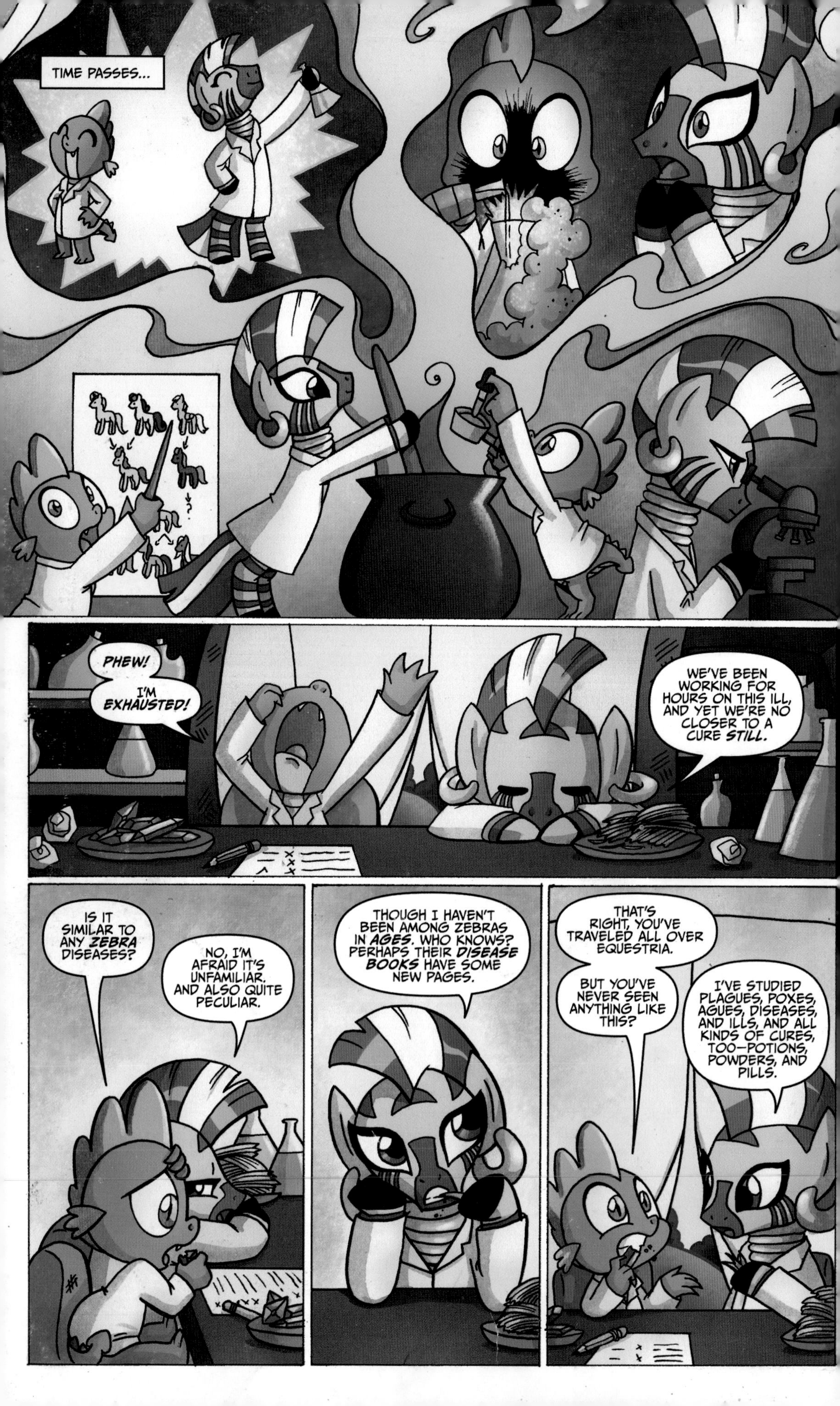
TIME PASSES...
PHEW!
I'M EXHAUSTED!
WE'VE BEEN WORKING FOR HOURS ON THIS ILL, AND YET WE'RE NO CLOSER TO A CURE STILL.
IS IT SIMILAR TO ANY ZEBRA DISEASES?
NO, I'M AFRAID IT'S UNFAMILIAR. AND ALSO QUITE PECULIAR.
THOUGH I HAVEN'T BEEN AMONG ZEBRAS IN AGES. WHO KNOWS? PERHAPS THEIR DISEASE BOOKS HAVE SOME NEW PAGES.
THAT'S RIGHT, YOU'VE TRAVELED ALL OVER EQUESTRIA.
BUT YOU'VE NEVER SEEN ANYTHING LIKE THIS?
I'VE STUDIED PLAGUES, POXES, AGUES, DISEASES, AND ILLS, AND ALL KINDS OF CURES, TOO—POTIONS, POWDERS, AND PILLS.

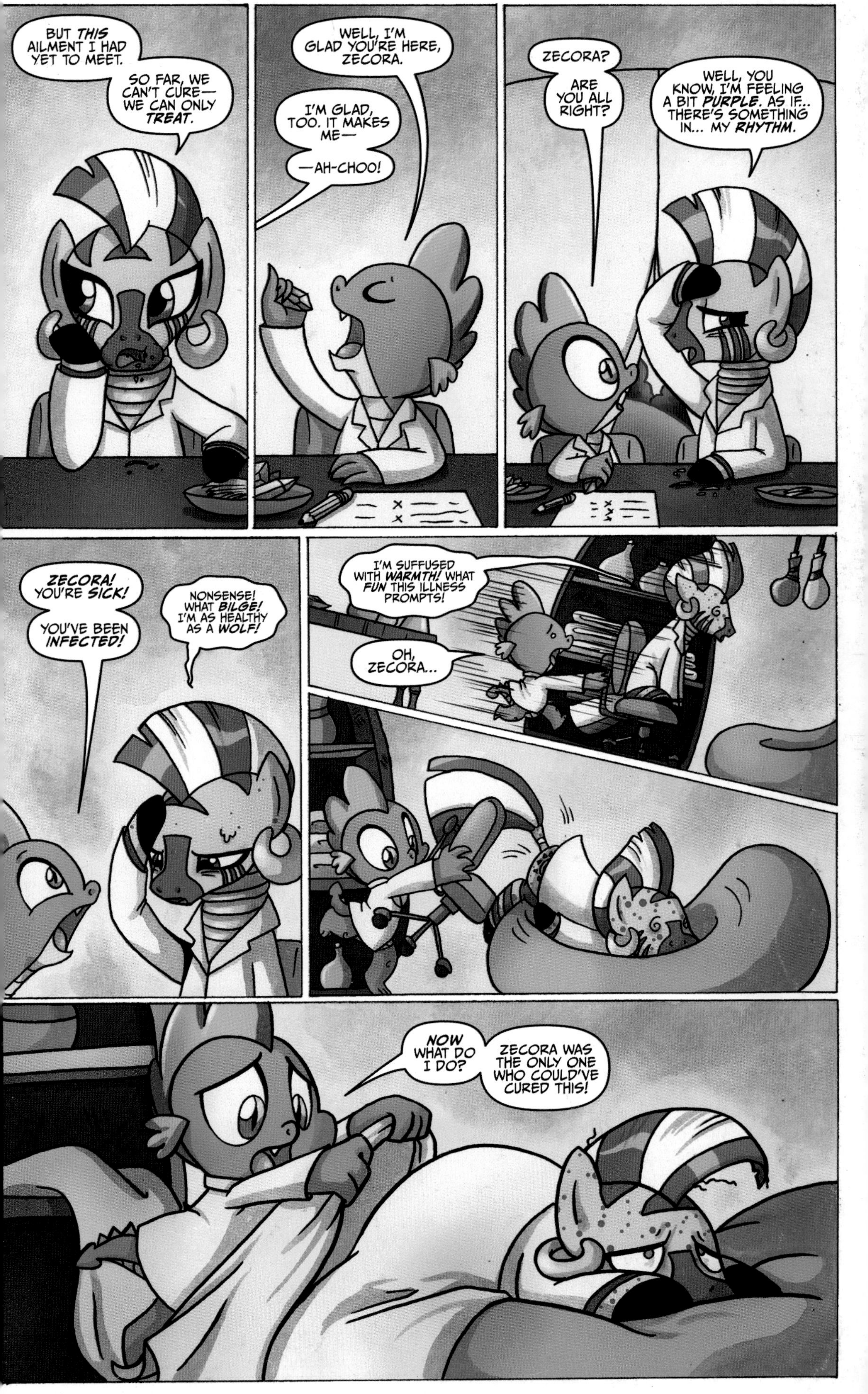
BUT THIS AILMENT I HAD YET TO MEET.
SO FAR, WE CAN'T CURE— WE CAN ONLY TREAT.
WELL, I'M GLAD YOU'RE HERE, ZECORA.
I'M GLAD, TOO. IT MAKES ME—
—AH-CHOO!
ZECORA?
ARE YOU ALL RIGHT?
WELL, YOU KNOW, I'M FEELING A BIT PURPLE. AS IF... THERE'S SOMETHING IN... MY RHYTHM.
ZECORA! YOU'RE SICK!
YOU'VE BEEN INFECTED!
NONSENSE! WHAT BILGE! I'M AS HEALTHY AS A WOLF!
I'M SUFFUSED WITH WARMTH! WHAT FUN THIS ILLNESS PROMPTS!
OH, ZECORA...
NOW WHAT DO I DO?
ZECORA WAS THE ONLY ONE WHO COULD'VE CURED THIS!

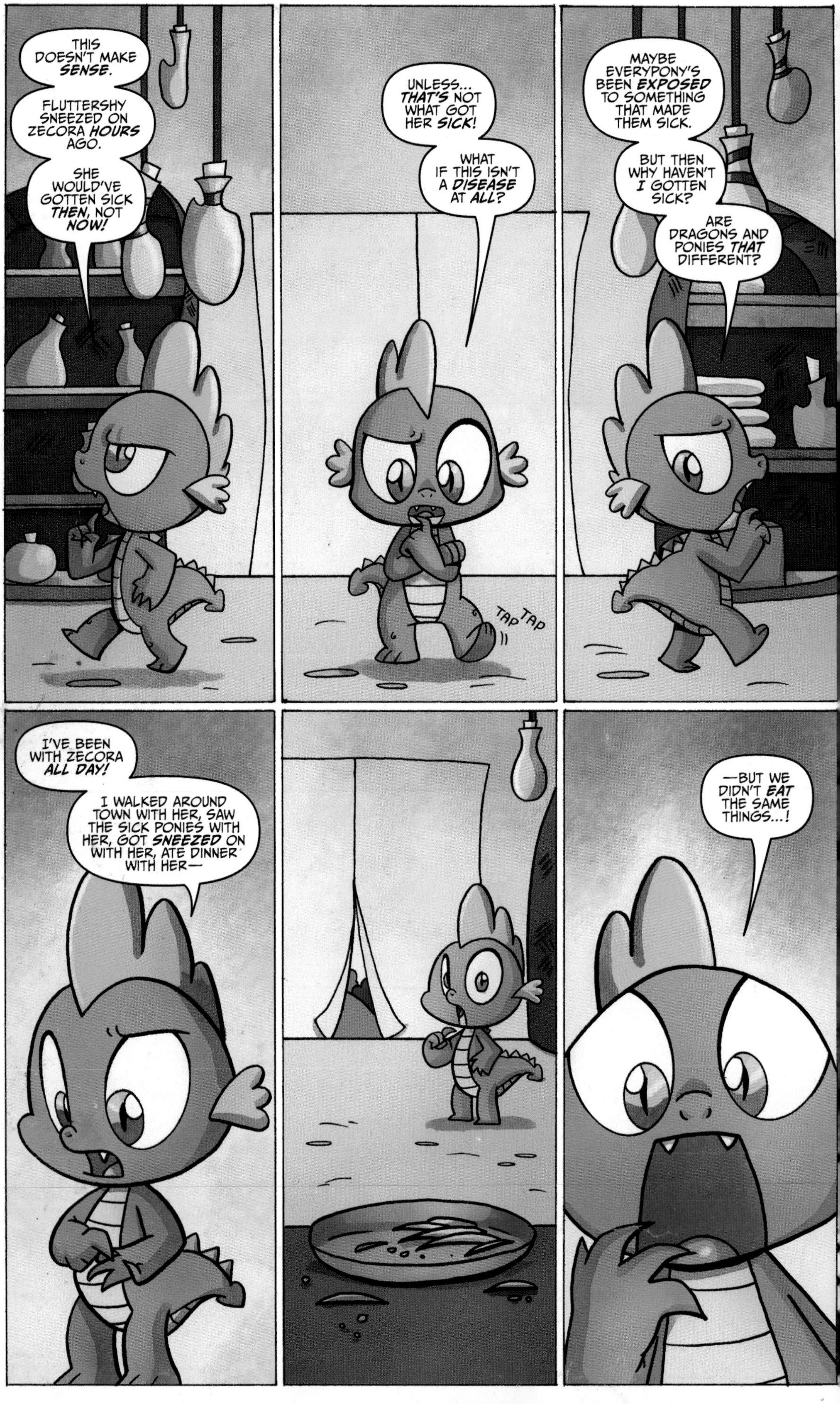
THIS DOESN'T MAKE SENSE.
FLUTTERSHY SNEEZED ON ZECORA HOURS AGO.
SHE WOULD'VE GOTTEN SICK THEN, NOT NOW!
UNLESS... THAT'S NOT WHAT GOT HER SICK!
WHAT IF THIS ISN'T A DISEASE AT ALL?
TAP TAP
MAYBE EVERYPONY'S BEEN EXPOSED TO SOMETHING THAT MADE THEM SICK.
BUT THEN WHY HAVEN'T I GOTTEN SICK?
ARE DRAGONS AND PONIES THAT DIFFERENT?
I'VE BEEN WITH ZECORA ALL DAY!
I WALKED AROUND TOWN WITH HER, SAW THE SICK PONIES WITH HER, GOT SNEEZED ON WITH HER, ATE DINNER WITH HER—
—BUT WE DIDN'T EAT THE SAME THINGS...!

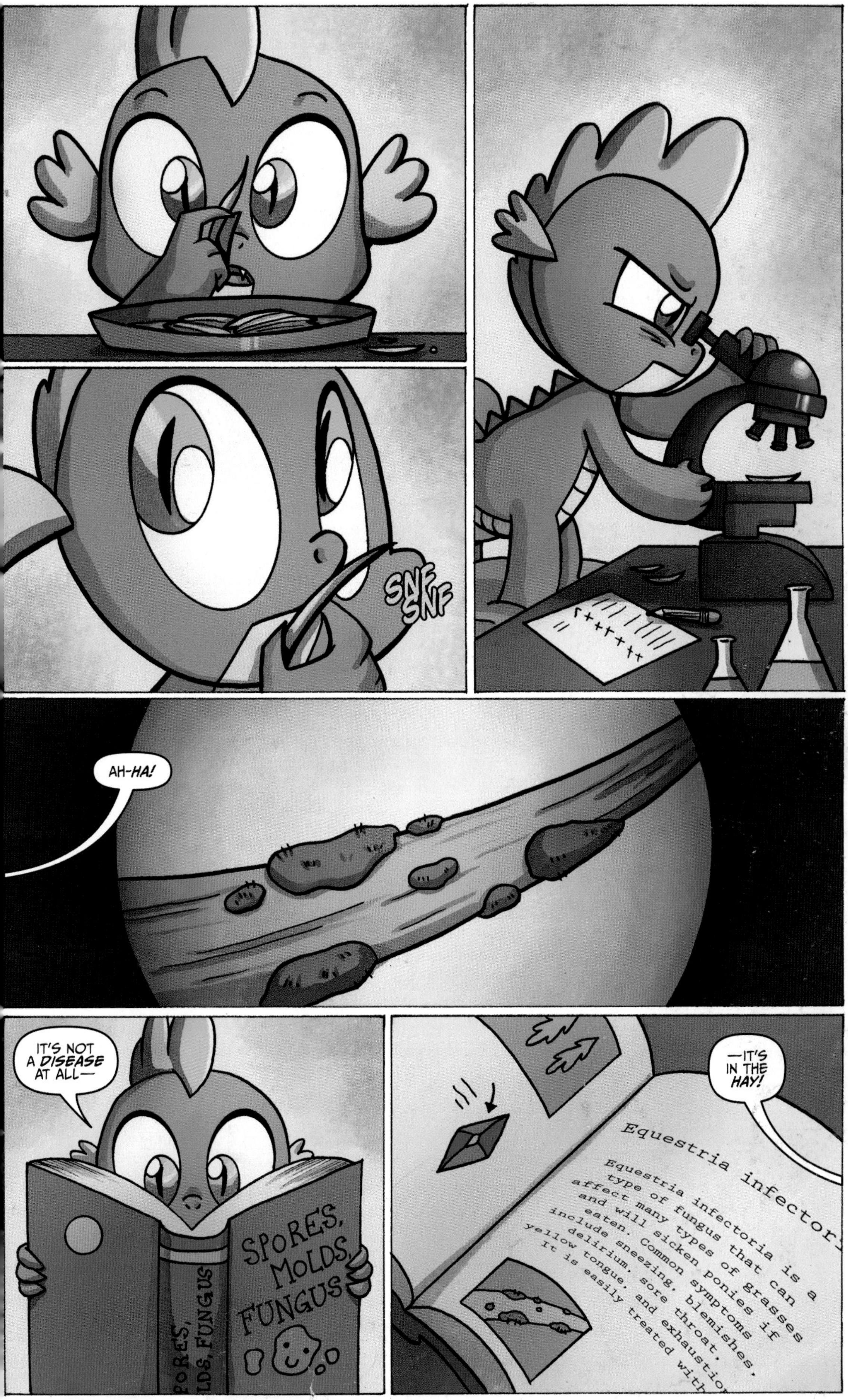
SNF SNF
AH-HA!
IT'S NOT A DISEASE AT ALL—
SPORES, MOLDS, FUNGUS
—IT'S IN THE HAY!
Equestria infectori
Equestria infectoria is a
type of fungus that can
affect many types of grasses
and will sicken ponies if
eaten. Common symptoms
include sneezing, blemishes,
delirium, sore throat,
yellow tongue, and exhaustio
It is easily treated with

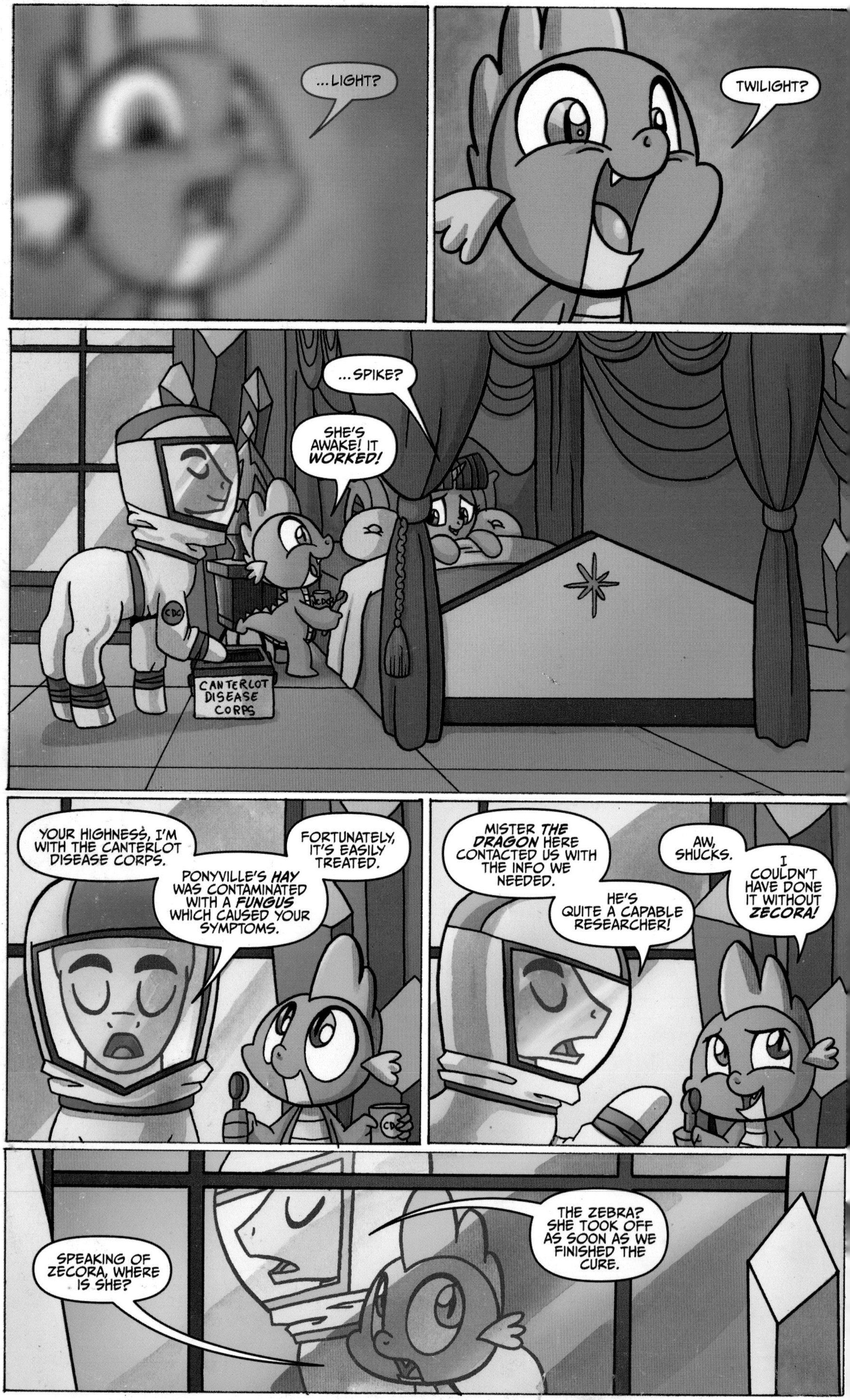
...LIGHT?
TWILIGHT?
...SPIKE?
SHE'S AWAKE! IT WORKED!
CANTERLOT DISEASE CORPS
YOUR HIGHNESS, I'M WITH THE CANTERLOT DISEASE CORPS.
PONYVILLE'S HAY WAS CONTAMINATED WITH A FUNGUS WHICH CAUSED YOUR SYMPTOMS.
FORTUNATELY, IT'S EASILY TREATED.
MISTER THE DRAGON HERE CONTACTED US WITH THE INFO WE NEEDED.
HE'S QUITE A CAPABLE RESEARCHER!
AW, SHUCKS.
I COULDN'T HAVE DONE IT WITHOUT ZECORA!
SPEAKING OF ZECORA, WHERE IS SHE?
THE ZEBRA? SHE TOOK OFF AS SOON AS WE FINISHED THE CURE.

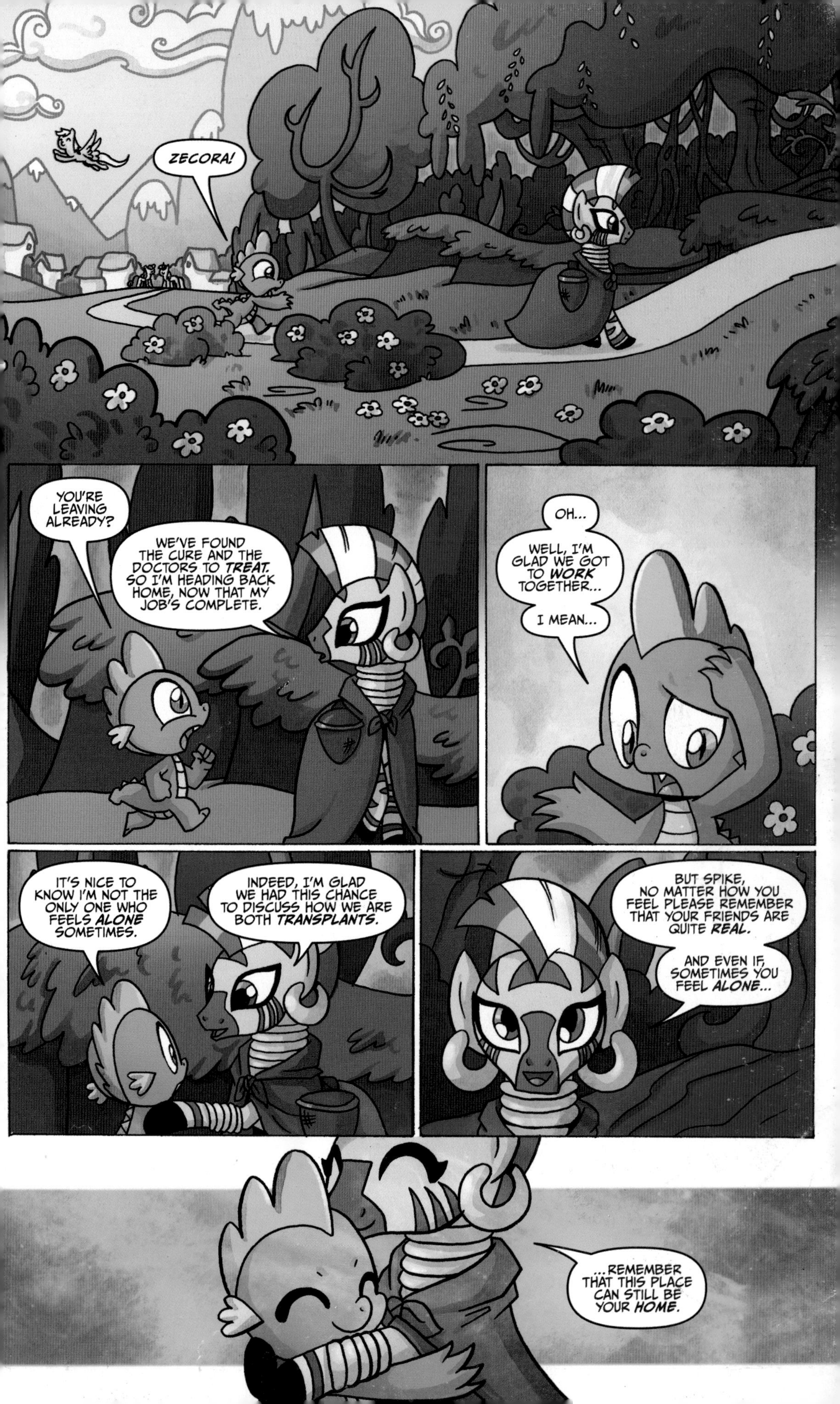
ZECORA!
YOU'RE LEAVING ALREADY?
WE'VE FOUND THE CURE AND THE DOCTORS TO *TREAT*. SO I'M HEADING BACK HOME, NOW THAT MY JOB'S COMPLETE.
OH...
WELL, I'M GLAD WE GOT TO *WORK* TOGETHER...
I MEAN...
IT'S NICE TO KNOW I'M NOT THE ONLY ONE WHO FEELS *ALONE* SOMETIMES.
INDEED, I'M GLAD WE HAD THIS CHANCE TO DISCUSS HOW WE ARE BOTH *TRANSPLANTS*.
BUT SPIKE, NO MATTER HOW YOU FEEL PLEASE REMEMBER THAT YOUR FRIENDS ARE QUITE *REAL*.
AND EVEN IF, SOMETIMES YOU FEEL *ALONE*...
...REMEMBER THAT THIS PLACE CAN STILL BE YOUR *HOME*.

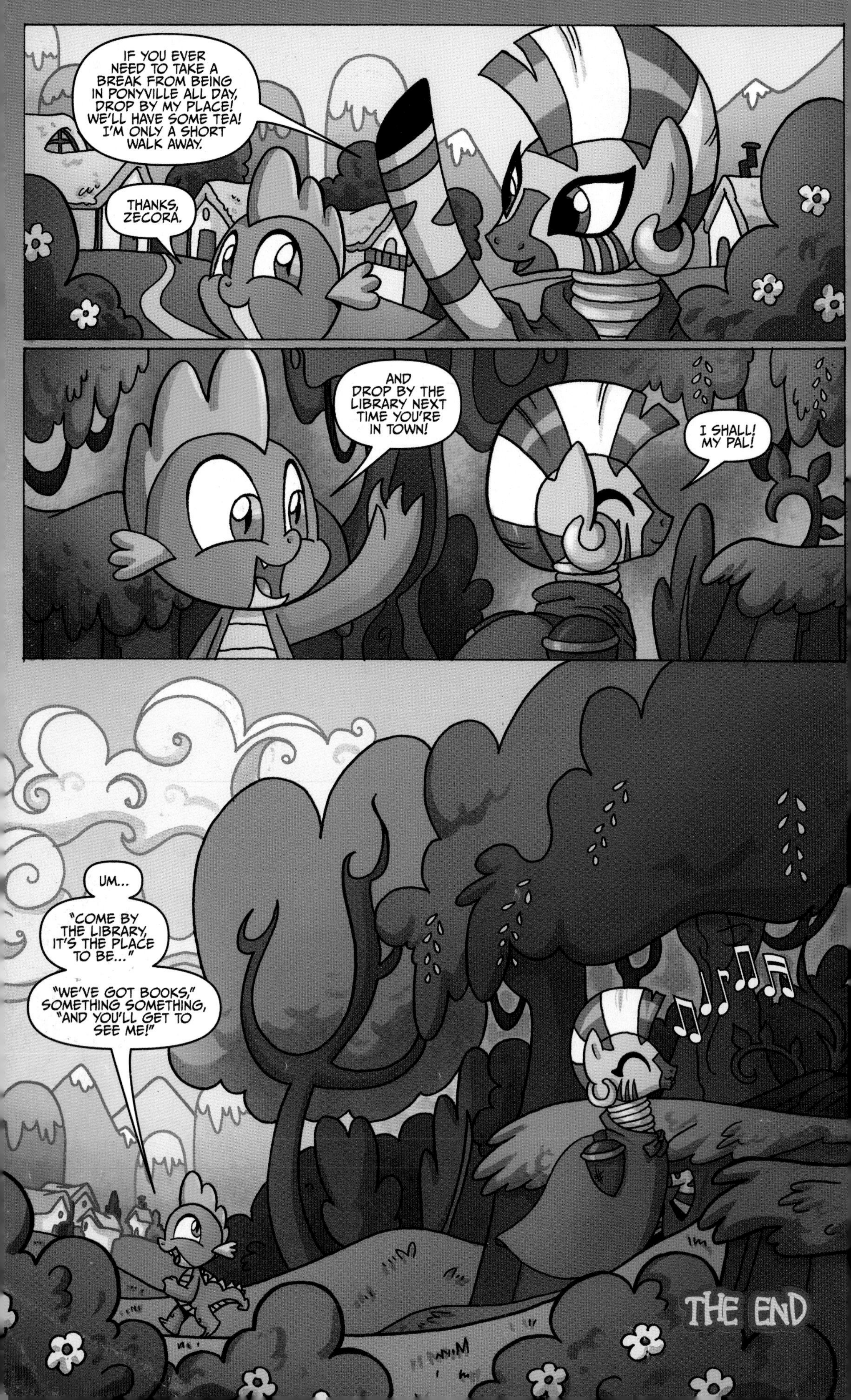
IF YOU EVER NEED TO TAKE A BREAK FROM BEING IN PONYVILLE ALL DAY, DROP BY MY PLACE! WE'LL HAVE SOME TEA! I'M ONLY A SHORT WALK AWAY.
THANKS, ZECORA.
AND DROP BY THE LIBRARY NEXT TIME YOU'RE IN TOWN!
I SHALL! MY PAL!
UM...
"COME BY THE LIBRARY, IT'S THE PLACE TO BE..."
"WE'VE GOT BOOKS," SOMETHING SOMETHING, "AND YOU'LL GET TO SEE ME!"
THE END

my LITTLE PONY

FRIENDS FOREVER

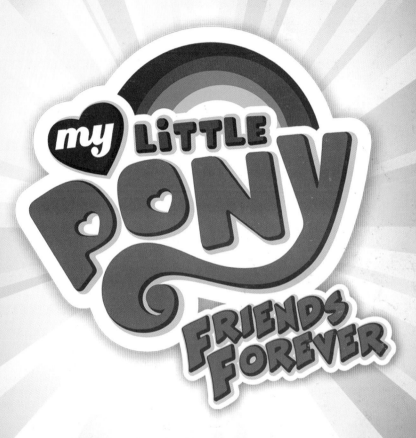

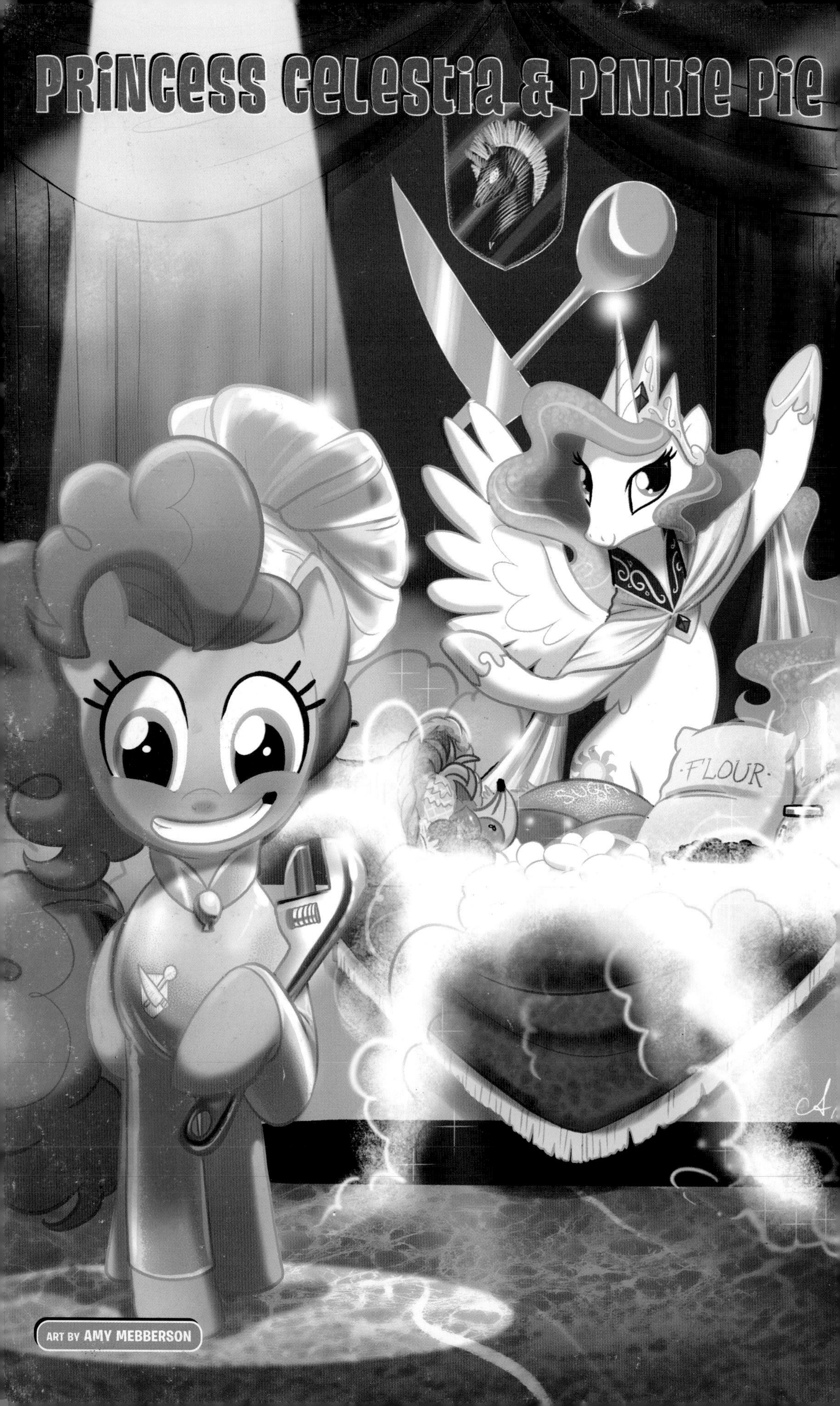
Princess Celestia & Pinkie Pie
·FLOUR·
ART BY AMY MEBBERSON

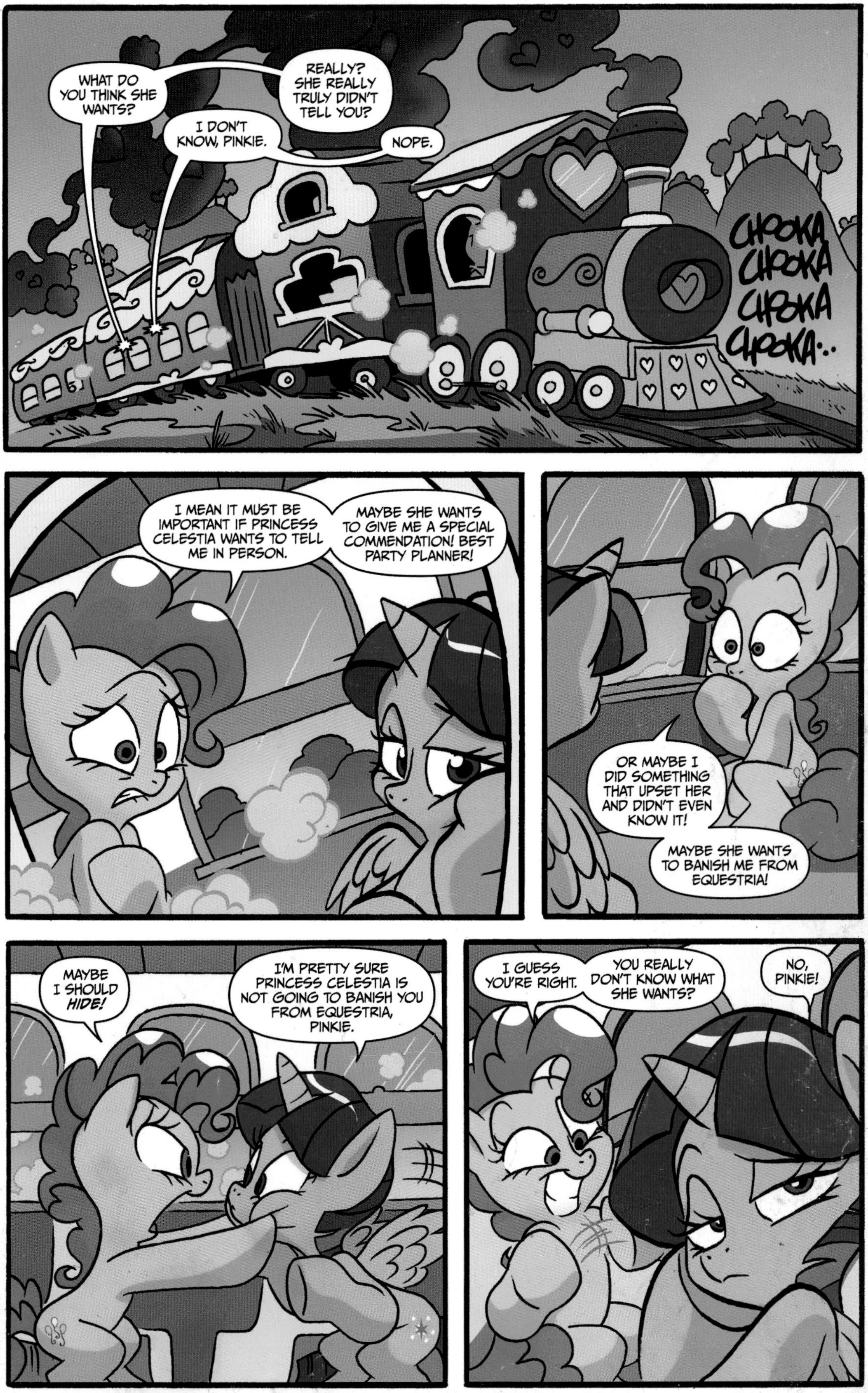
WHAT DO YOU THINK SHE WANTS?
I DON'T KNOW, PINKIE.
REALLY? SHE REALLY TRULY DIDN'T TELL YOU?
NOPE.
CHOOKA CHOOKA CHOOKA CHOOKA...
I MEAN IT MUST BE IMPORTANT IF PRINCESS CELESTIA WANTS TO TELL ME IN PERSON.
MAYBE SHE WANTS TO GIVE ME A SPECIAL COMMENDATION! BEST PARTY PLANNER!
OR MAYBE I DID SOMETHING THAT UPSET HER AND DIDN'T EVEN KNOW IT!
MAYBE SHE WANTS TO BANISH ME FROM EQUESTRIA!
MAYBE I SHOULD *HIDE!*
I'M PRETTY SURE PRINCESS CELESTIA IS NOT GOING TO BANISH YOU FROM EQUESTRIA, PINKIE.
I GUESS YOU'RE RIGHT.
YOU REALLY DON'T KNOW WHAT SHE WANTS?
NO, PINKIE!

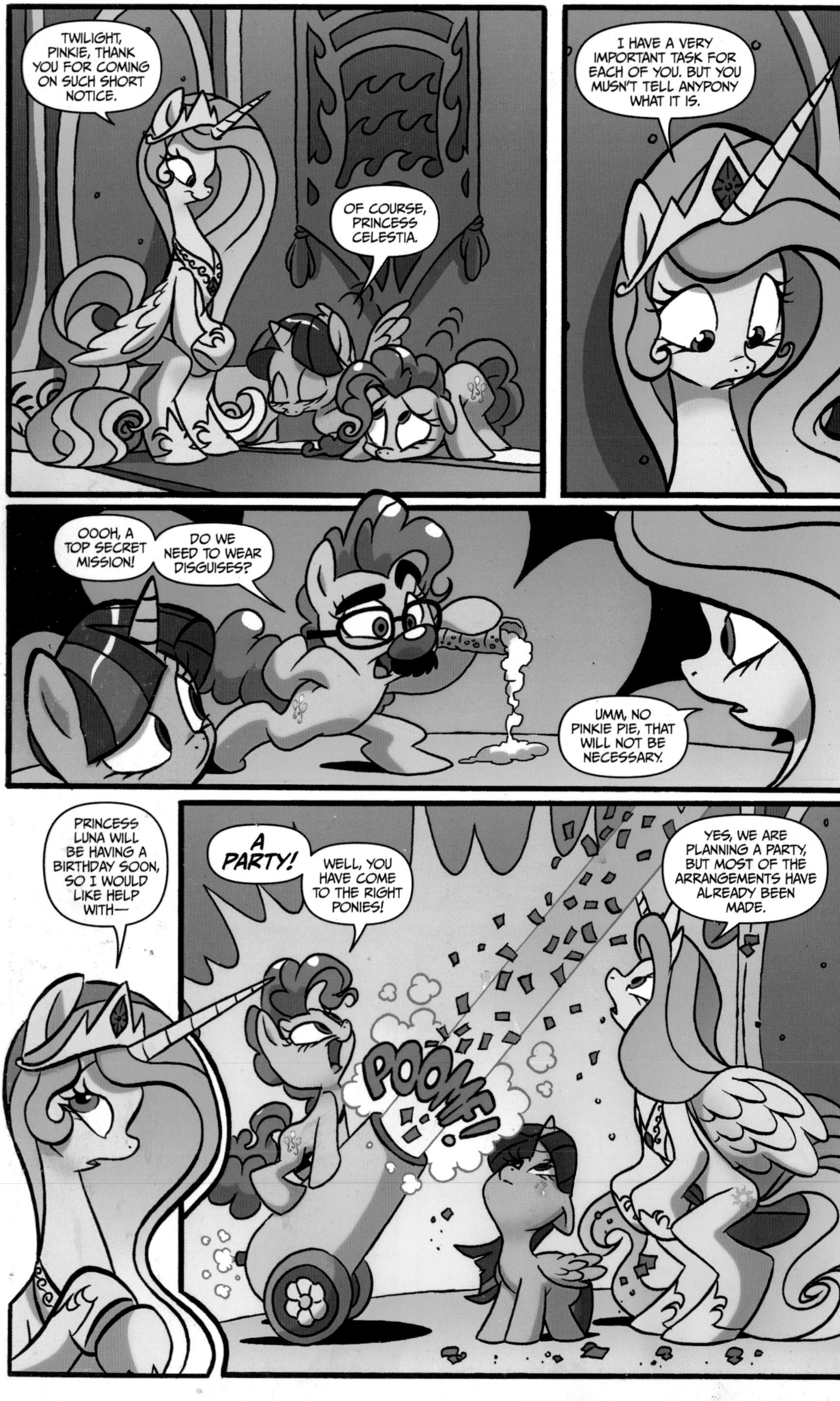

TWILIGHT, PINKIE, THANK YOU FOR COMING ON SUCH SHORT NOTICE.
OF COURSE, PRINCESS CELESTIA.
I HAVE A VERY IMPORTANT TASK FOR EACH OF YOU. BUT YOU MUSN'T TELL ANYPONY WHAT IT IS.
OOOH, A TOP SECRET MISSION!
DO WE NEED TO WEAR DISGUISES?
UMM, NO PINKIE PIE, THAT WILL NOT BE NECESSARY.
PRINCESS LUNA WILL BE HAVING A BIRTHDAY SOON, SO I WOULD LIKE HELP WITH—
A PARTY!
WELL, YOU HAVE COME TO THE RIGHT PONIES!
POOMF!
YES, WE ARE PLANNING A PARTY, BUT MOST OF THE ARRANGEMENTS HAVE ALREADY BEEN MADE.

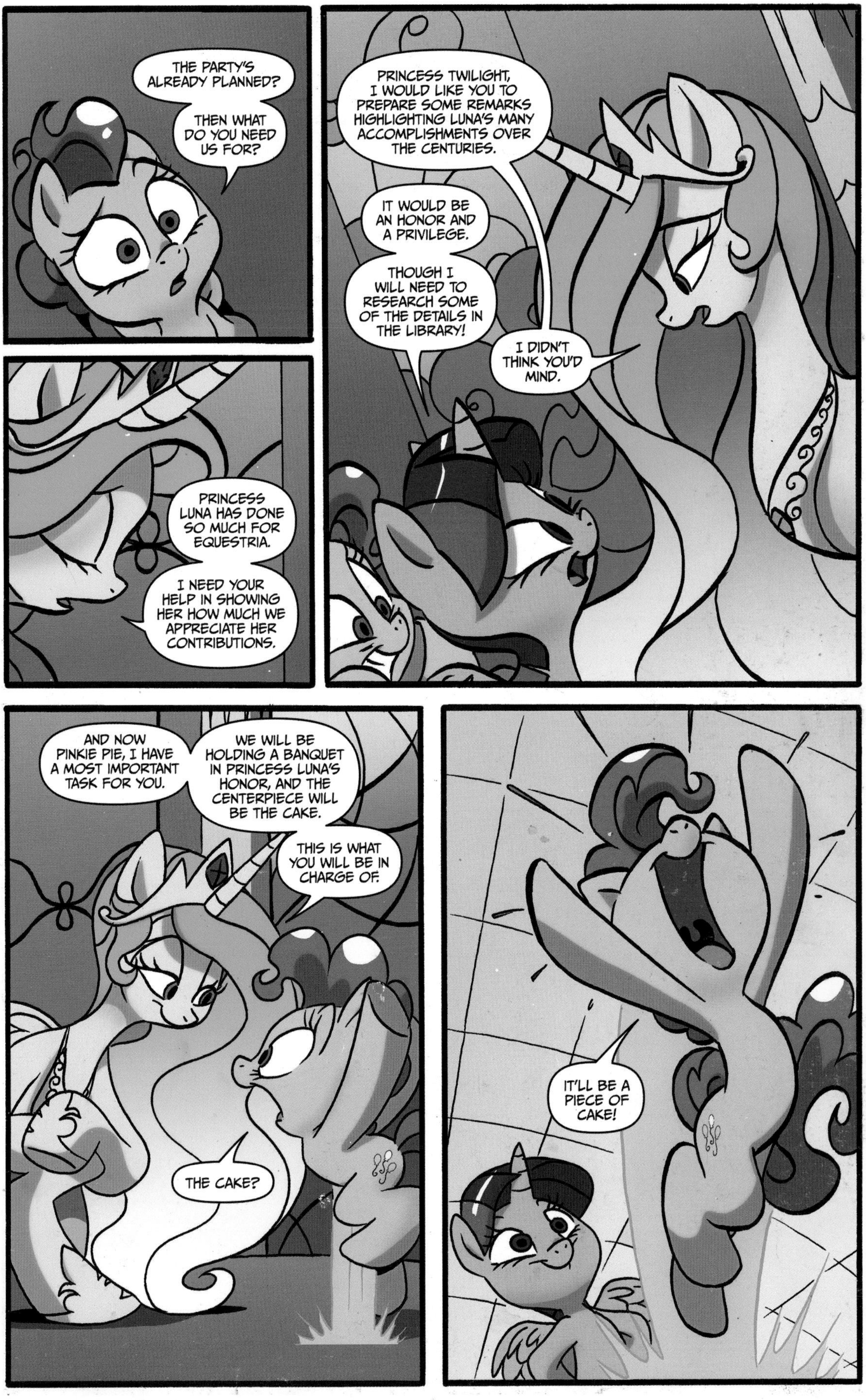
THE PARTY'S ALREADY PLANNED?
THEN WHAT DO YOU NEED US FOR?
PRINCESS LUNA HAS DONE SO MUCH FOR EQUESTRIA.
I NEED YOUR HELP IN SHOWING HER HOW MUCH WE APPRECIATE HER CONTRIBUTIONS.
PRINCESS TWILIGHT, I WOULD LIKE YOU TO PREPARE SOME REMARKS HIGHLIGHTING LUNA'S MANY ACCOMPLISHMENTS OVER THE CENTURIES.
IT WOULD BE AN HONOR AND A PRIVILEGE.
THOUGH I WILL NEED TO RESEARCH SOME OF THE DETAILS IN THE LIBRARY!
I DIDN'T THINK YOU'D MIND.
AND NOW PINKIE PIE, I HAVE A MOST IMPORTANT TASK FOR YOU.
WE WILL BE HOLDING A BANQUET IN PRINCESS LUNA'S HONOR, AND THE CENTERPIECE WILL BE THE CAKE.
THIS IS WHAT YOU WILL BE IN CHARGE OF.
THE CAKE?
IT'LL BE A PIECE OF CAKE!

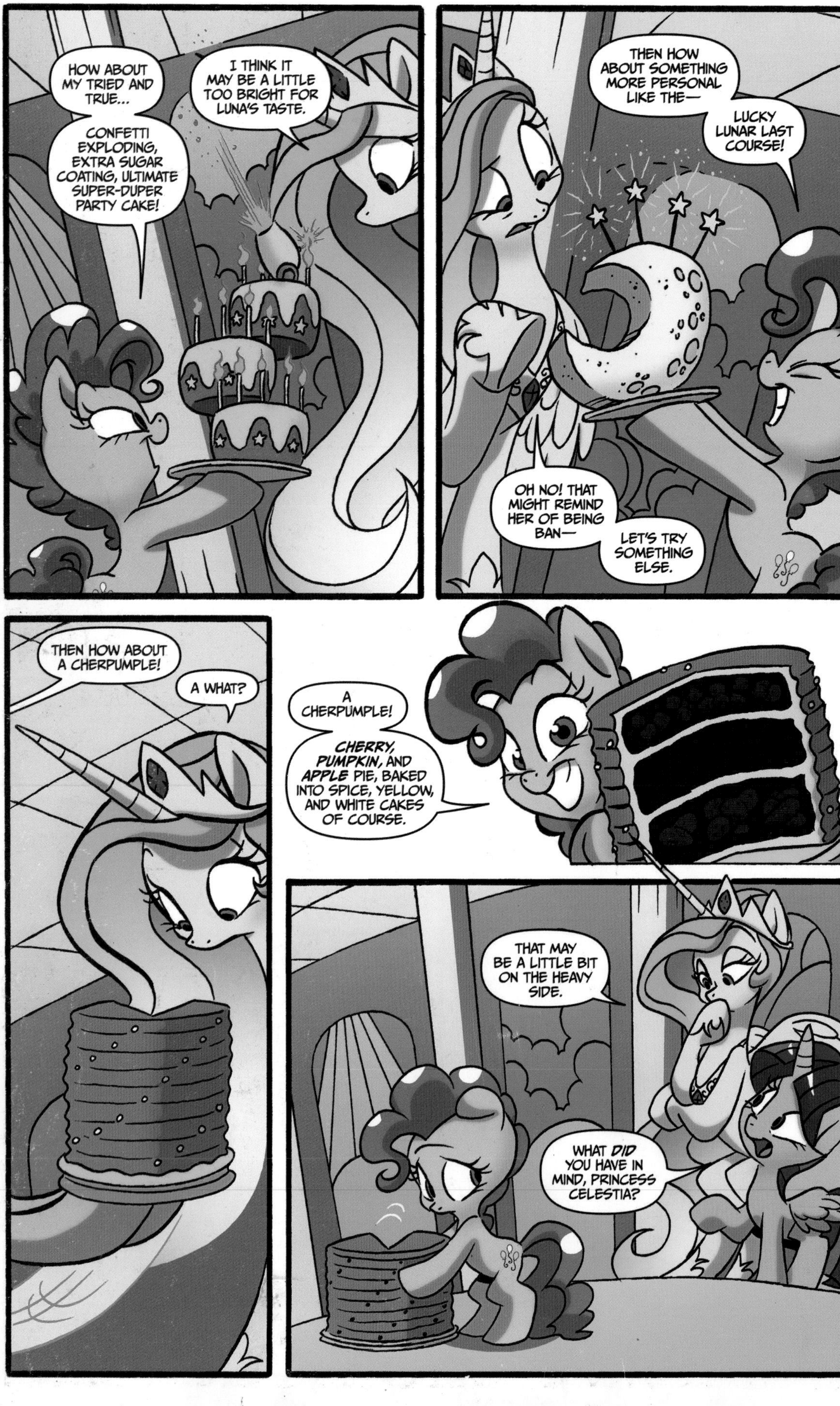
HOW ABOUT MY TRIED AND TRUE...
CONFETTI EXPLODING, EXTRA SUGAR COATING, ULTIMATE SUPER-DUPER PARTY CAKE!
I THINK IT MAY BE A LITTLE TOO BRIGHT FOR LUNA'S TASTE.
THEN HOW ABOUT SOMETHING MORE PERSONAL LIKE THE—
LUCKY LUNAR LAST COURSE!
OH NO! THAT MIGHT REMIND HER OF BEING BAN—
LET'S TRY SOMETHING ELSE.
THEN HOW ABOUT A CHERPUMPLE!
A WHAT?
A CHERPUMPLE!
CHERRY, PUMPKIN, AND *APPLE* PIE, BAKED INTO SPICE, YELLOW, AND WHITE CAKES OF COURSE.
THAT MAY BE A LITTLE BIT ON THE HEAVY SIDE.
WHAT *DID* YOU HAVE IN MIND, PRINCESS CELESTIA?

JUST SOMETHING FUN, EXCITING, AND GRAND.

YET ELEGANT AND BEFITTING EQUESTRIAN ROYALTY.

YOU BOTH HAVE THE RESOURCES OF CANTERLOT AT YOUR DISPOSAL.

I HAVE EVERY BIT OF CONFIDENCE IN BOTH OF YOU.

NOW, IF YOU'LL EXCUSE ME, I HAVE MUCH TO ATTEND TO, BUT WILL CHECK IN SHORTLY.

FUN, EXCITING, AND GRAND, YET ELEGANT AND BEFITTING ROYALTY?

WHAT DOES THAT EVEN MEAN?

I'M SURE YOU'LL FIGURE IT OUT, PINKIE.

I'M NOT SO SURE, TWILIGHT.

I SHOWED HER SOME OF MY BEST STUFF BACK THERE AND SHE DIDN'T SEEM TO LIKE ANY OF IT.

NOW, PINKIE, OUT OF EVERYPONY IN EQUESTRIA, SHE PICKED YOU TO DO THIS.

YOU'RE THE PERFECT PONY!

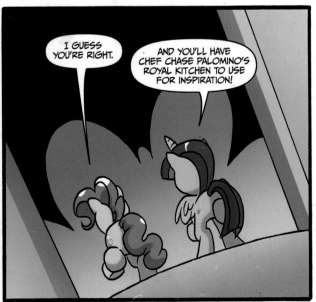

I GUESS YOU'RE RIGHT.

AND YOU'LL HAVE CHEF CHASE PALOMINO'S ROYAL KITCHEN TO USE FOR INSPIRATION!

YOU'LL BE FINE, PINKIE!

I'LL BE AT THE LIBRARY IF YOU NEED ME!

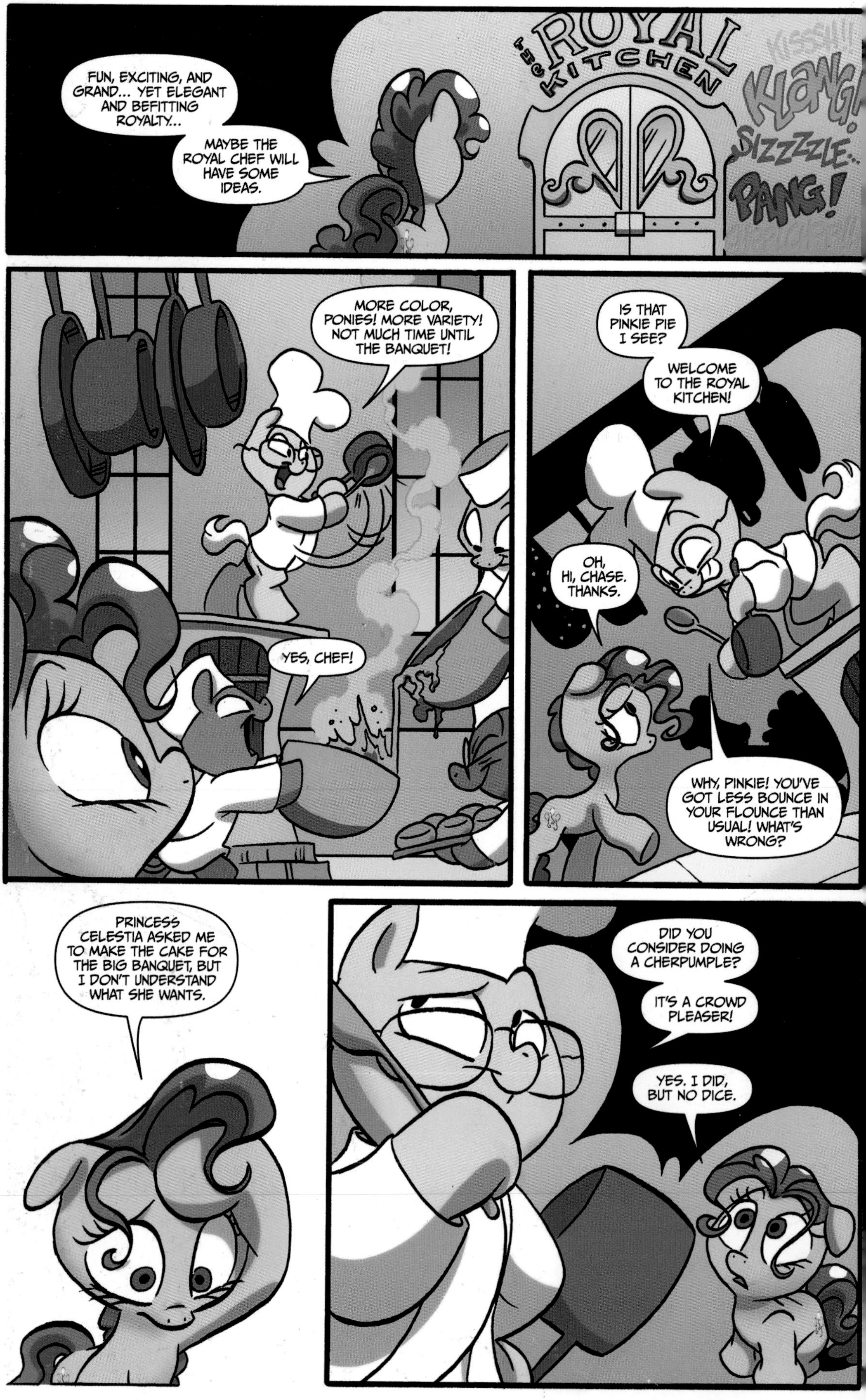
FUN, EXCITING, AND GRAND... YET ELEGANT AND BEFITTING ROYALTY...
MAYBE THE ROYAL CHEF WILL HAVE SOME IDEAS.
ROYAL KITCHEN
KISSSH!!
KLANG!
SIZZZZLE...
PANG!
MORE COLOR, PONIES! MORE VARIETY! NOT MUCH TIME UNTIL THE BANQUET!
YES, CHEF!
IS THAT PINKIE PIE I SEE?
WELCOME TO THE ROYAL KITCHEN!
OH, HI, CHASE. THANKS.
WHY, PINKIE! YOU'VE GOT LESS BOUNCE IN YOUR FLOUNCE THAN USUAL! WHAT'S WRONG?
PRINCESS CELESTIA ASKED ME TO MAKE THE CAKE FOR THE BIG BANQUET, BUT I DON'T UNDERSTAND WHAT SHE WANTS.
DID YOU CONSIDER DOING A CHERPUMPLE?
IT'S A CROWD PLEASER!
YES. I DID, BUT NO DICE.

GEE, PINKIE, I DON'T KNOW WHAT TO TELL YOU.

WE'VE GOT OUR HOOVES FULL TRYING TO GET ALL THE FOOD TOGETHER FOR THE BANQUET.

BUT YOU'RE ONE OF EQUESTRIA'S MOST FABULOUS PONIES.

I'M SURE YOU'LL COME UP WITH SOMETHING.

YOU REALLY THINK SO?

THINK? I KNOW SO!

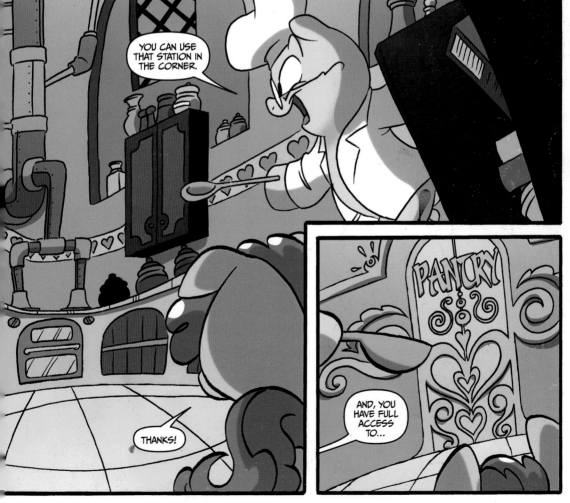

YOU CAN USE THAT STATION IN THE CORNER.

THANKS!

PANTRY

AND, YOU HAVE FULL ACCESS TO...

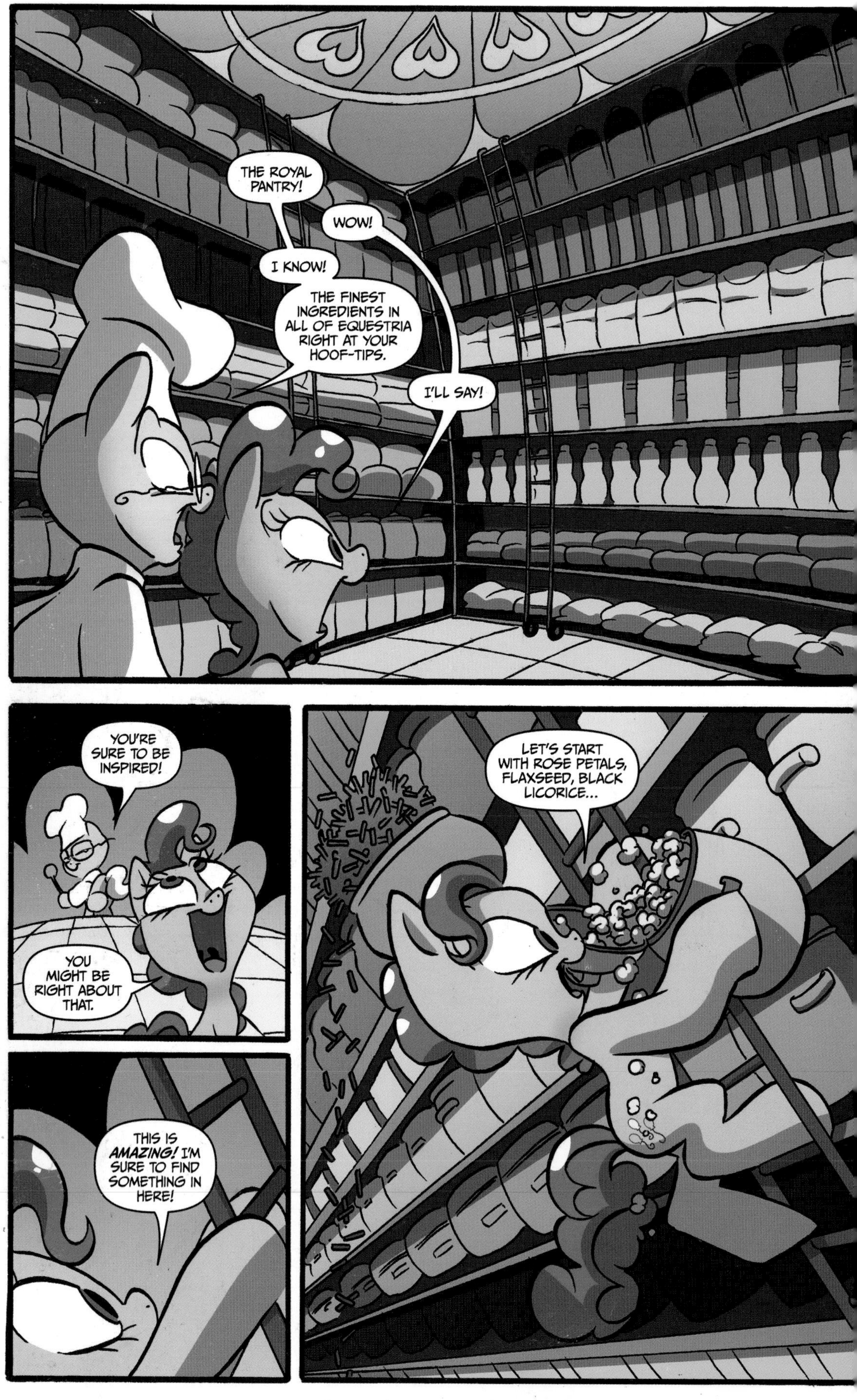
THE ROYAL PANTRY!
WOW!
I KNOW!
THE FINEST INGREDIENTS IN ALL OF EQUESTRIA RIGHT AT YOUR HOOF-TIPS.
I'LL SAY!
YOU'RE SURE TO BE INSPIRED!
YOU MIGHT BE RIGHT ABOUT THAT.
THIS IS *AMAZING!* I'M SURE TO FIND SOMETHING IN HERE!
LET'S START WITH ROSE PETALS, FLAXSEED, BLACK LICORICE...

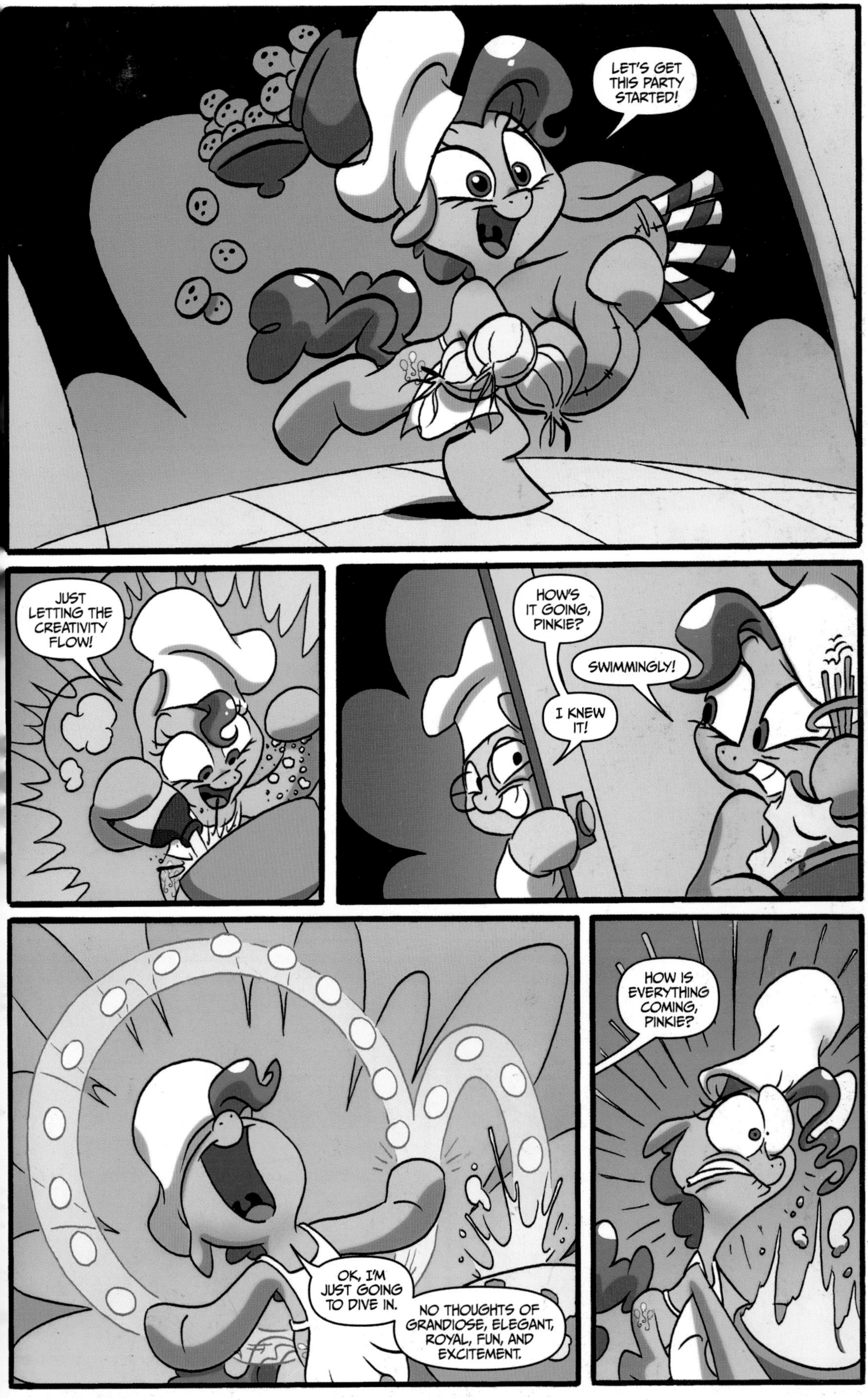
LET'S GET THIS PARTY STARTED!
JUST LETTING THE CREATIVITY FLOW!
HOW'S IT GOING, PINKIE?
SWIMMINGLY!
I KNEW IT!
OK, I'M JUST GOING TO DIVE IN.
NO THOUGHTS OF GRANDIOSE, ELEGANT, ROYAL, FUN, AND EXCITEMENT.
HOW IS EVERYTHING COMING, PINKIE?

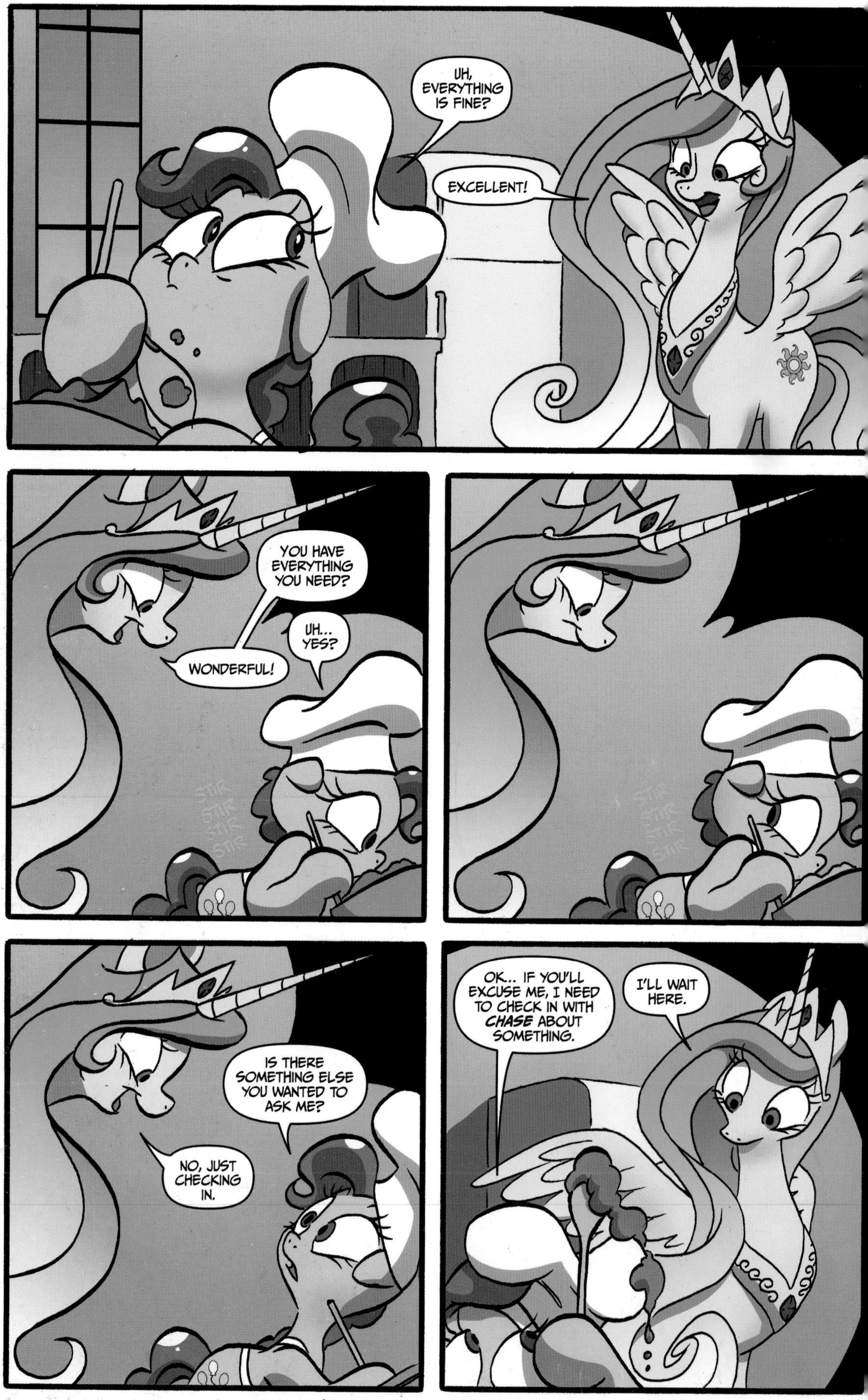

UH, EVERYTHING IS FINE?
EXCELLENT!
YOU HAVE EVERYTHING YOU NEED?
UH... YES?
WONDERFUL!
STIR STIR STIR STIR
STIR STIR STIR STIR
IS THERE SOMETHING ELSE YOU WANTED TO ASK ME?
NO, JUST CHECKING IN.
OK... IF YOU'LL EXCUSE ME, I NEED TO CHECK IN WITH *CHASE* ABOUT SOMETHING.
I'LL WAIT HERE.

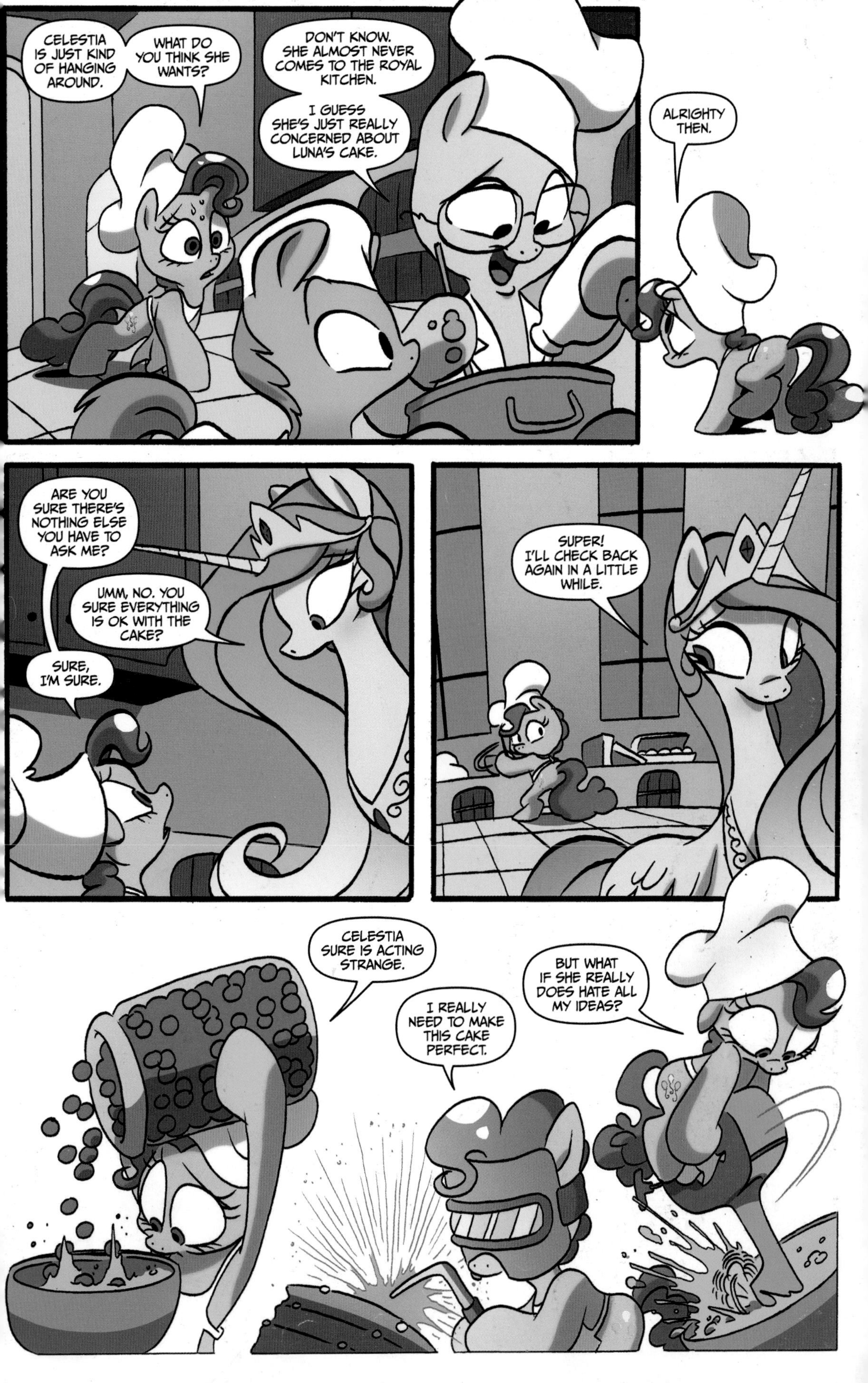
CELESTIA IS JUST KIND OF HANGING AROUND.
WHAT DO YOU THINK SHE WANTS?
DON'T KNOW. SHE ALMOST NEVER COMES TO THE ROYAL KITCHEN.
I GUESS SHE'S JUST REALLY CONCERNED ABOUT LUNA'S CAKE.
ALRIGHTY THEN.
ARE YOU SURE THERE'S NOTHING ELSE YOU HAVE TO ASK ME?
UMM, NO. YOU SURE EVERYTHING IS OK WITH THE CAKE?
SURE, I'M SURE.
SUPER! I'LL CHECK BACK AGAIN IN A LITTLE WHILE.
CELESTIA SURE IS ACTING STRANGE.
I REALLY NEED TO MAKE THIS CAKE PERFECT.
BUT WHAT IF SHE REALLY DOES HATE ALL MY IDEAS?

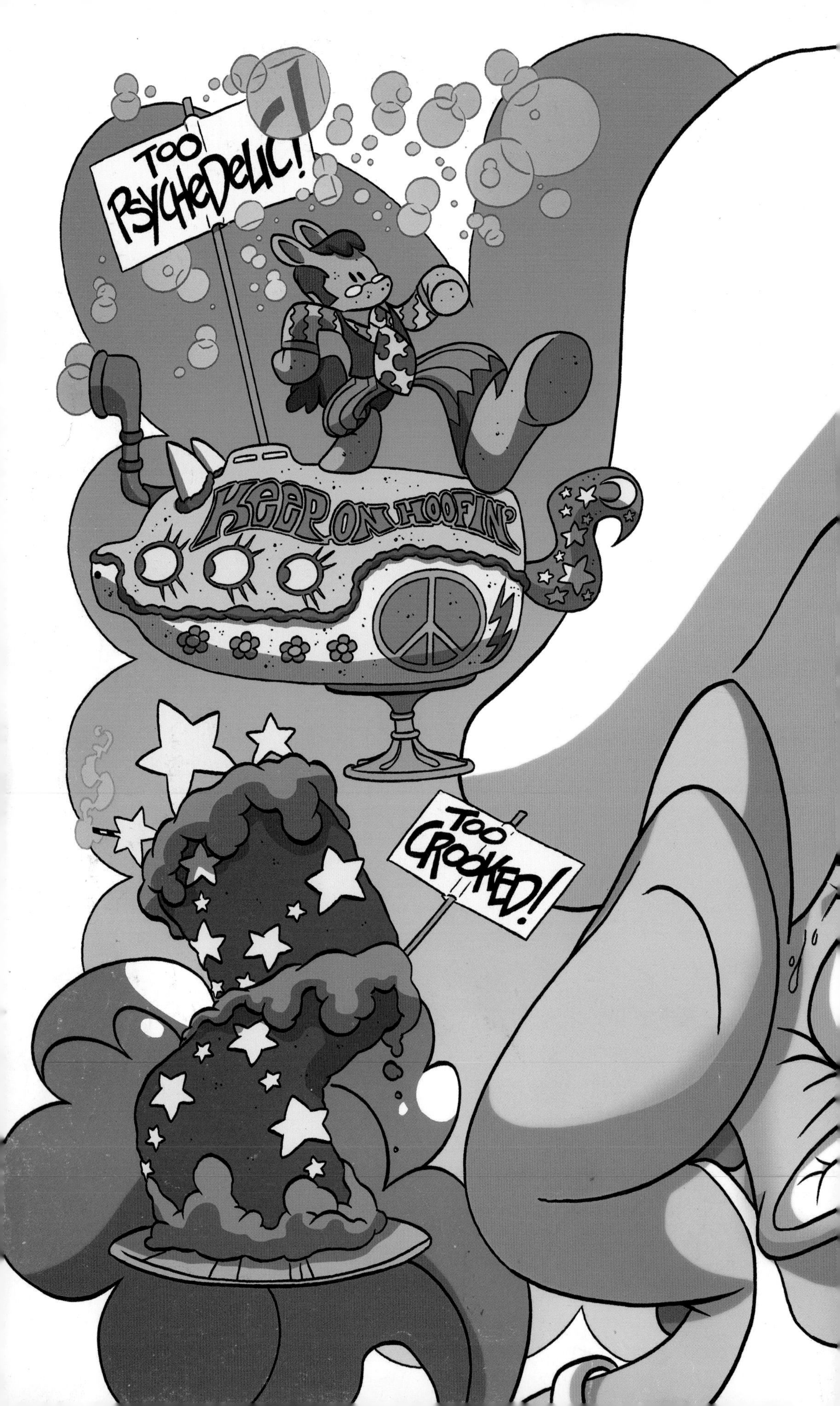
TOO PSYCHEDELIC!
KEEP ON HOOFIN'
TOO CROOKED!

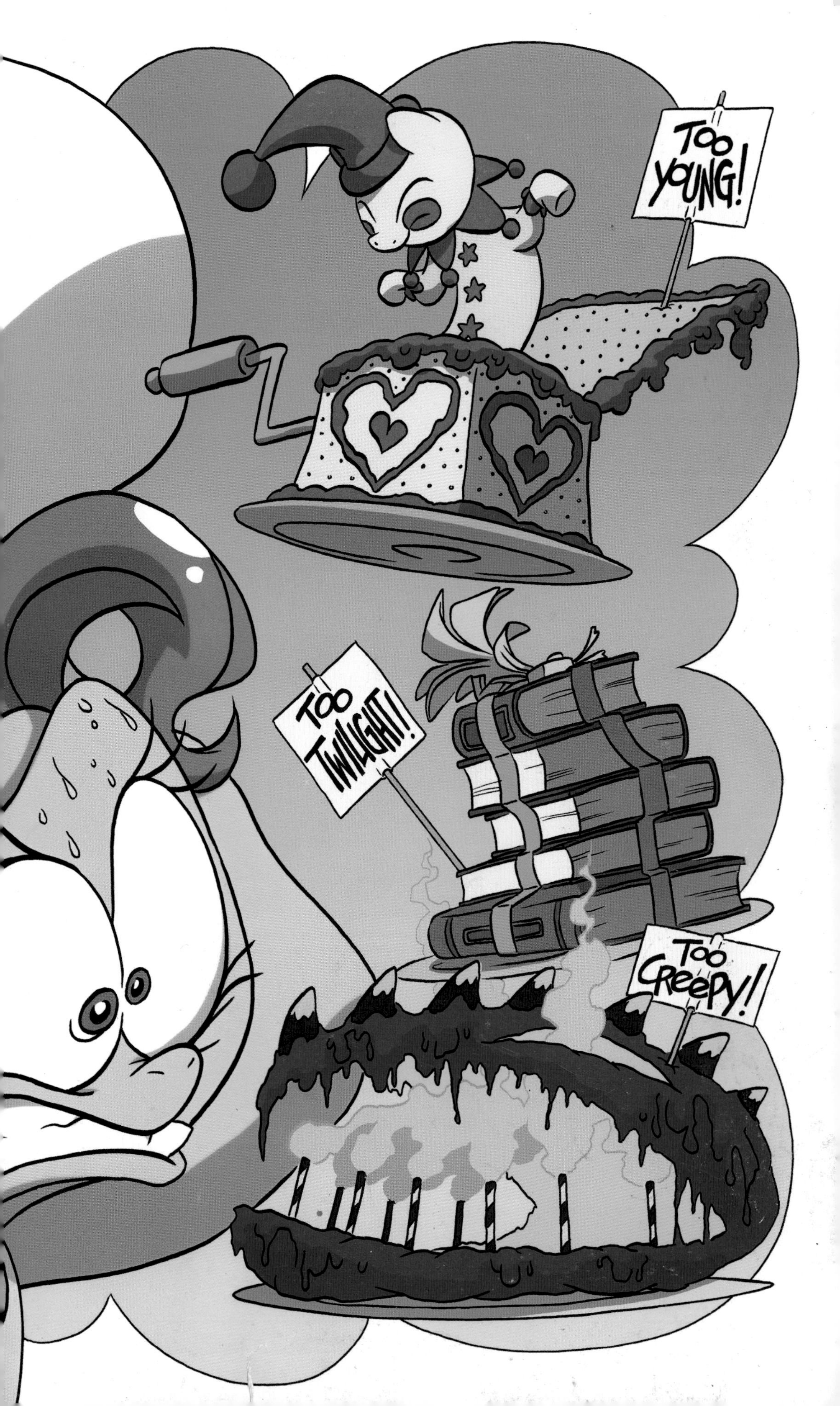
TOO YOUNG!
TOO TWILIGHT!
TOO CREEPY!

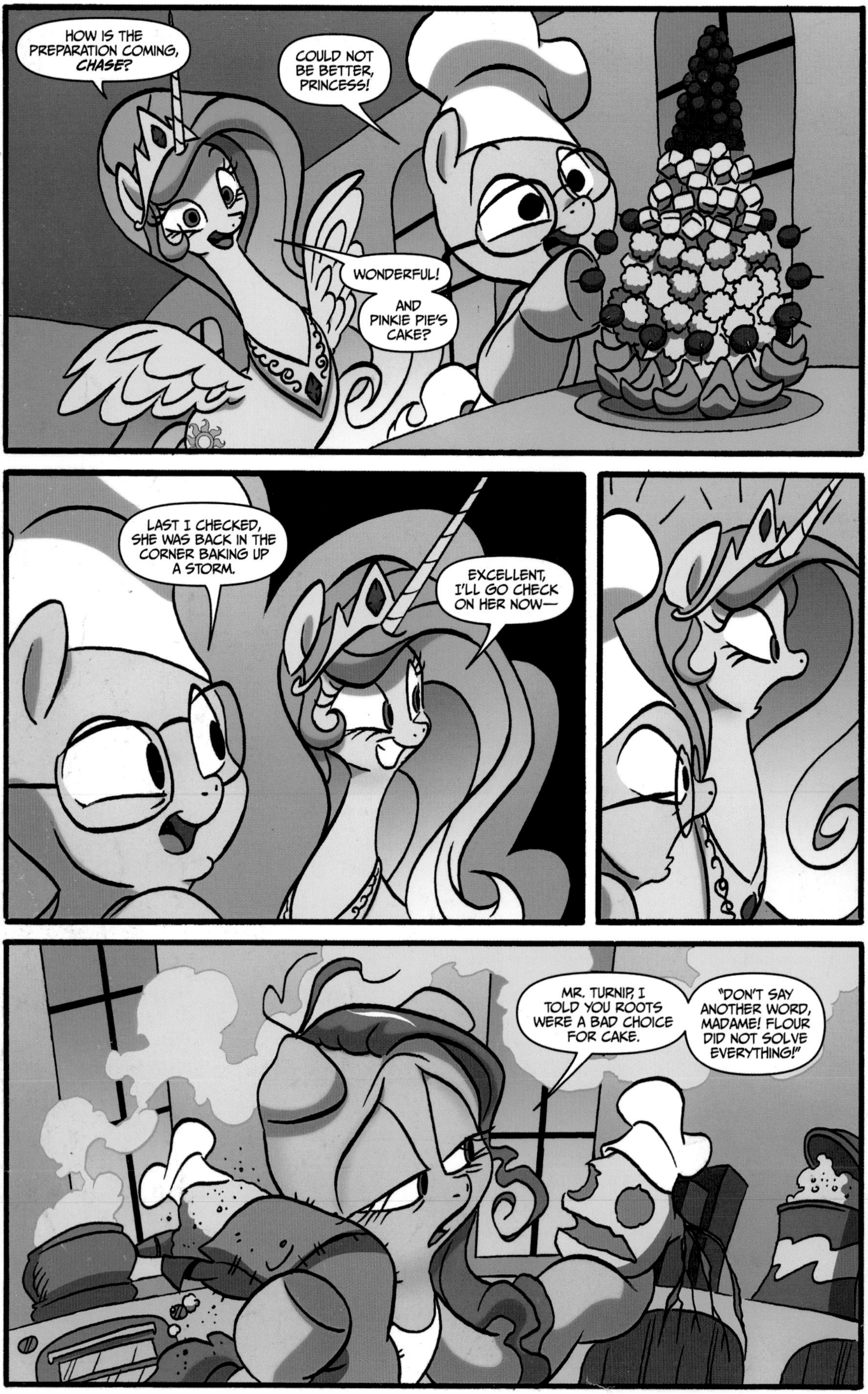

HOW IS THE PREPARATION COMING, *CHASE?*
COULD NOT BE BETTER, PRINCESS!
WONDERFUL!
AND PINKIE PIE'S CAKE?
LAST I CHECKED, SHE WAS BACK IN THE CORNER BAKING UP A STORM.
EXCELLENT, I'LL GO CHECK ON HER NOW—
MR. TURNIP, I TOLD YOU ROOTS WERE A BAD CHOICE FOR CAKE.
"DON'T SAY ANOTHER WORD, MADAME! FLOUR DID NOT SOLVE EVERYTHING!"

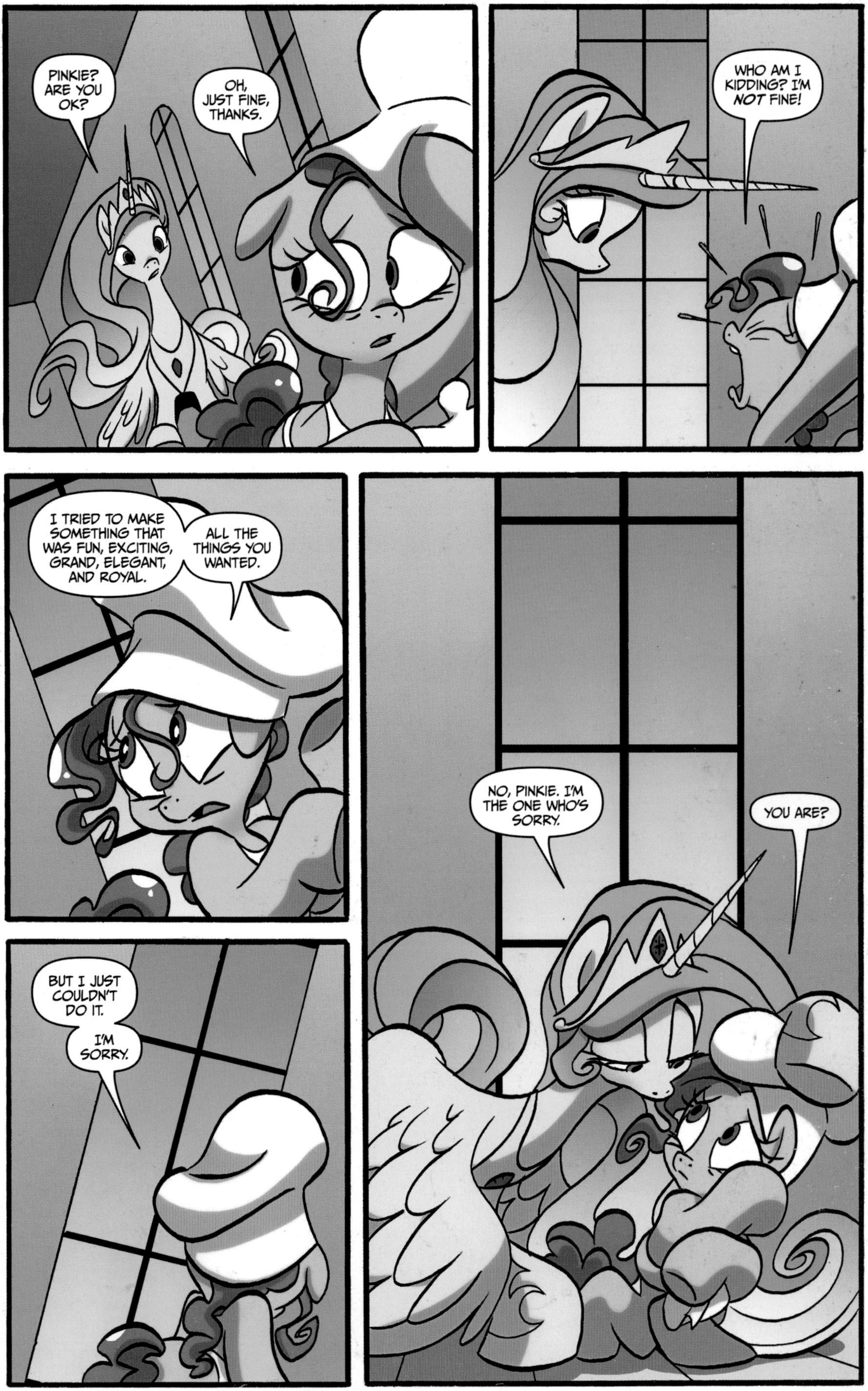
PINKIE? ARE YOU OK?
OH, JUST FINE, THANKS.
WHO AM I KIDDING? I'M *NOT* FINE!
I TRIED TO MAKE SOMETHING THAT WAS FUN, EXCITING, GRAND, ELEGANT, AND ROYAL.
ALL THE THINGS YOU WANTED.
BUT I JUST COULDN'T DO IT.
I'M SORRY.
NO, PINKIE. I'M THE ONE WHO'S SORRY.
YOU ARE?

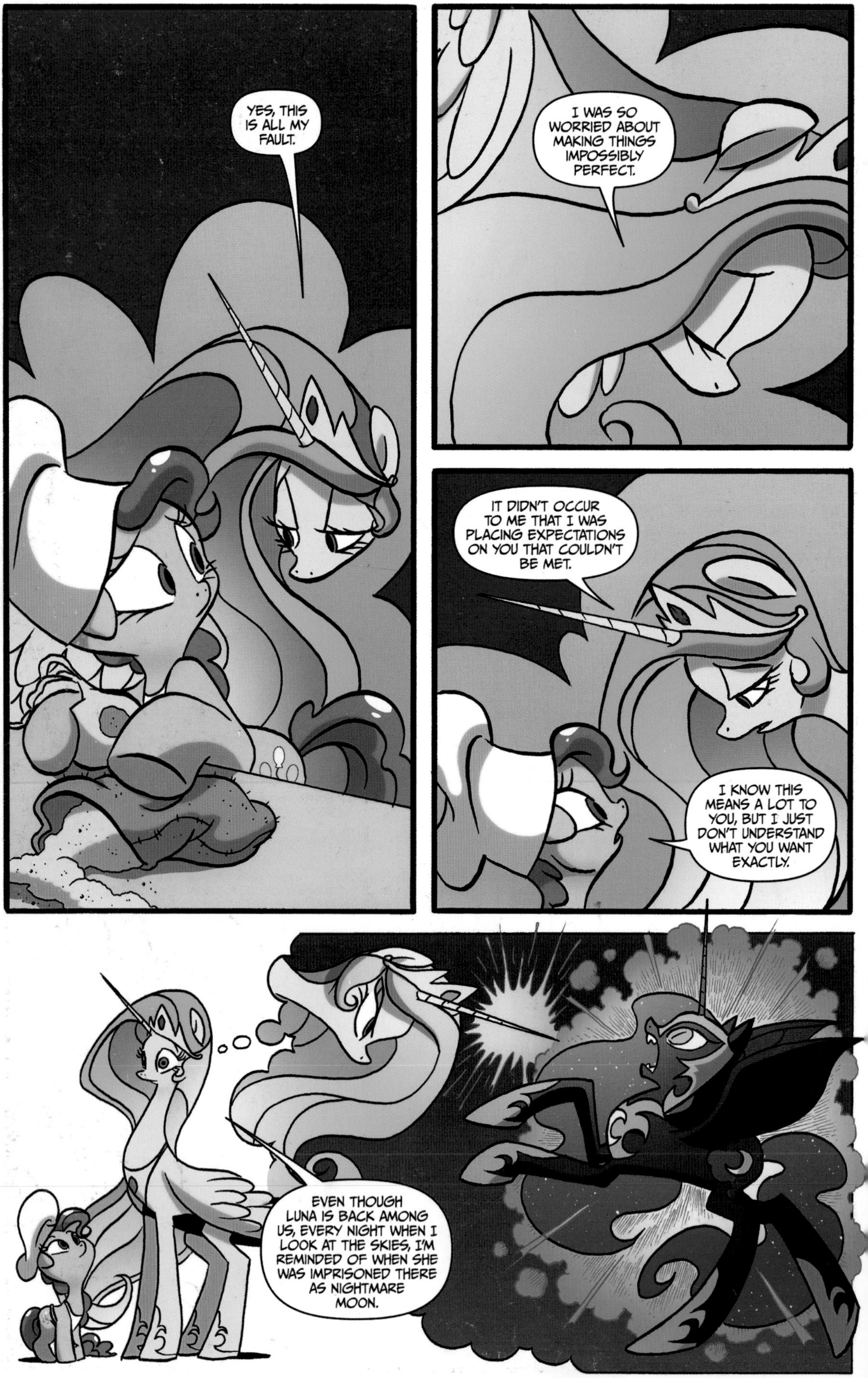
YES, THIS IS ALL MY FAULT.
I WAS SO WORRIED ABOUT MAKING THINGS IMPOSSIBLY PERFECT.
IT DIDN'T OCCUR TO ME THAT I WAS PLACING EXPECTATIONS ON YOU THAT COULDN'T BE MET.
I KNOW THIS MEANS A LOT TO YOU, BUT I JUST DON'T UNDERSTAND WHAT YOU WANT EXACTLY.
EVEN THOUGH LUNA IS BACK AMONG US, EVERY NIGHT WHEN I LOOK AT THE SKIES, I'M REMINDED OF WHEN SHE WAS IMPRISONED THERE AS NIGHTMARE MOON.

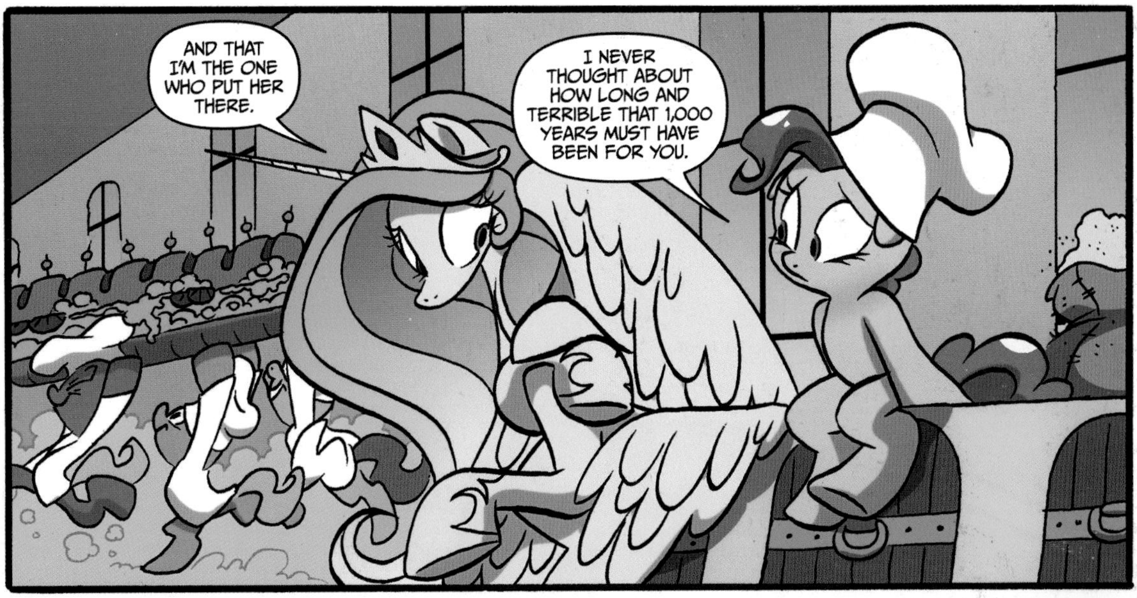
AND THAT I'M THE ONE WHO PUT HER THERE.
I NEVER THOUGHT ABOUT HOW LONG AND TERRIBLE THAT 1,000 YEARS MUST HAVE BEEN FOR YOU.

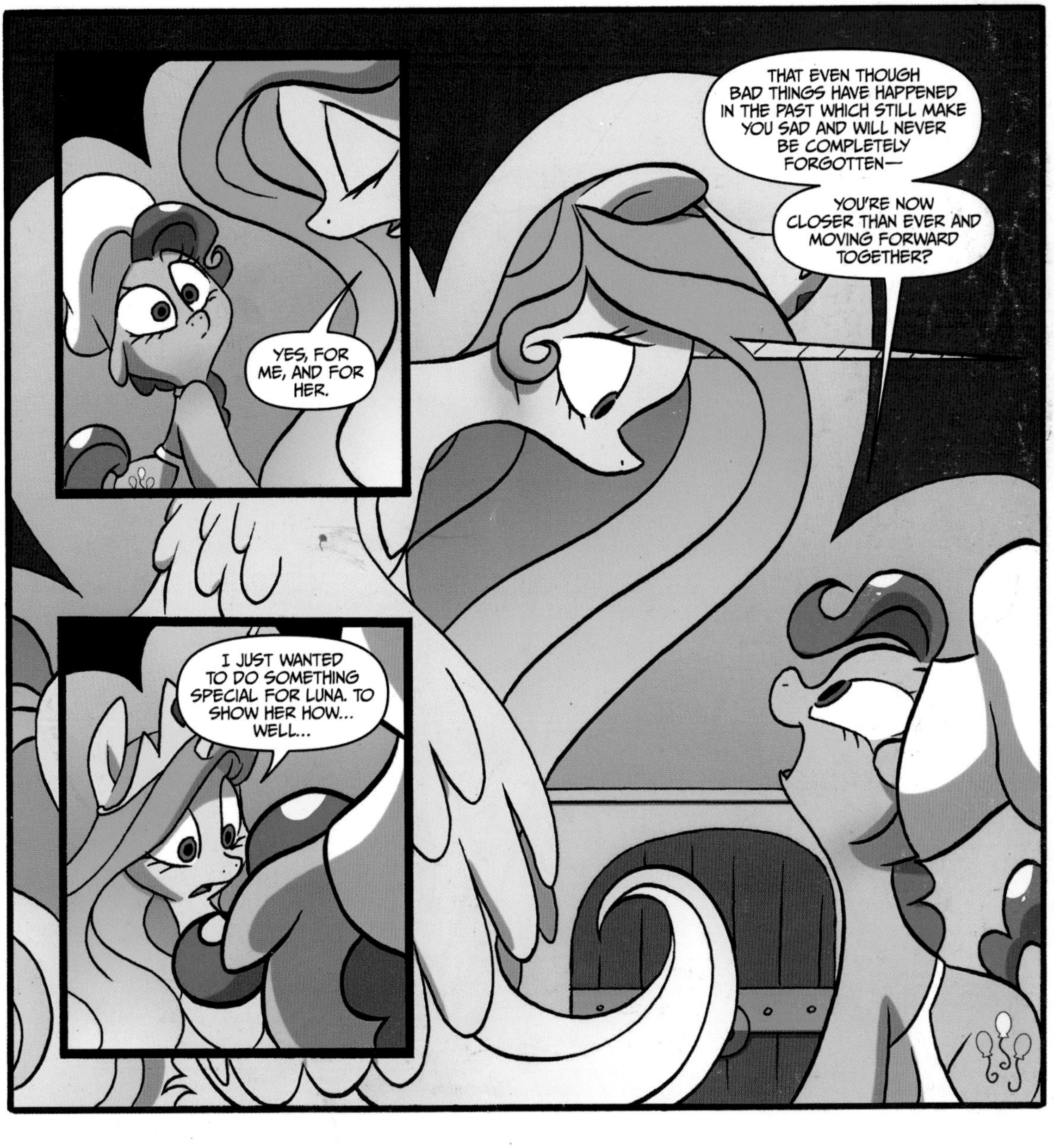
YES, FOR ME, AND FOR HER.
THAT EVEN THOUGH BAD THINGS HAVE HAPPENED IN THE PAST WHICH STILL MAKE YOU SAD AND WILL NEVER BE COMPLETELY FORGOTTEN—
YOU'RE NOW CLOSER THAN EVER AND MOVING FORWARD TOGETHER?
I JUST WANTED TO DO SOMETHING SPECIAL FOR LUNA. TO SHOW HER HOW... WELL...

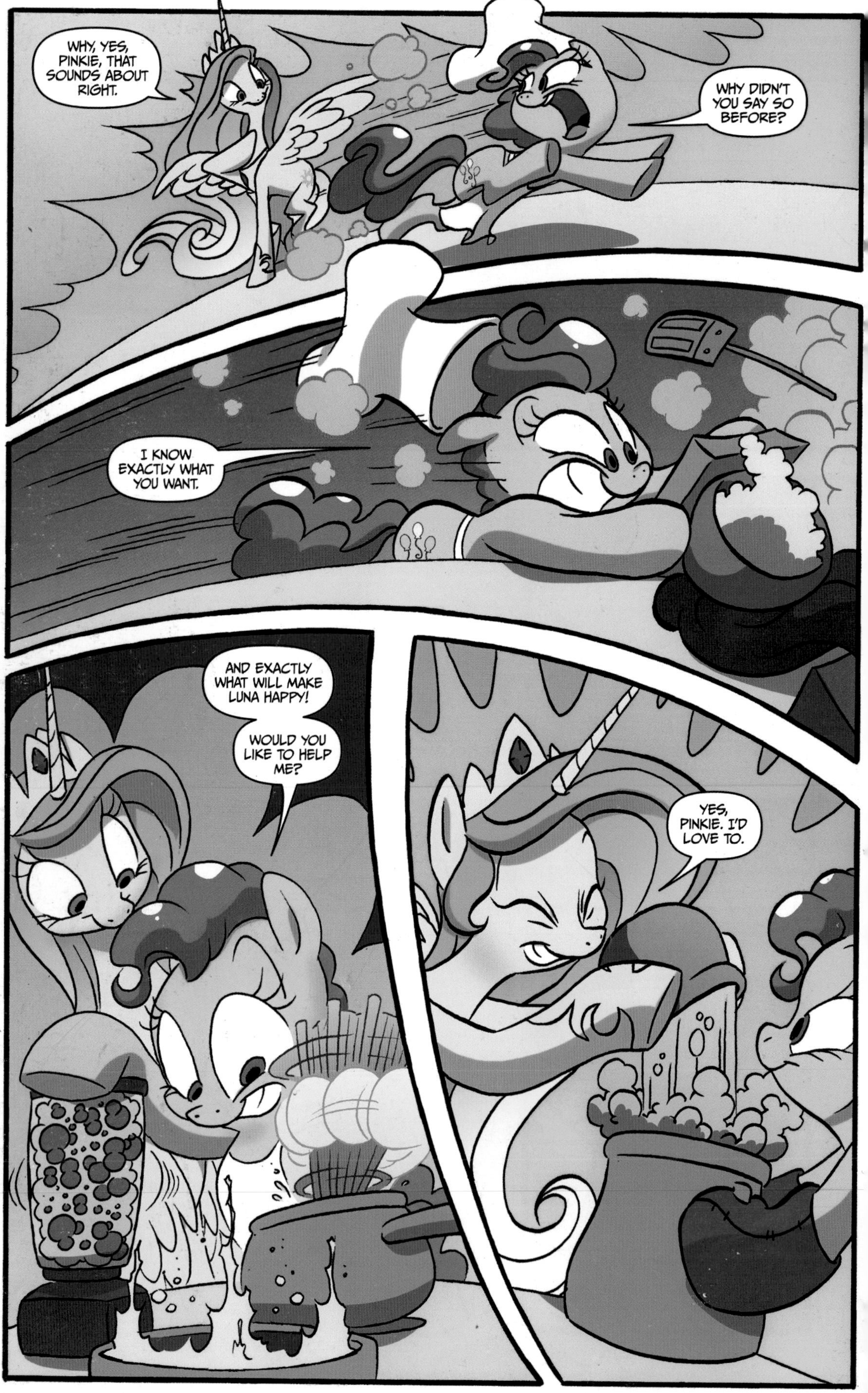
WHY, YES, PINKIE, THAT SOUNDS ABOUT RIGHT.
WHY DIDN'T YOU SAY SO BEFORE?
I KNOW EXACTLY WHAT YOU WANT.
AND EXACTLY WHAT WILL MAKE LUNA HAPPY!
WOULD YOU LIKE TO HELP ME?
YES, PINKIE. I'D LOVE TO.

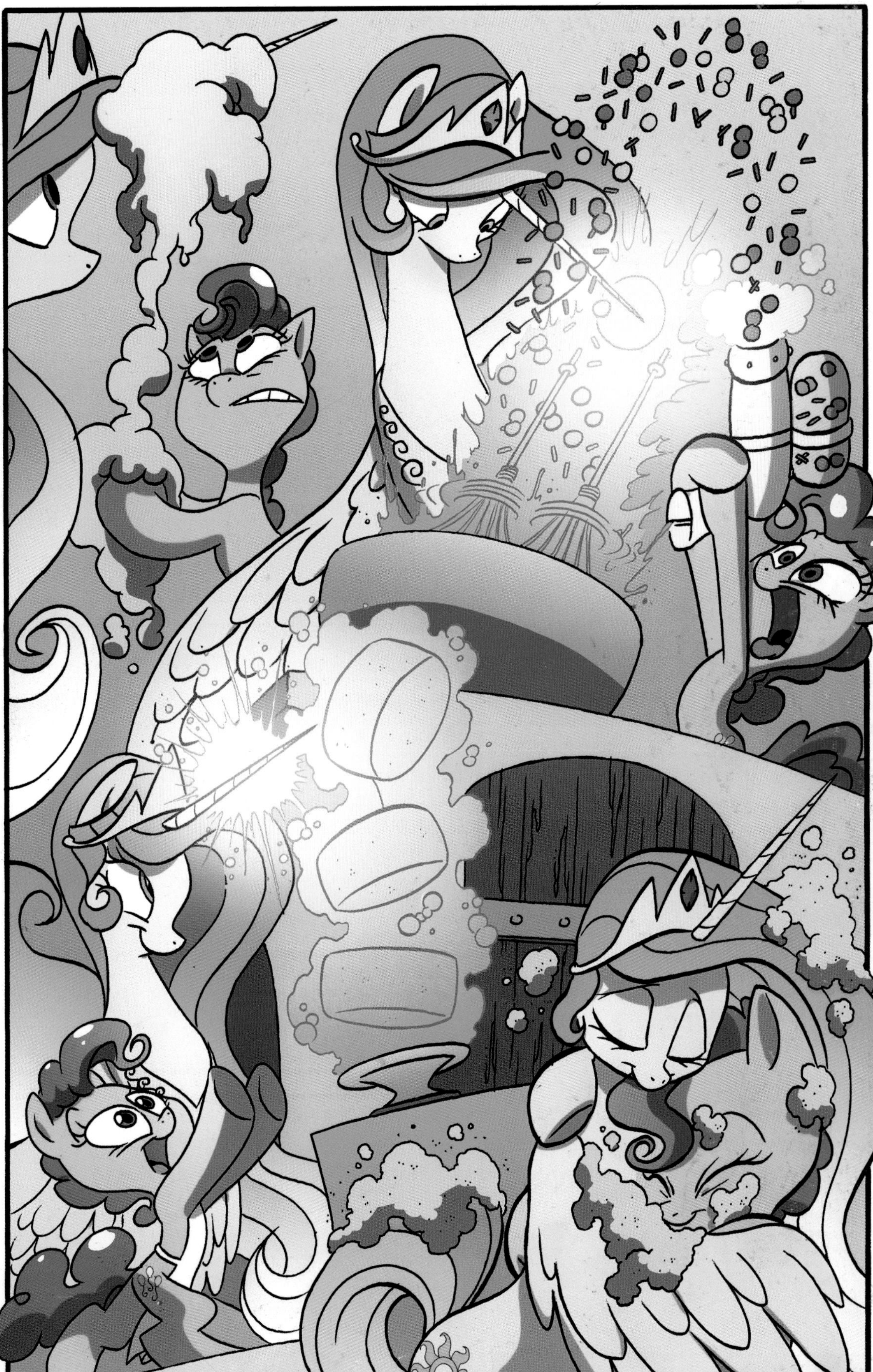

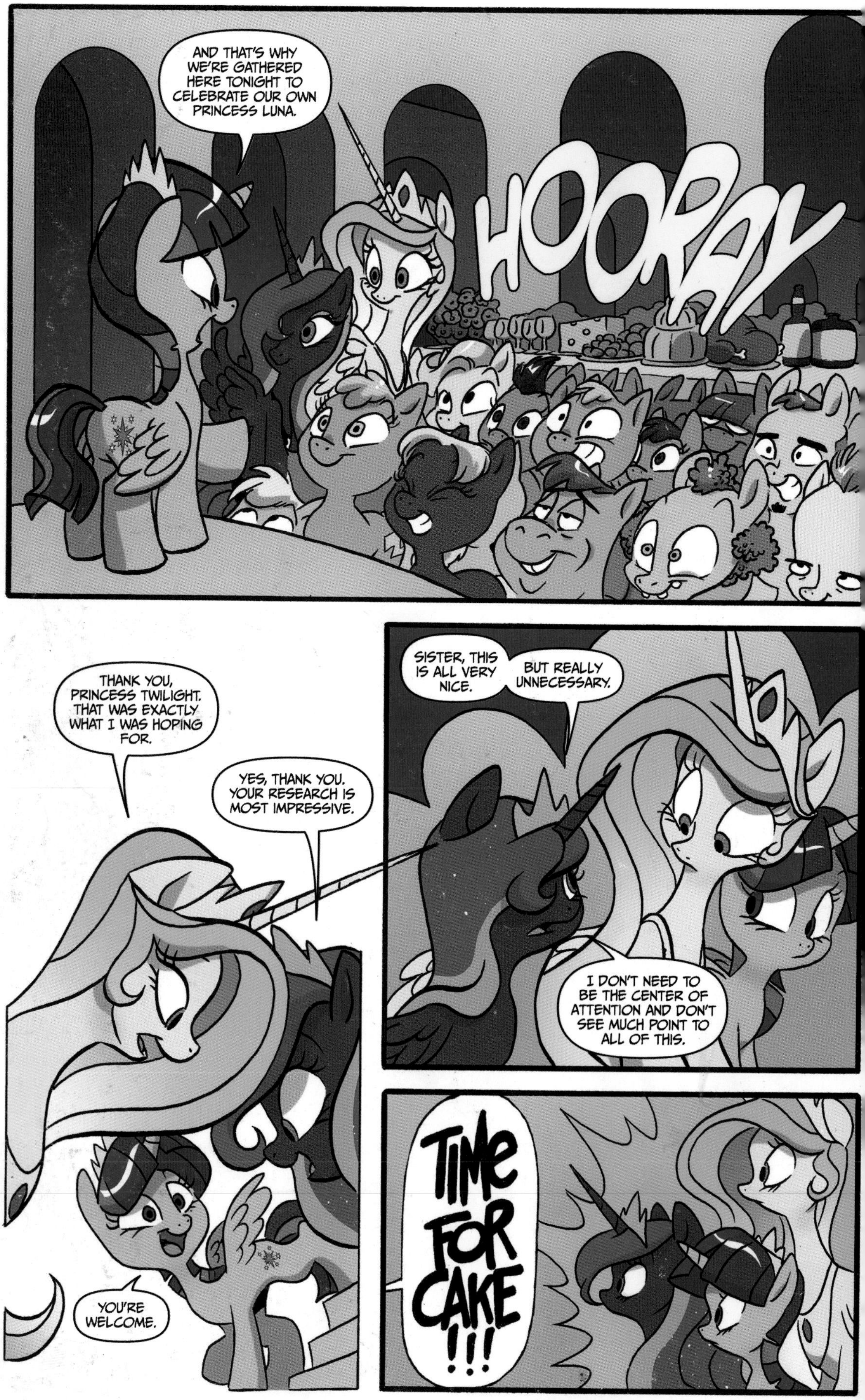
AND THAT'S WHY WE'RE GATHERED HERE TONIGHT TO CELEBRATE OUR OWN PRINCESS LUNA.
HOORAY
THANK YOU, PRINCESS TWILIGHT. THAT WAS EXACTLY WHAT I WAS HOPING FOR.
YES, THANK YOU. YOUR RESEARCH IS MOST IMPRESSIVE.
YOU'RE WELCOME.
SISTER, THIS IS ALL VERY NICE.
BUT REALLY UNNECESSARY.
I DON'T NEED TO BE THE CENTER OF ATTENTION AND DON'T SEE MUCH POINT TO ALL OF THIS.
TIME FOR CAKE!!!

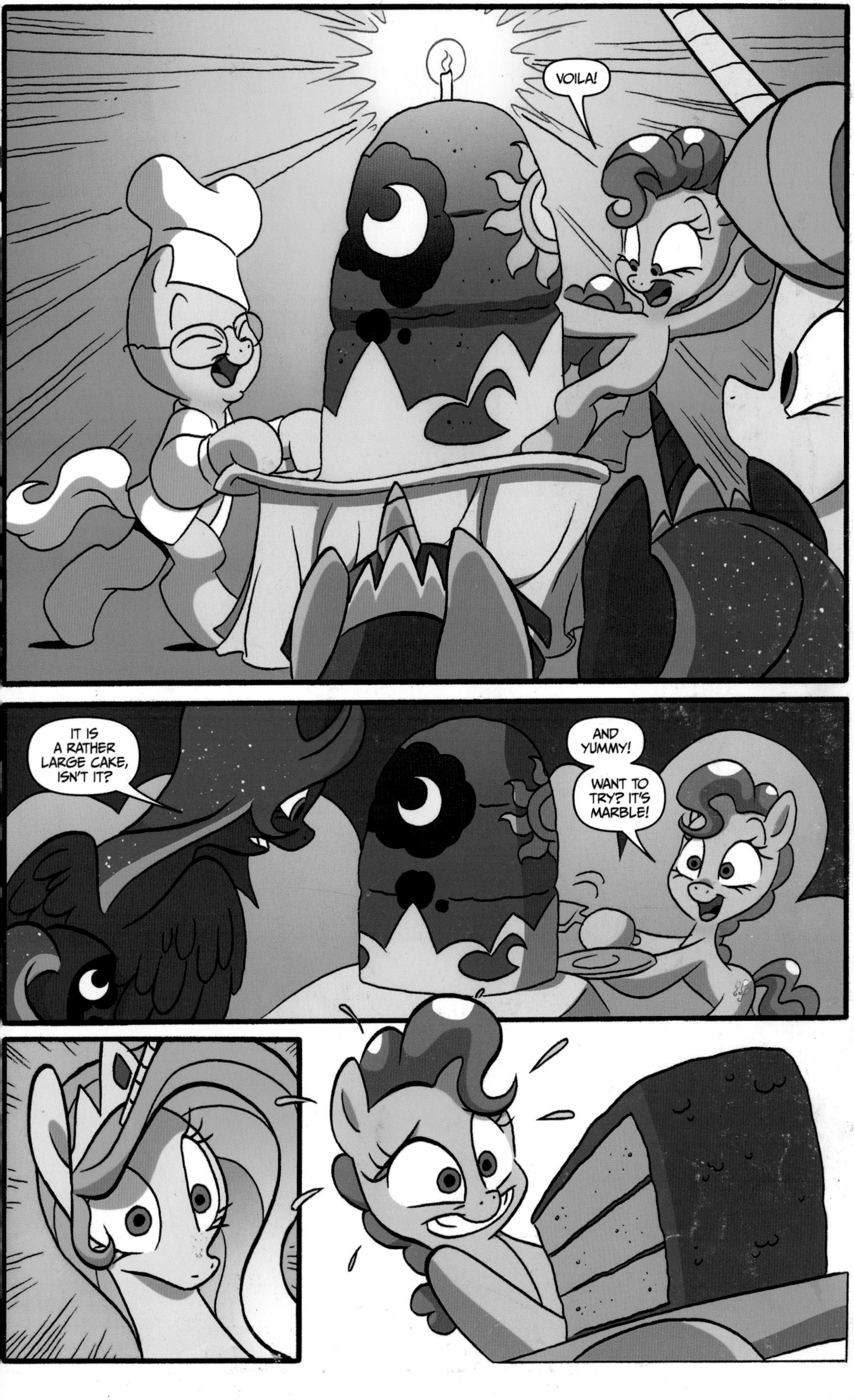
VOILA!
IT IS A RATHER LARGE CAKE, ISN'T IT?
AND YUMMY!
WANT TO TRY? IT'S MARBLE!

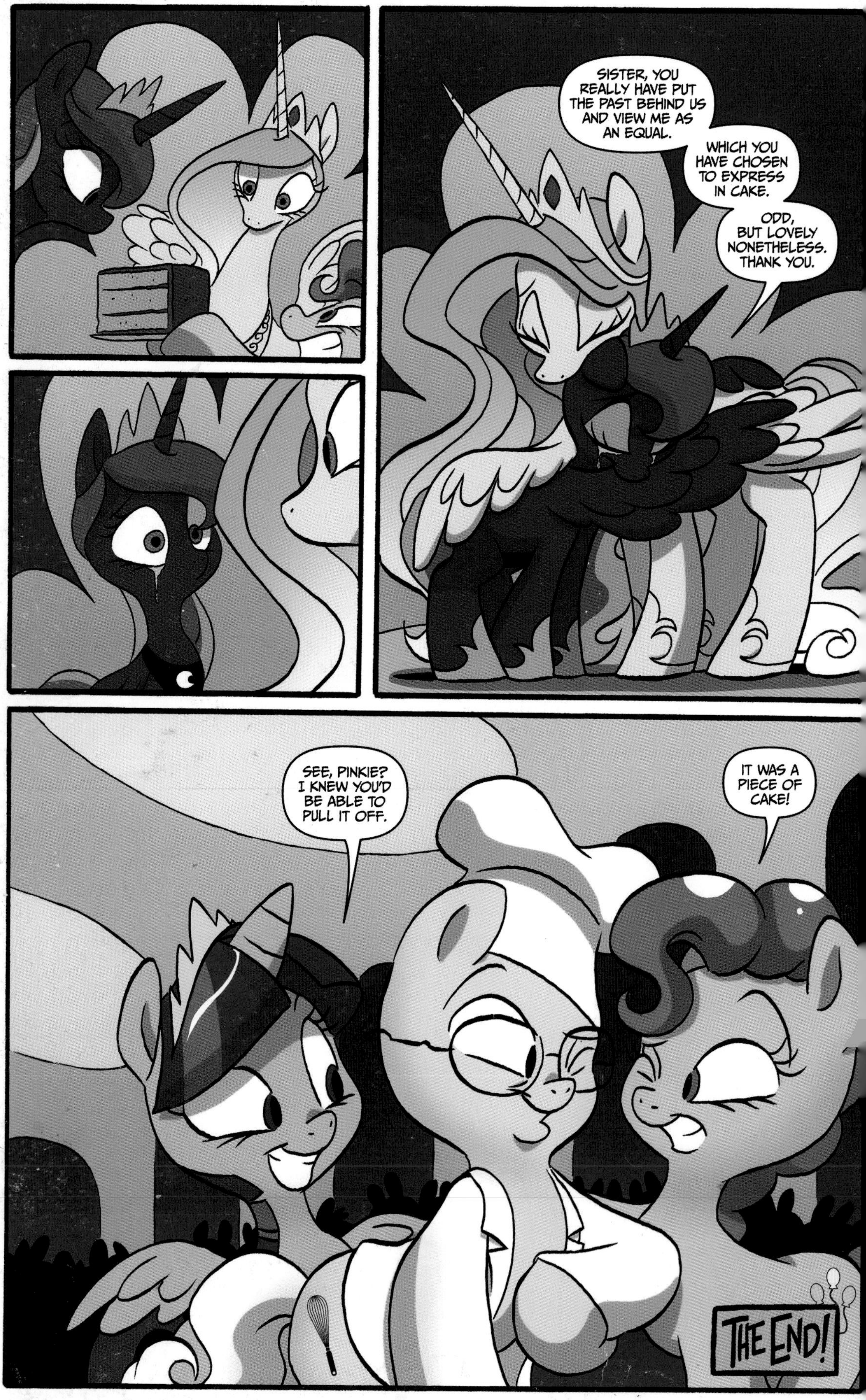
SISTER, YOU REALLY HAVE PUT THE PAST BEHIND US AND VIEW ME AS AN EQUAL.
WHICH YOU HAVE CHOSEN TO EXPRESS IN CAKE.
ODD, BUT LOVELY NONETHELESS. THANK YOU.
SEE, PINKIE? I KNEW YOU'D BE ABLE TO PULL IT OFF.
IT WAS A PIECE OF CAKE!
THE END!

my LITTLE PONY

FRIENDS FOREVER

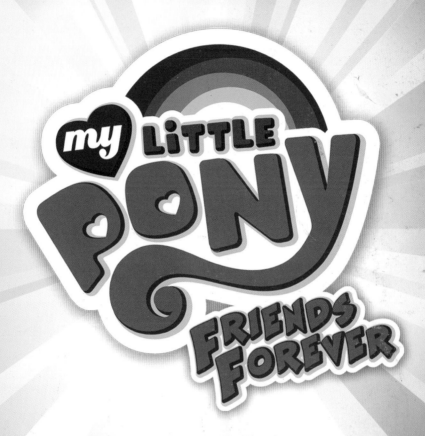

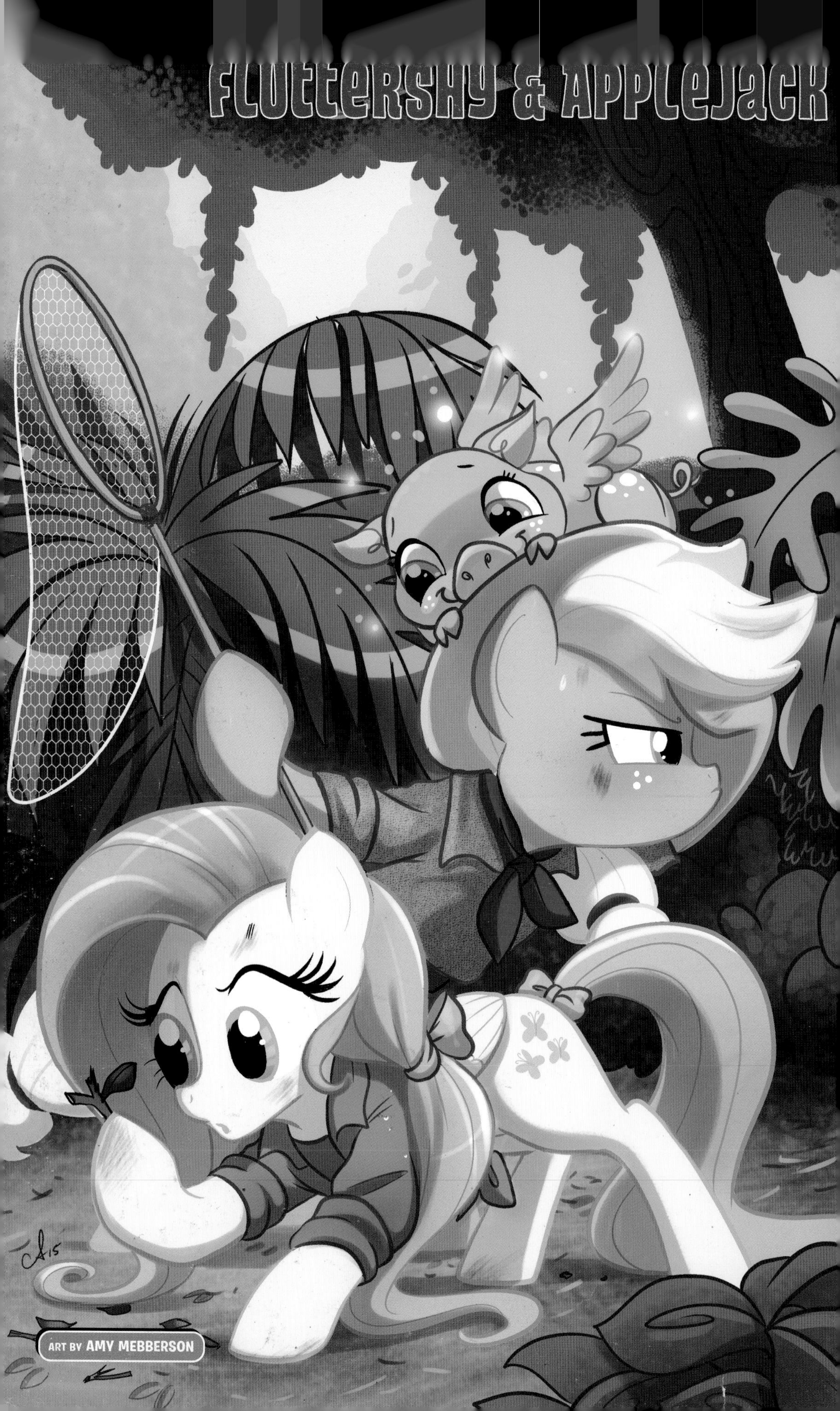
FLUTTERSHY & APPLEJACK
ART BY AMY MEBBERSON

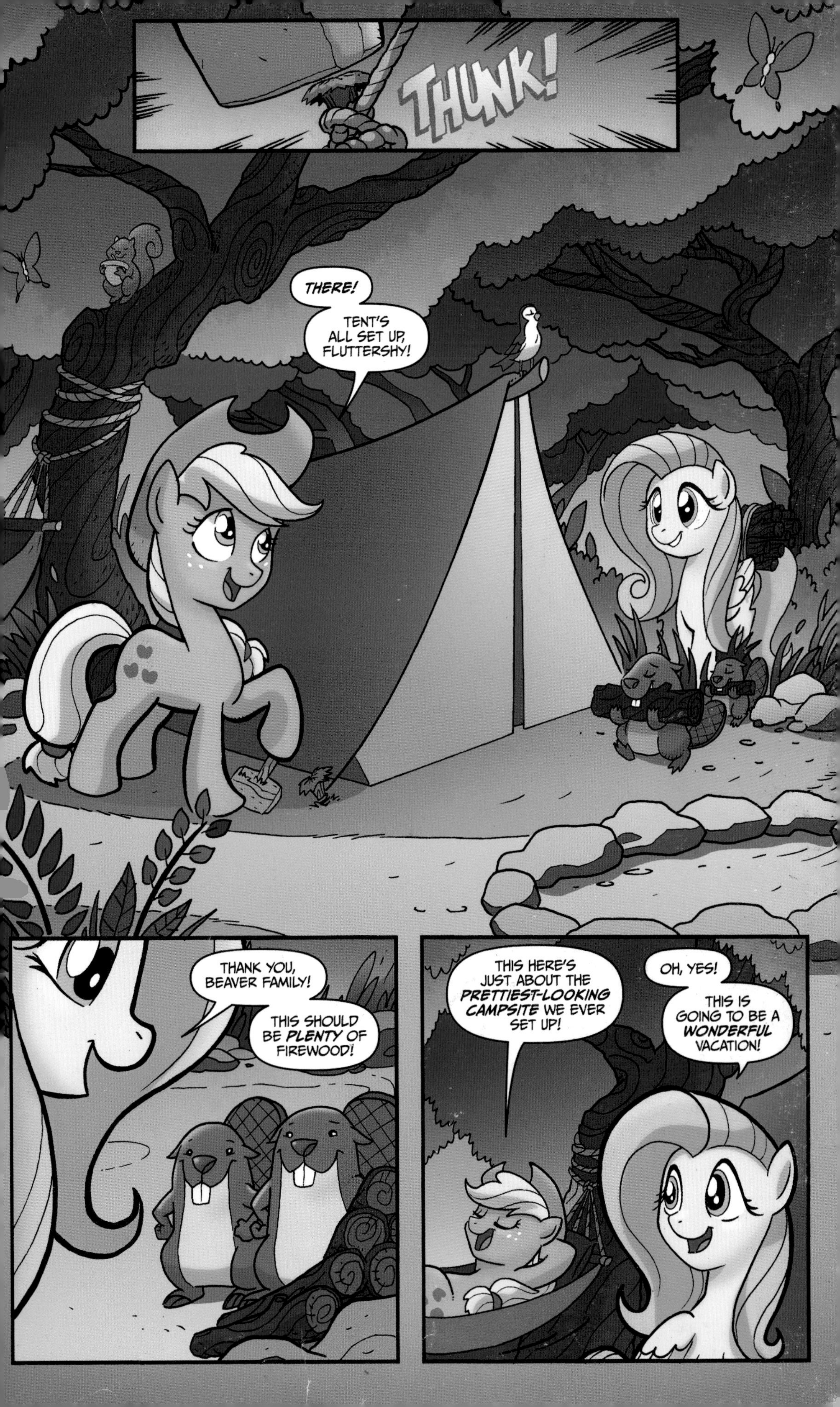

THUNK!
THERE!
TENT'S ALL SET UP, FLUTTERSHY!
THANK YOU, BEAVER FAMILY!
THIS SHOULD BE PLENTY OF FIREWOOD!
THIS HERE'S JUST ABOUT THE PRETTIEST-LOOKING CAMPSITE WE EVER SET UP!
OH, YES!
THIS IS GOING TO BE A WONDERFUL VACATION!

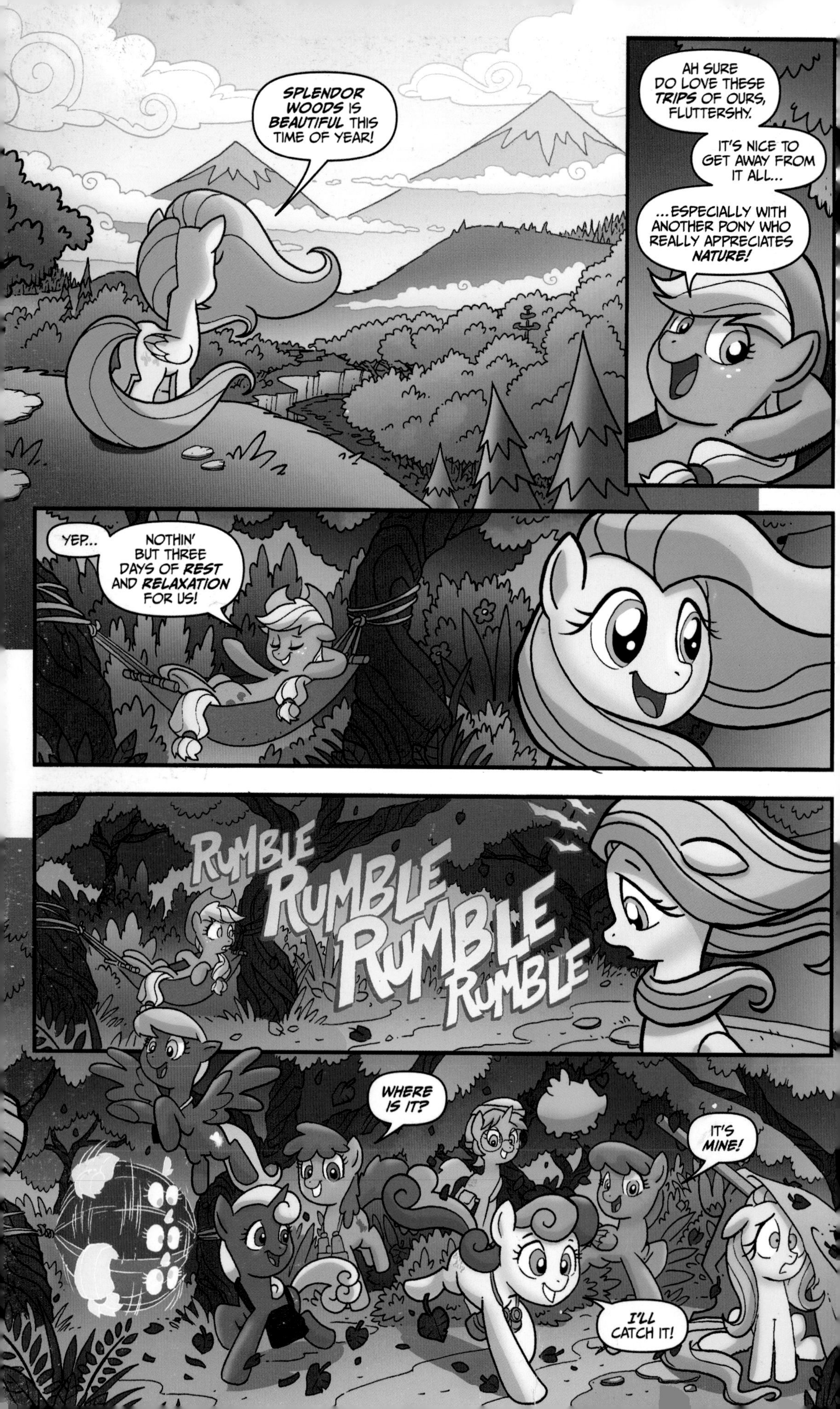
SPLENDOR WOODS IS BEAUTIFUL THIS TIME OF YEAR!
AH SURE DO LOVE THESE TRIPS OF OURS, FLUTTERSHY.
IT'S NICE TO GET AWAY FROM IT ALL...
...ESPECIALLY WITH ANOTHER PONY WHO REALLY APPRECIATES NATURE!
YEP...
NOTHIN' BUT THREE DAYS OF REST AND RELAXATION FOR US!
RUMBLE RUMBLE RUMBLE RUMBLE
WHERE IS IT?
IT'S MINE!
I'LL CATCH IT!

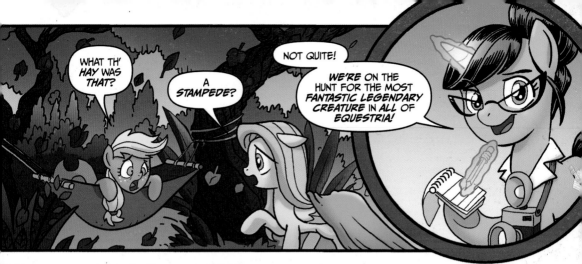

WHAT TH' HAY WAS THAT?

A STAMPEDE?

NOT QUITE!

WE'RE ON THE HUNT FOR THE MOST *FANTASTIC LEGENDARY CREATURE* IN ALL OF *EQUESTRIA!*

"*LEGENDARY CREATURE*"?

AN' JUST *WHO* ARE *YOU?*

THE NAME'S *NOSEY NEWS*, REPORTER FOR *CANTERLOT DAILY*, AND I'M HERE INVESTIGATING A RECENT *SIGHTING* OF—

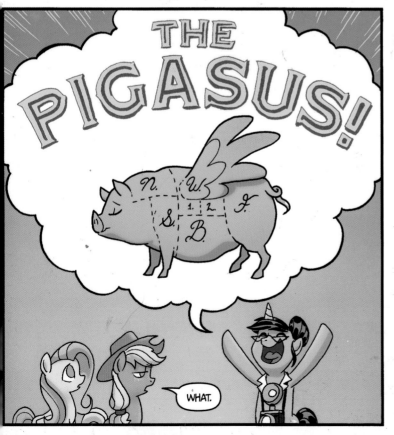

THE **PIGASUS!**

WHAT.

A *NOBLE BEAST* WITH THE BODY OF A *PIG* AND THE WINGS OF A *BIRD!*

I TOOK THIS PICTURE JUST *LAST WEEK*, HERE IN *SPLENDOR WOODS!*

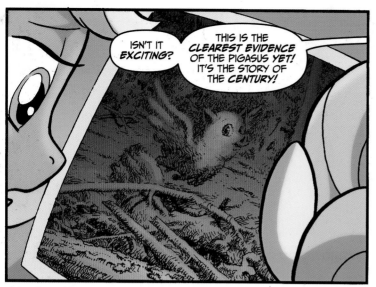

ISN'T IT *EXCITING?*

THIS IS THE *CLEAREST EVIDENCE* OF THE *PIGASUS YET!* IT'S THE STORY OF THE *CENTURY!*

THIS IS YER *"PROOF"?*

THIS DON'T LOOK ANYTHING *LIKE* A PIGASUS!

LOOKS MORE LIKE... A *SQUIRREL* WEARIN' A *TRENCHCOAT* TO ME.

IF YOU TURN IT *SIDEWAYS,* IT LOOKS KIND OF LIKE *TWO HEDGEHOGS* DANCING...

YES! *WELL!*

SNATCH!

REGARDLESS OF HOW *YOU* MAY FEEL ABOUT MY *PROOF—*

—PLENTY OF *OTHER* PONIES BELIEVE IN THE PIGASUS!

PLUSHIE HUT

PIGASUS HUNT!

WH—! TH—! HOW—!

WHAT IN TH' NAME OF *HAY BALES* IS THIS?!

OTHER *PIGASUS-CATCHERS,* OF COURSE!

ALL THESE PONIES HAVE BEEN *INSPIRED* BY MY PICTURE TO COME AND *SEARCH* FOR THE PIGASUS!

AND *WE* WON'T *LEAVE* UNTIL WE *FIND* IT!

PLUSHIE HUT

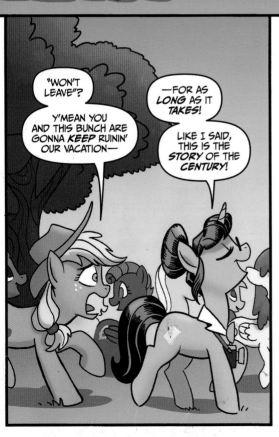

"*WON'T LEAVE*"?

Y'MEAN YOU AND THIS BUNCH ARE GONNA *KEEP* RUININ' OUR VACATION—

—FOR AS *LONG* AS IT *TAKES!*

LIKE I SAID, THIS IS THE *STORY* OF THE *CENTURY!*

NOW, IF YOU'LL *EXCUSE* ME, I'D LIKE TO TRY AN OFFICIAL PIGASUS *FUNNEL CAKE!*

UM... DON'T WORRY, APPLEJACK!

I'M SURE THEY WON'T BE *TOO* MUCH OF A DISRUPTION TO OUR... VACATION...

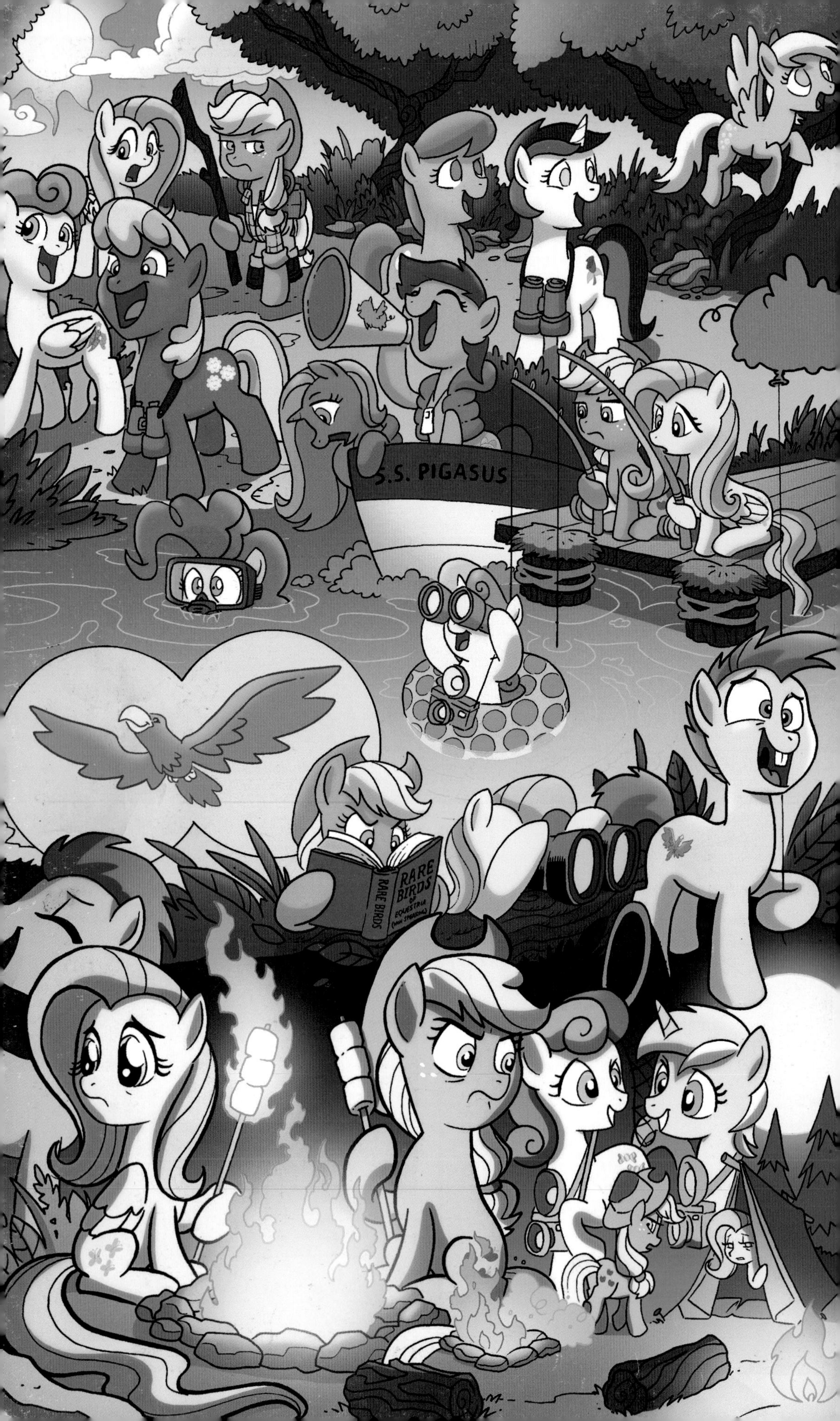
S.S. PIGASUS
RARE BIRDS
RARE BIRDS OF EQUESTRIA (NON SPEAKING)

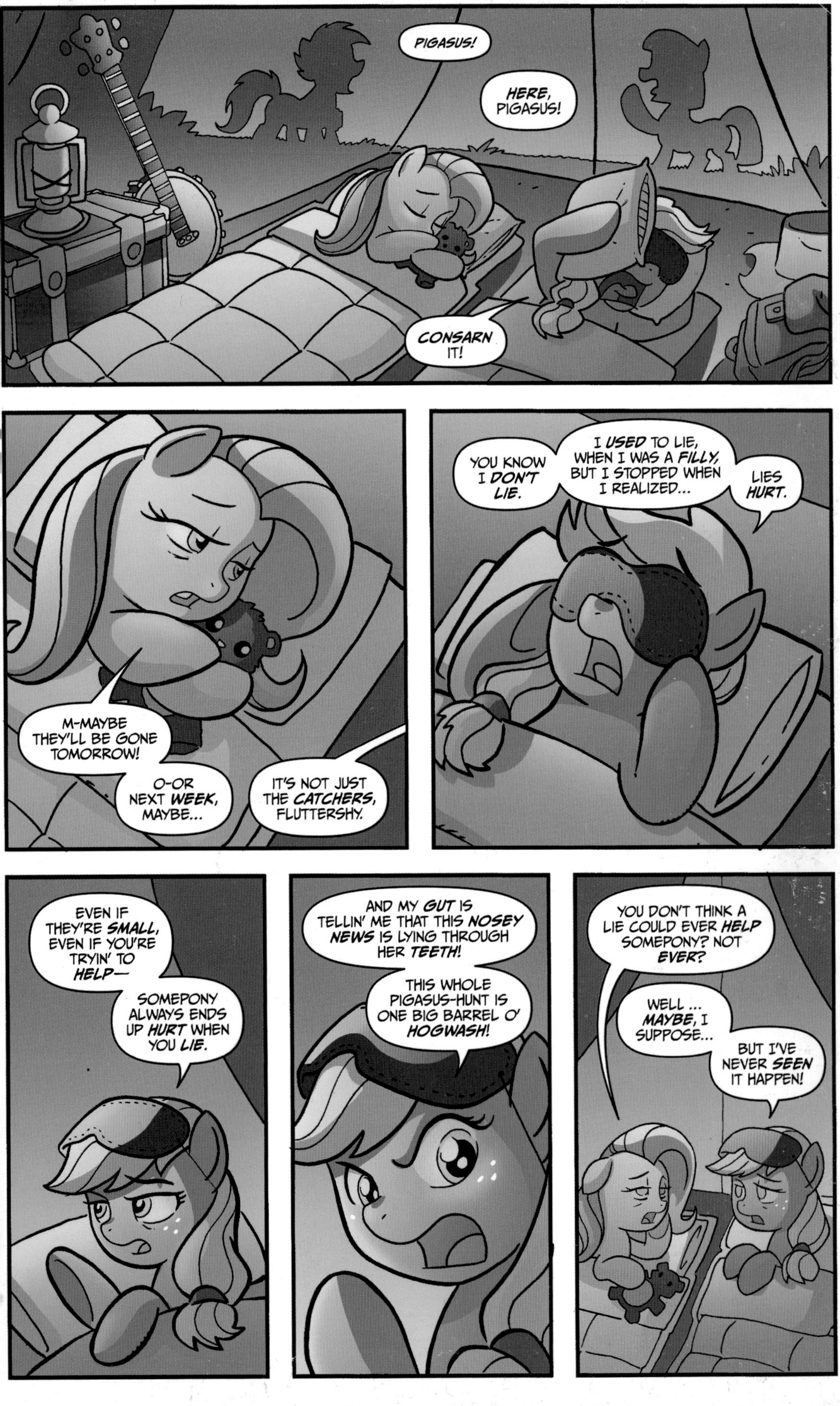
PIGASUS!
HERE, PIGASUS!
CONSARN IT!
M-MAYBE THEY'LL BE GONE TOMORROW!
O-OR NEXT WEEK, MAYBE...
IT'S NOT JUST THE CATCHERS, FLUTTERSHY.
YOU KNOW I DON'T LIE.
I USED TO LIE, WHEN I WAS A FILLY, BUT I STOPPED WHEN I REALIZED...
LIES HURT.
EVEN IF THEY'RE SMALL, EVEN IF YOU'RE TRYIN' TO HELP—
SOMEPONY ALWAYS ENDS UP HURT WHEN YOU LIE.
AND MY GUT IS TELLIN' ME THAT THIS NOSEY NEWS IS LYING THROUGH HER TEETH!
THIS WHOLE PIGASUS-HUNT IS ONE BIG BARREL O' HOGWASH!
YOU DON'T THINK A LIE COULD EVER HELP SOMEPONY? NOT EVER?
WELL ... MAYBE, I SUPPOSE...
BUT I'VE NEVER SEEN IT HAPPEN!

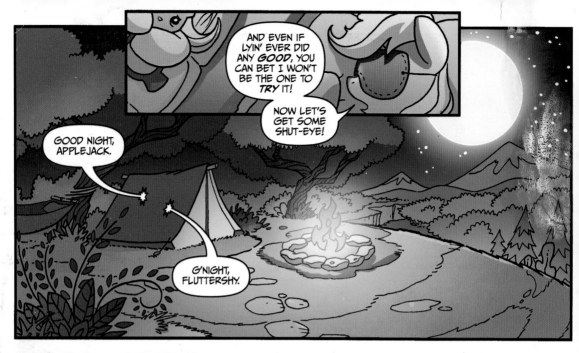

AND EVEN IF LYIN' EVER DID ANY *GOOD*, YOU CAN BET I WON'T BE THE ONE TO *TRY* IT!

NOW LET'S GET SOME SHUT-EYE!

GOOD NIGHT, APPLEJACK.

G'NIGHT, FLUTTERSHY.

YAAAWWWNN...

smack smack

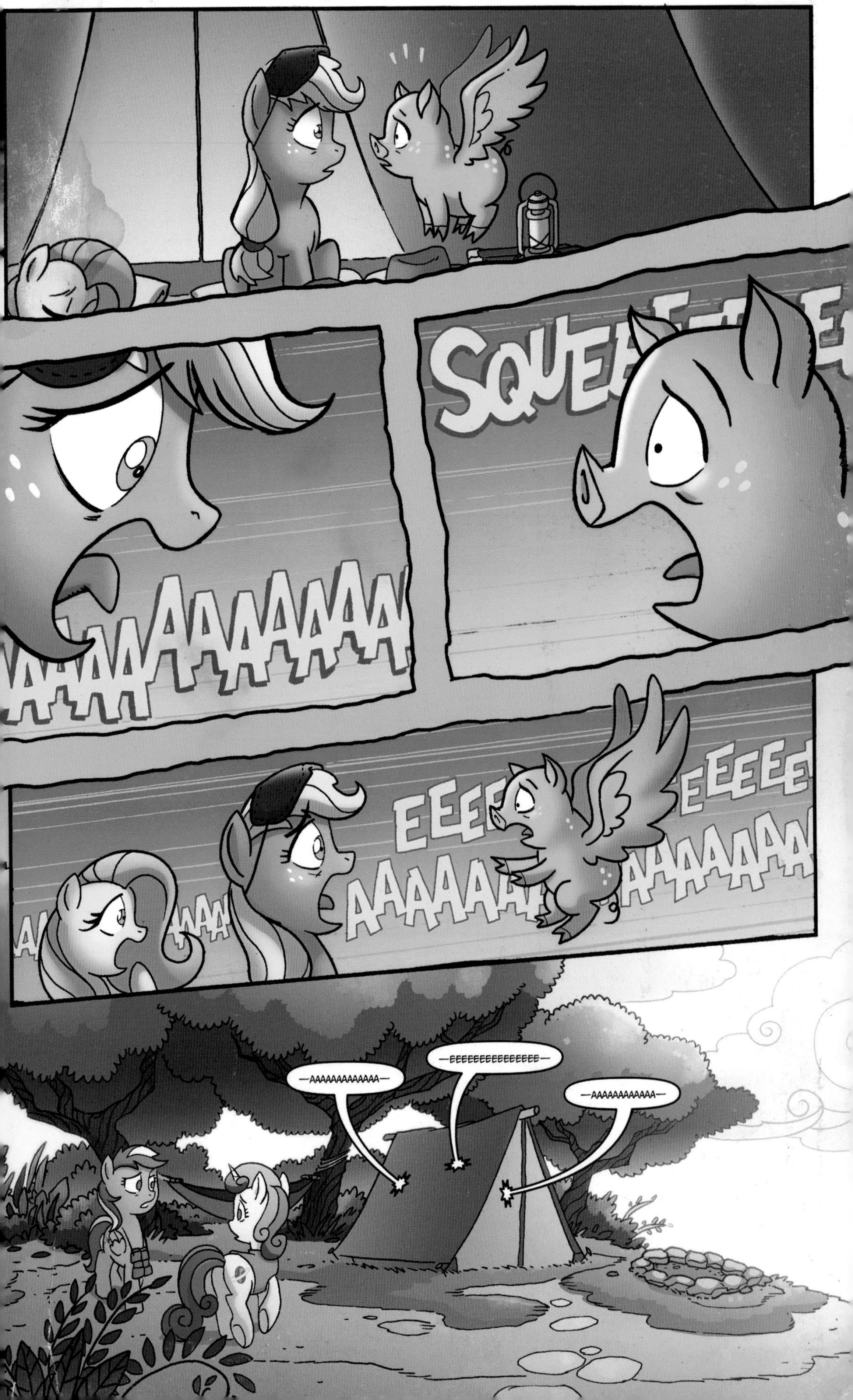

SQUE
AAAAAAAAAAA
EEEEEEEE
AAAAAAAAAAAAAA
—AAAAAAAAAAAAA—
—EEEEEEEEEEEEEEE—
—AAAAAAAAAAAA—

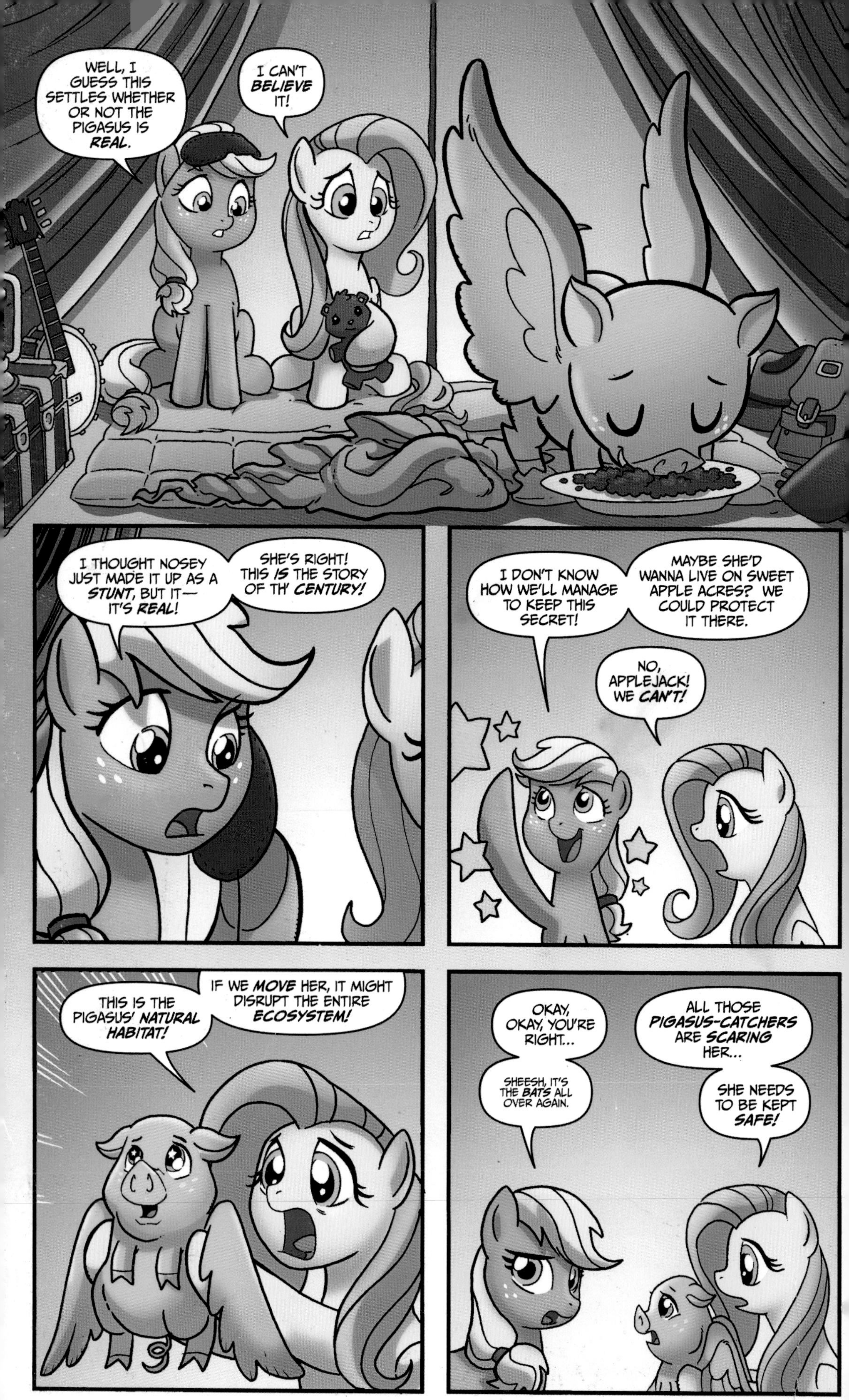
WELL, I GUESS THIS SETTLES WHETHER OR NOT THE PIGASUS IS REAL.
I CAN'T BELIEVE IT!
I THOUGHT NOSEY JUST MADE IT UP AS A STUNT, BUT IT— IT'S REAL!
SHE'S RIGHT! THIS IS THE STORY OF TH' CENTURY!
I DON'T KNOW HOW WE'LL MANAGE TO KEEP THIS SECRET!
MAYBE SHE'D WANNA LIVE ON SWEET APPLE ACRES? WE COULD PROTECT IT THERE.
NO, APPLEJACK! WE CAN'T!
THIS IS THE PIGASUS' NATURAL HABITAT!
IF WE MOVE HER, IT MIGHT DISRUPT THE ENTIRE ECOSYSTEM!
OKAY, OKAY, YOU'RE RIGHT...
SHEESH, IT'S THE BATS ALL OVER AGAIN.
ALL THOSE PIGASUS-CATCHERS ARE SCARING HER...
SHE NEEDS TO BE KEPT SAFE!

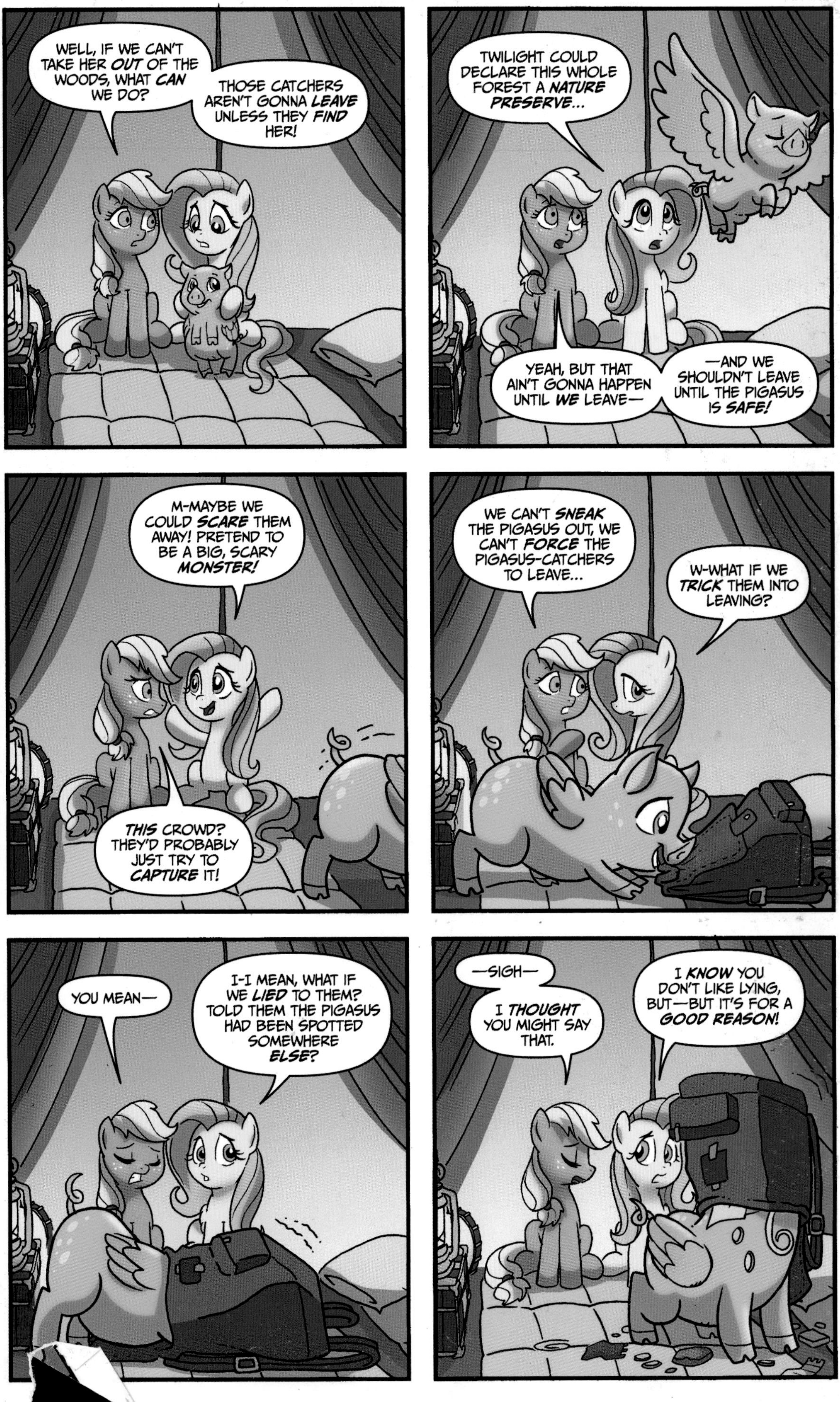
WELL, IF WE CAN'T TAKE HER OUT OF THE WOODS, WHAT CAN WE DO?
THOSE CATCHERS AREN'T GONNA LEAVE UNLESS THEY FIND HER!
TWILIGHT COULD DECLARE THIS WHOLE FOREST A NATURE PRESERVE...
YEAH, BUT THAT AIN'T GONNA HAPPEN UNTIL WE LEAVE—
—AND WE SHOULDN'T LEAVE UNTIL THE PIGASUS IS SAFE!
M-MAYBE WE COULD SCARE THEM AWAY! PRETEND TO BE A BIG, SCARY MONSTER!
THIS CROWD? THEY'D PROBABLY JUST TRY TO CAPTURE IT!
WE CAN'T SNEAK THE PIGASUS OUT, WE CAN'T FORCE THE PIGASUS-CATCHERS TO LEAVE...
W-WHAT IF WE TRICK THEM INTO LEAVING?
YOU MEAN—
I-I MEAN, WHAT IF WE LIED TO THEM? TOLD THEM THE PIGASUS HAD BEEN SPOTTED SOMEWHERE ELSE?
—SIGH—
I THOUGHT YOU MIGHT SAY THAT.
I KNOW YOU DON'T LIKE LYING, BUT—BUT IT'S FOR A GOOD REASON!

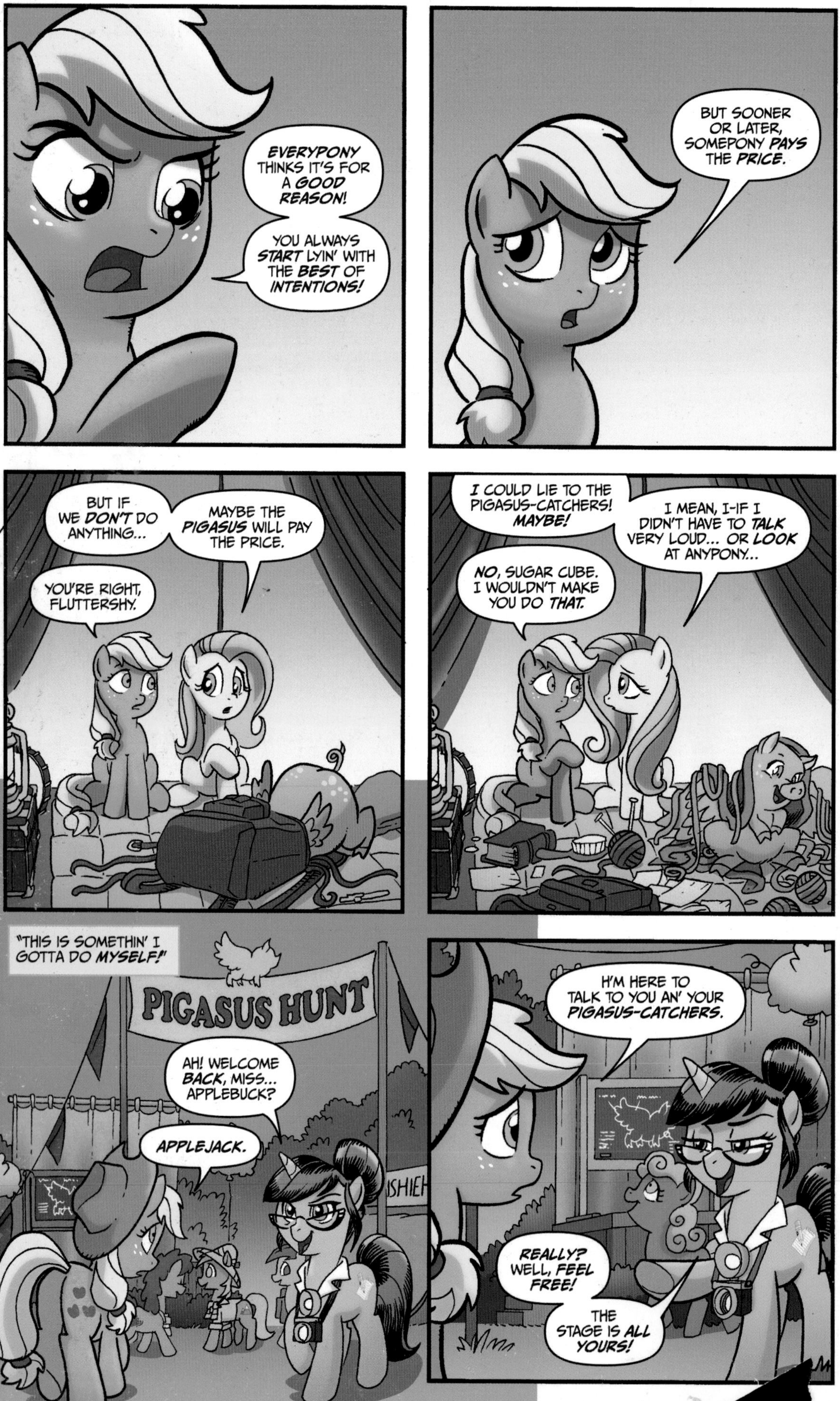

EVERYPONY THINKS IT'S FOR A GOOD REASON!
YOU ALWAYS START LYIN' WITH THE BEST OF INTENTIONS!
BUT SOONER OR LATER, SOMEPONY PAYS THE PRICE.
BUT IF WE DON'T DO ANYTHING...
MAYBE THE PIGASUS WILL PAY THE PRICE.
YOU'RE RIGHT, FLUTTERSHY.
I COULD LIE TO THE PIGASUS-CATCHERS! MAYBE!
I MEAN, I-IF I DIDN'T HAVE TO TALK VERY LOUD... OR LOOK AT ANYPONY...
NO, SUGAR CUBE. I WOULDN'T MAKE YOU DO THAT.
"THIS IS SOMETHIN' I GOTTA DO MYSELF!"
PIGASUS HUNT
AH! WELCOME BACK, MISS... APPLEBUCK?
APPLEJACK.
H'M HERE TO TALK TO YOU AN' YOUR PIGASUS-CATCHERS.
REALLY? WELL, FEEL FREE!
THE STAGE IS ALL YOURS!

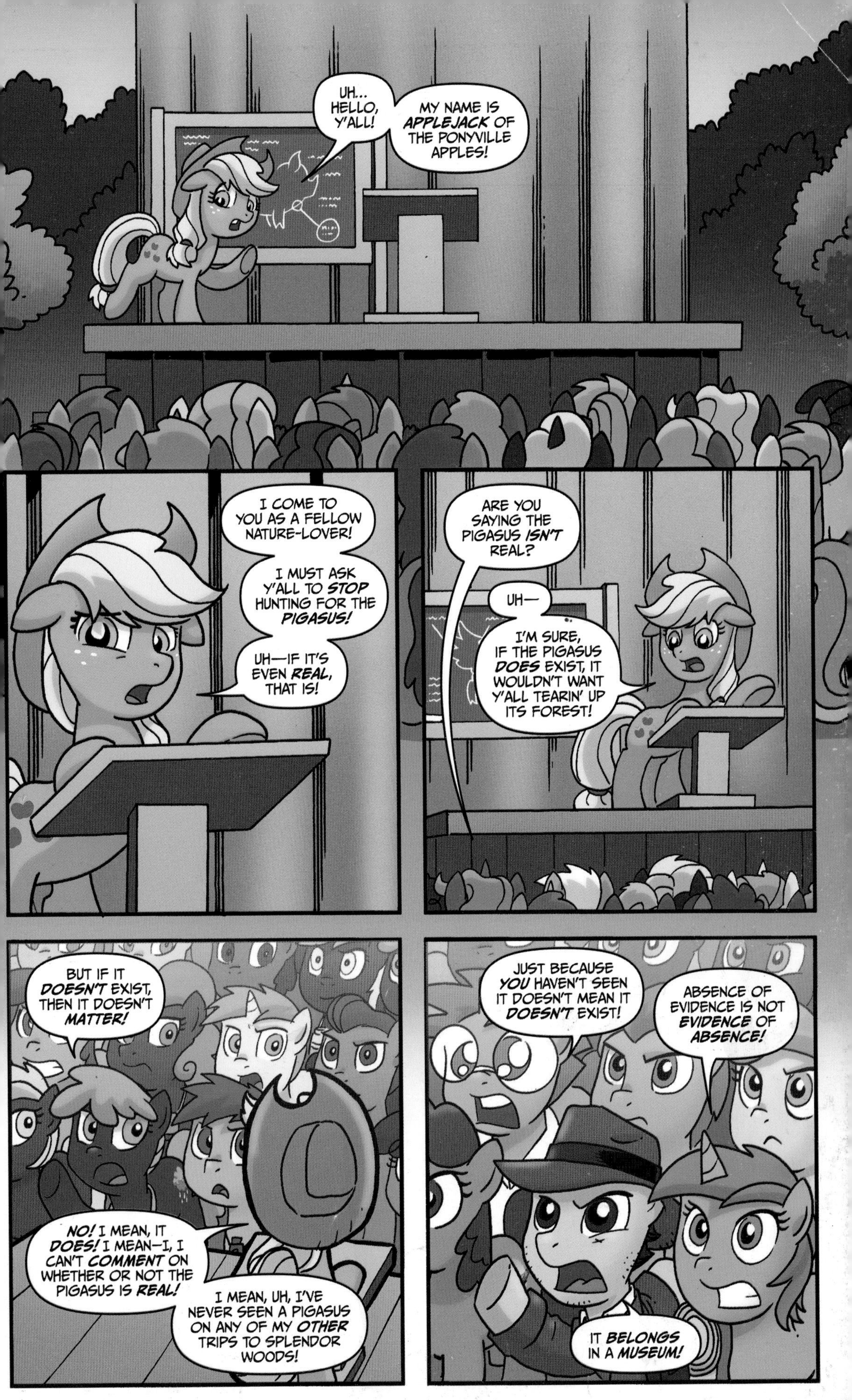

UH... HELLO, Y'ALL!
MY NAME IS APPLEJACK OF THE PONYVILLE APPLES!
I COME TO YOU AS A FELLOW NATURE-LOVER!
I MUST ASK Y'ALL TO STOP HUNTING FOR THE PIGASUS!
UH—IF IT'S EVEN REAL, THAT IS!
ARE YOU SAYING THE PIGASUS ISN'T REAL?
UH—
I'M SURE, IF THE PIGASUS DOES EXIST, IT WOULDN'T WANT Y'ALL TEARIN' UP ITS FOREST!
BUT IF IT DOESN'T EXIST, THEN IT DOESN'T MATTER!
NO! I MEAN, IT DOES! I MEAN—I, I CAN'T COMMENT ON WHETHER OR NOT THE PIGASUS IS REAL!
I MEAN, UH, I'VE NEVER SEEN A PIGASUS ON ANY OF MY OTHER TRIPS TO SPLENDOR WOODS!
JUST BECAUSE YOU HAVEN'T SEEN IT DOESN'T MEAN IT DOESN'T EXIST!
ABSENCE OF EVIDENCE IS NOT EVIDENCE OF ABSENCE!
IT BELONGS IN A MUSEUM!

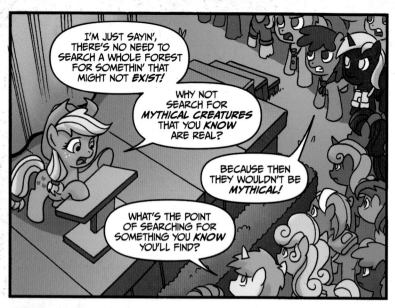

I'M JUST SAYIN', THERE'S NO NEED TO SEARCH A WHOLE FOREST FOR SOMETHIN' THAT MIGHT NOT *EXIST*!

WHY NOT SEARCH FOR *MYTHICAL CREATURES* THAT YOU *KNOW* ARE REAL?

BECAUSE THEN THEY WOULDN'T BE *MYTHICAL*!

WHAT'S THE POINT OF SEARCHING FOR SOMETHING YOU *KNOW* YOU'LL FIND?

BUT—ER—THAT IS TO SAY, UH—

I SURE DON'T *SEE* ANY PIGASUS AROUND HERE RIGHT *NOW*!

SO, UH...

OH, NO...

...THIS ISN'T WORKING WELL AT *ALL*.

I *KNEW* THIS WOULD BE HARD FOR HER!

APPLEJACK TRYING TO *LIE* IS LIKE A *PIG* TRYING TO *FLY*!

OH, UM—

ANY *OTHER* PIG, I MEAN.

SNERK?

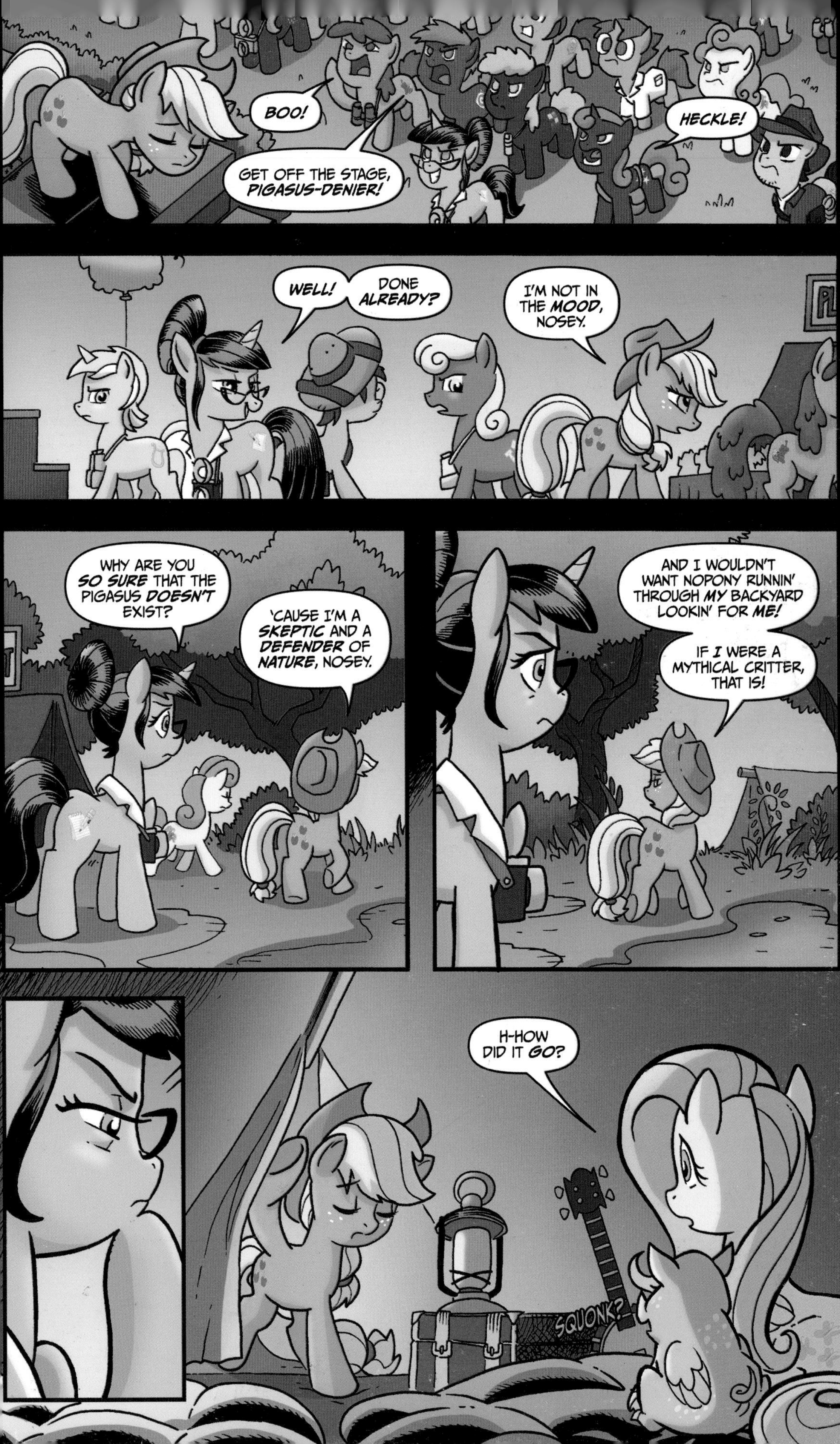
BOO!
GET OFF THE STAGE, PIGASUS-DENIER!
HECKLE!
WELL!
DONE ALREADY?
I'M NOT IN THE MOOD, NOSEY.
WHY ARE YOU SO SURE THAT THE PIGASUS DOESN'T EXIST?
'CAUSE I'M A SKEPTIC AND A DEFENDER OF NATURE, NOSEY.
AND I WOULDN'T WANT NOPONY RUNNIN' THROUGH MY BACKYARD LOOKIN' FOR ME!
IF I WERE A MYTHICAL CRITTER, THAT IS!
H-HOW DID IT GO?
SQUONK?

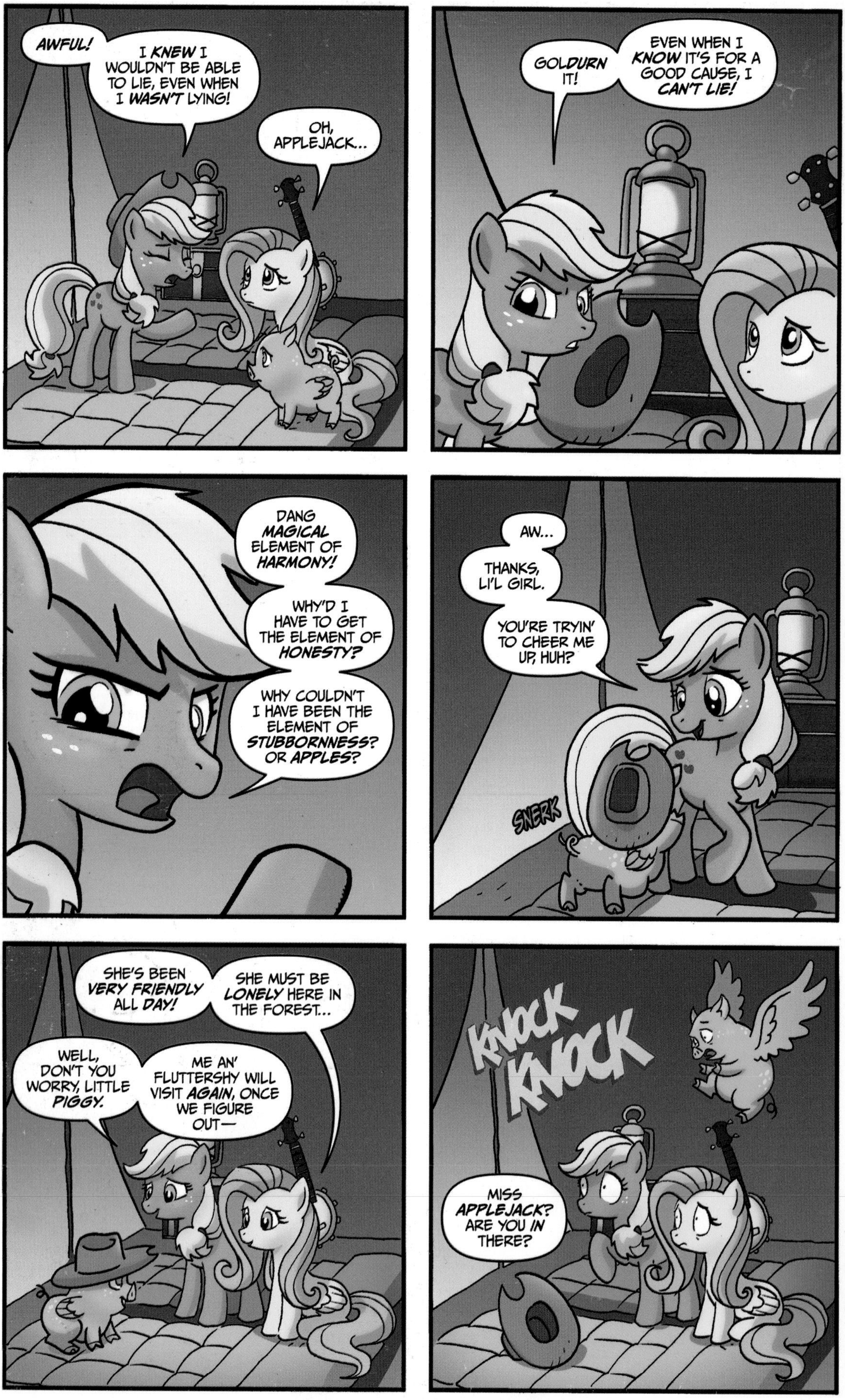
AWFUL!
I KNEW I WOULDN'T BE ABLE TO LIE, EVEN WHEN I WASN'T LYING!
OH, APPLEJACK...
GOLDURN IT!
EVEN WHEN I KNOW IT'S FOR A GOOD CAUSE, I CAN'T LIE!
DANG MAGICAL ELEMENT OF HARMONY!
WHY'D I HAVE TO GET THE ELEMENT OF HONESTY?
WHY COULDN'T I HAVE BEEN THE ELEMENT OF STUBBORNNESS? OR APPLES?
AW...
THANKS, LI'L GIRL.
YOU'RE TRYIN' TO CHEER ME UP, HUH?
SNERK
SHE'S BEEN VERY FRIENDLY ALL DAY!
SHE MUST BE LONELY HERE IN THE FOREST...
WELL, DON'T YOU WORRY, LITTLE PIGGY.
ME AN' FLUTTERSHY WILL VISIT AGAIN, ONCE WE FIGURE OUT—
KNOCK KNOCK
MISS APPLEJACK? ARE YOU IN THERE?

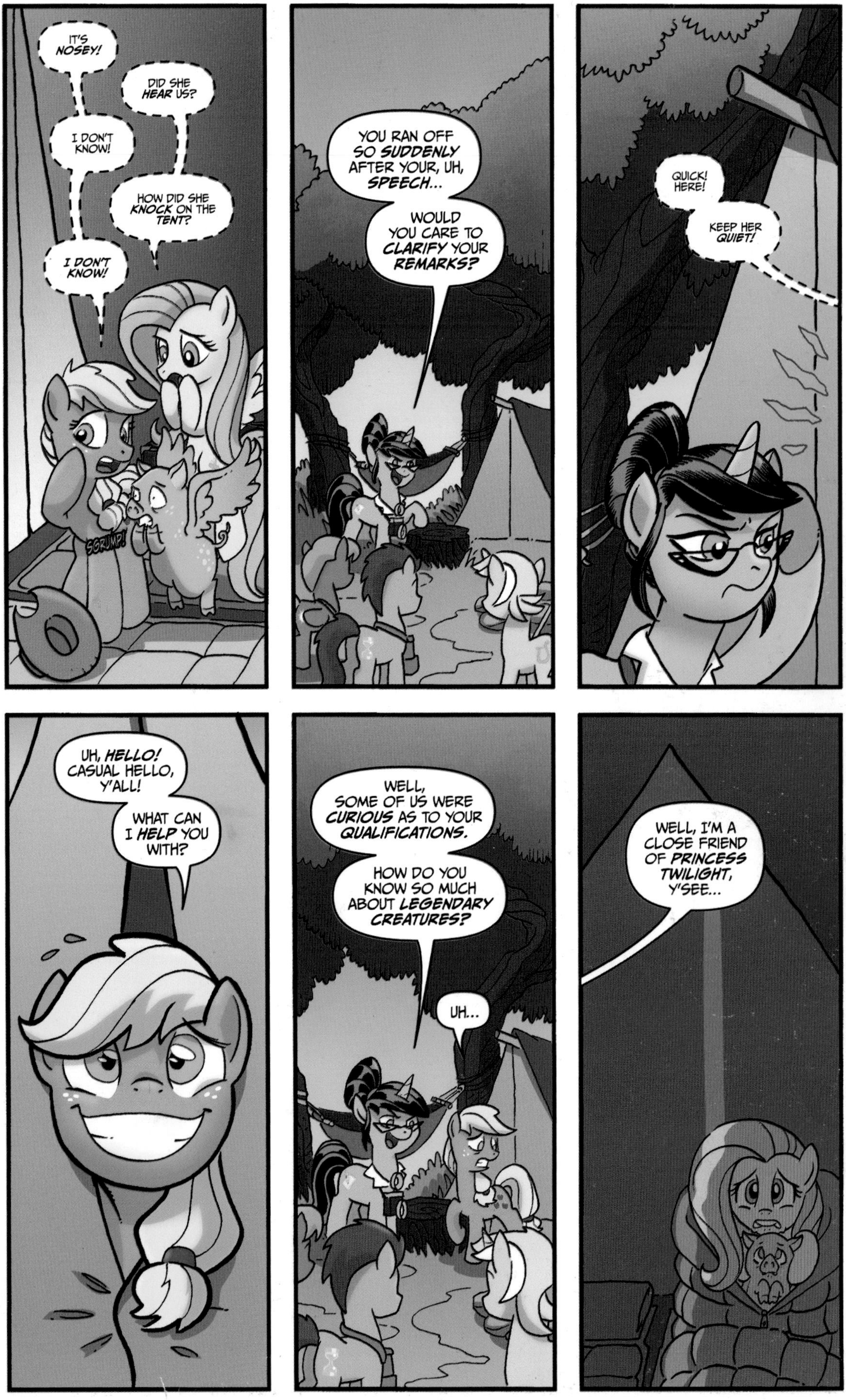
IT'S NOSEY!
DID SHE HEAR US?
I DON'T KNOW!
HOW DID SHE KNOCK ON THE TENT?
I DON'T KNOW!
SCRUMP!
YOU RAN OFF SO SUDDENLY AFTER YOUR, UH, SPEECH...
WOULD YOU CARE TO CLARIFY YOUR REMARKS?
QUICK! HERE!
KEEP HER QUIET!
UH, HELLO! CASUAL HELLO, Y'ALL!
WHAT CAN I HELP YOU WITH?
WELL, SOME OF US WERE CURIOUS AS TO YOUR QUALIFICATIONS.
HOW DO YOU KNOW SO MUCH ABOUT LEGENDARY CREATURES?
UH...
WELL, I'M A CLOSE FRIEND OF PRINCESS TWILIGHT, Y'SEE...

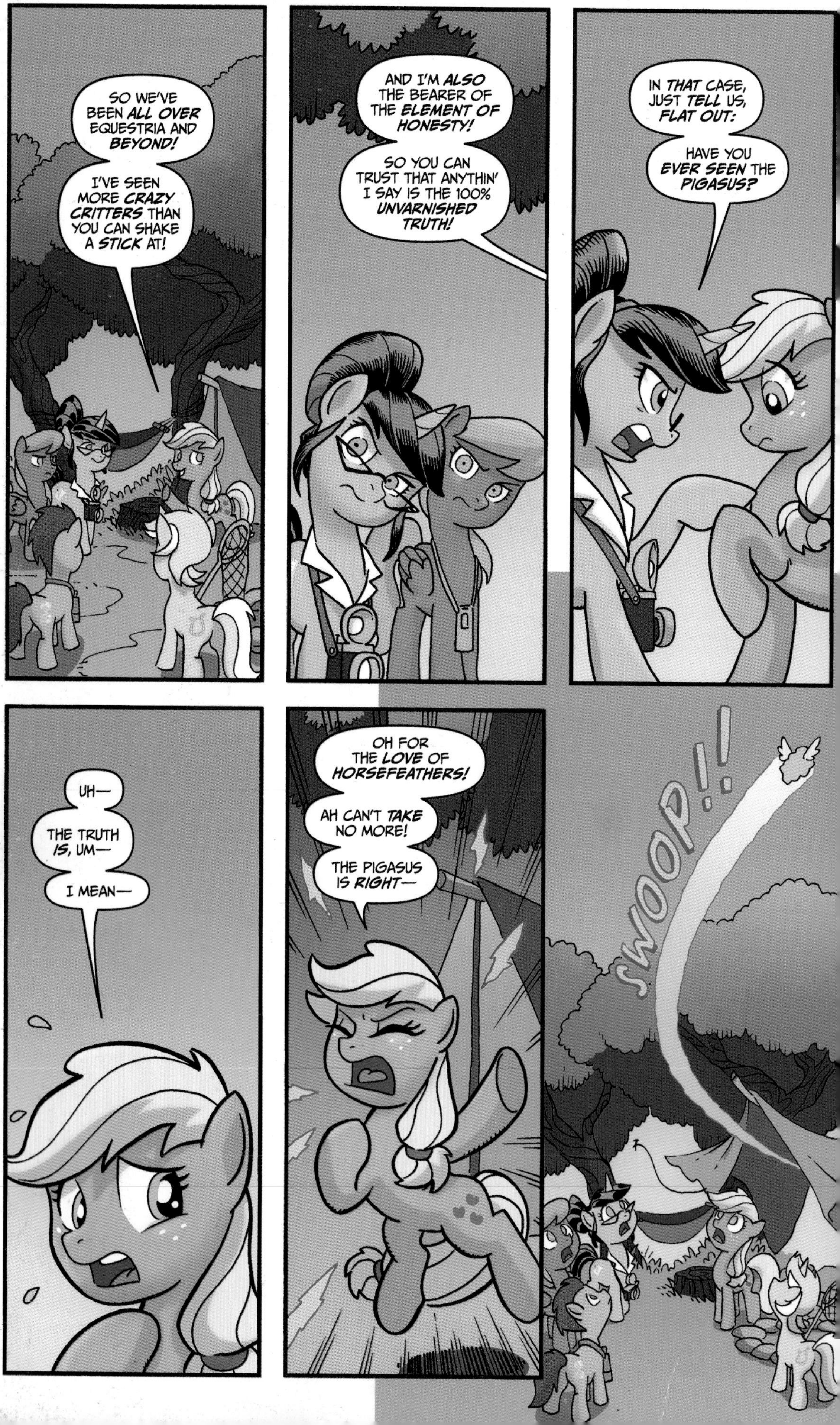

SO WE'VE BEEN ALL OVER EQUESTRIA AND BEYOND!
I'VE SEEN MORE CRAZY CRITTERS THAN YOU CAN SHAKE A STICK AT!
AND I'M ALSO THE BEARER OF THE ELEMENT OF HONESTY!
SO YOU CAN TRUST THAT ANYTHIN' I SAY IS THE 100% UNVARNISHED TRUTH!
IN THAT CASE, JUST TELL US, FLAT OUT:
HAVE YOU EVER SEEN THE PIGASUS?
UH—
THE TRUTH IS, UM—
I MEAN—
OH FOR THE LOVE OF HORSEFEATHERS!
AH CAN'T TAKE NO MORE!
THE PIGASUS IS RIGHT—
SWOOP!!

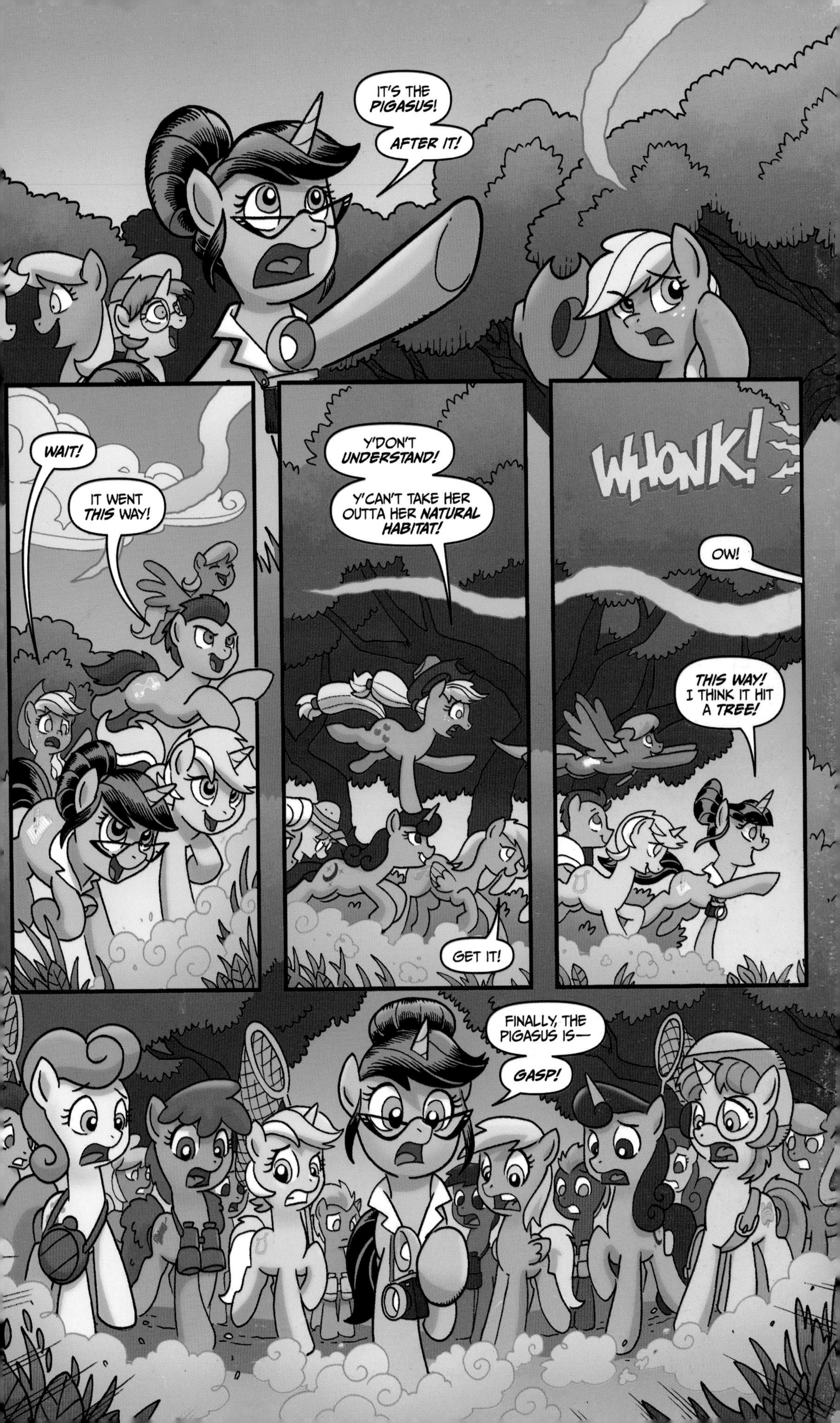
IT'S THE PIGASUS!
AFTER IT!
WAIT!
IT WENT THIS WAY!
Y'DON'T UNDERSTAND!
Y'CAN'T TAKE HER OUTTA HER NATURAL HABITAT!
GET IT!
WHONK!
OW!
THIS WAY! I THINK IT HIT A TREE!
FINALLY, THE PIGASUS IS—
GASP!

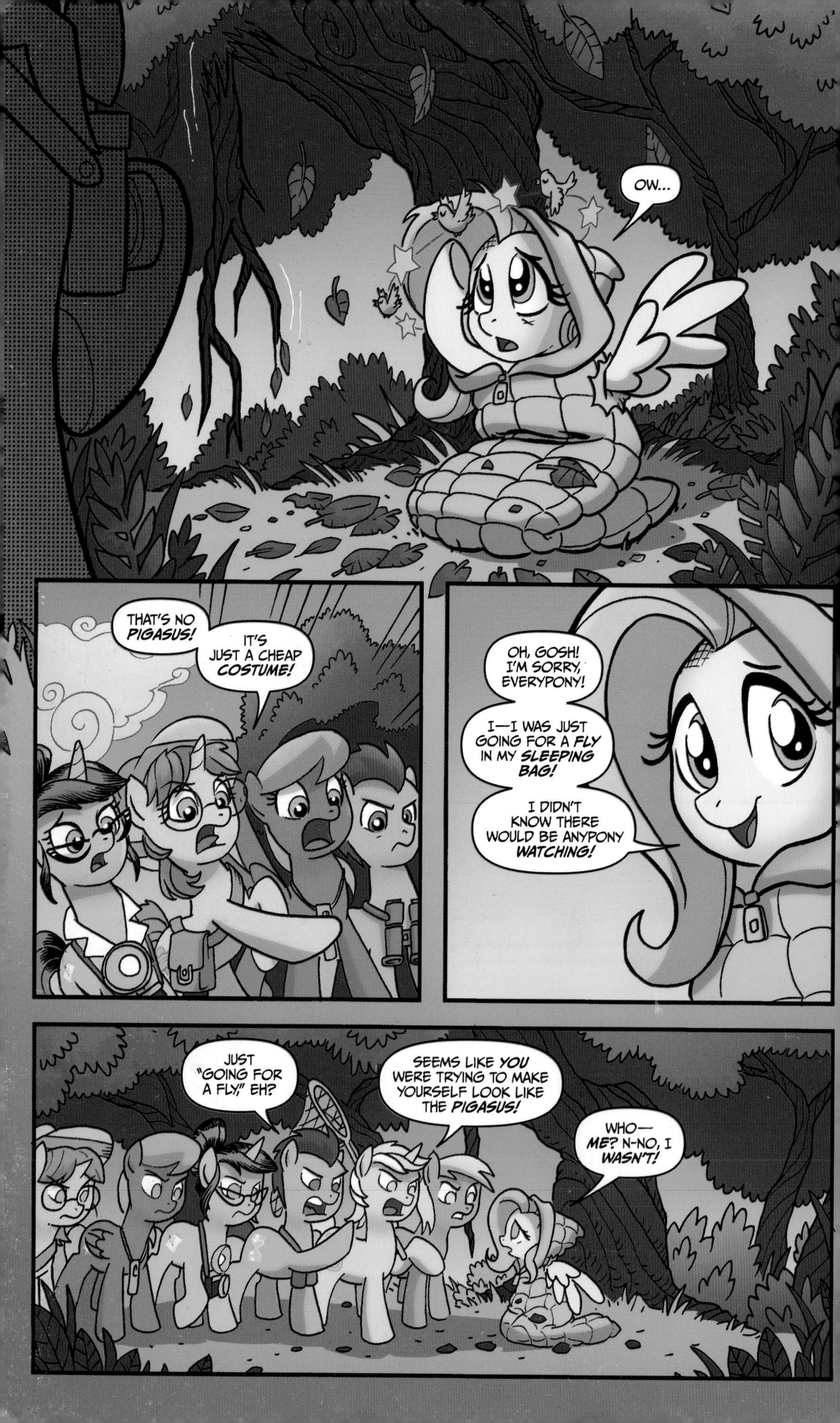
OW...
THAT'S NO PIGASUS!
IT'S JUST A CHEAP COSTUME!
OH, GOSH! I'M SORRY, EVERYPONY!
I—I WAS JUST GOING FOR A FLY IN MY SLEEPING BAG!
I DIDN'T KNOW THERE WOULD BE ANYPONY WATCHING!
JUST "GOING FOR A FLY," EH?
SEEMS LIKE YOU WERE TRYING TO MAKE YOURSELF LOOK LIKE THE PIGASUS!
WHO— ME? N-NO, I WASN'T!

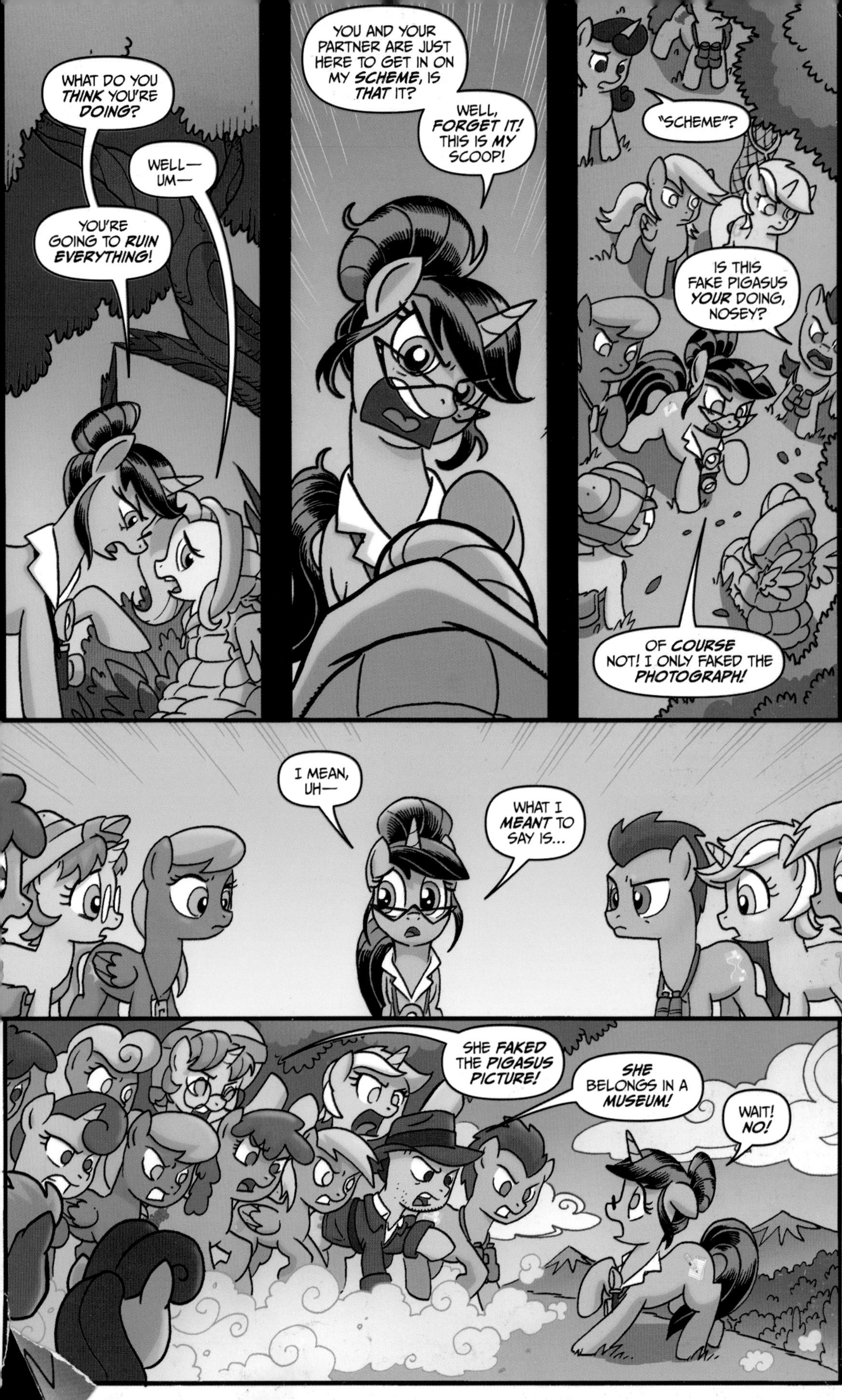
WHAT DO YOU *THINK* YOU'RE *DOING?*
WELL— UM—
YOU'RE GOING TO *RUIN EVERYTHING!*
YOU AND YOUR PARTNER ARE JUST HERE TO GET IN ON MY *SCHEME,* IS *THAT* IT?
WELL, *FORGET IT!* THIS IS *MY* SCOOP!
"SCHEME"?
IS THIS FAKE PIGASUS *YOUR* DOING, NOSEY?
OF *COURSE* NOT! I ONLY FAKED THE *PHOTOGRAPH!*
I MEAN, UH—
WHAT I *MEANT* TO SAY IS...
SHE *FAKED* THE *PIGASUS PICTURE!*
SHE BELONGS IN A *MUSEUM!*
WAIT! *NO!*

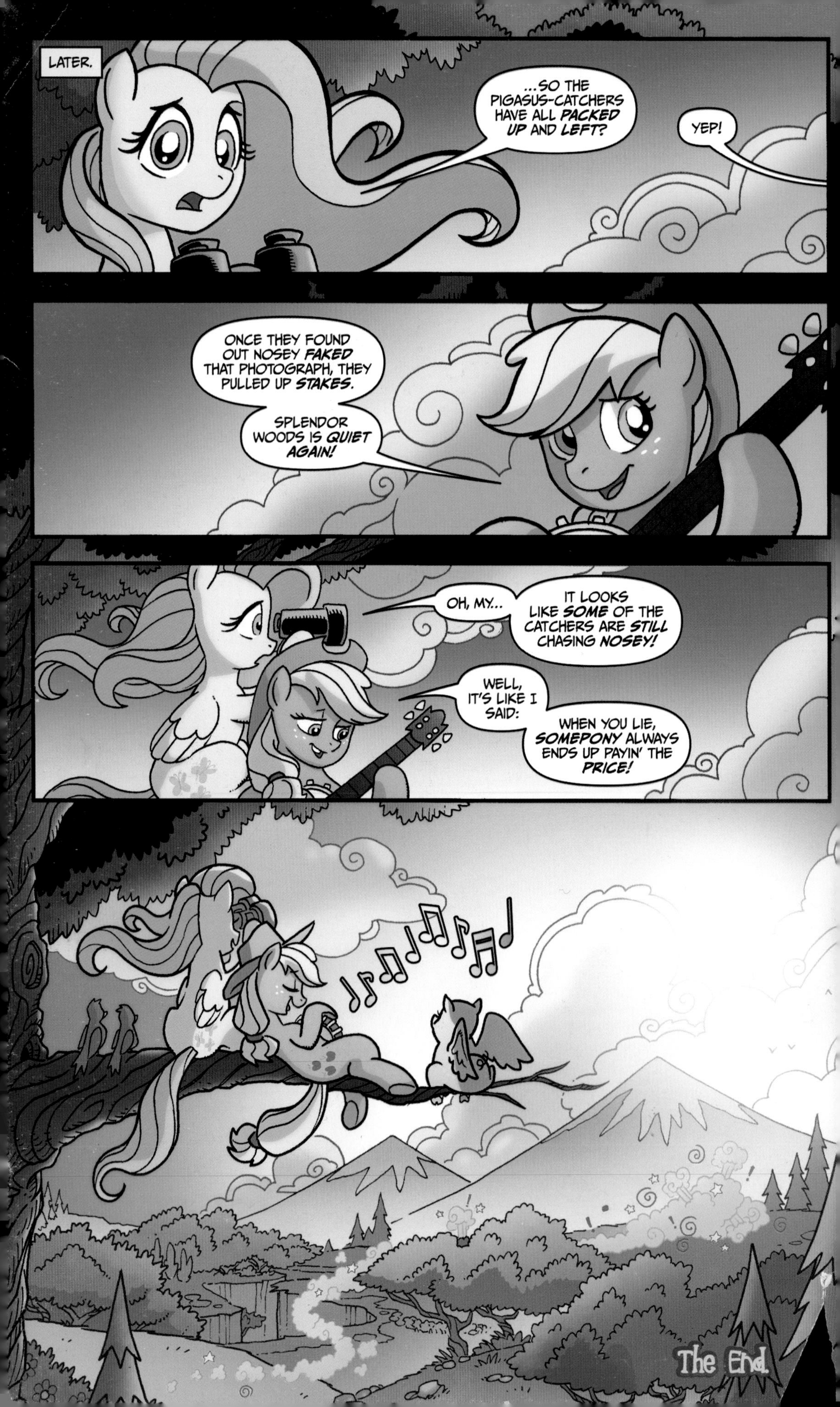
LATER.
...SO THE PIGASUS-CATCHERS HAVE ALL PACKED UP AND LEFT?
YEP!
ONCE THEY FOUND OUT NOSEY FAKED THAT PHOTOGRAPH, THEY PULLED UP STAKES.
SPLENDOR WOODS IS QUIET AGAIN!
OH, MY...
IT LOOKS LIKE SOME OF THE CATCHERS ARE STILL CHASING NOSEY!
WELL, IT'S LIKE I SAID:
WHEN YOU LIE, SOMEPONY ALWAYS ENDS UP PAYIN' THE PRICE!
The End.

my LITTLE PONY

FRIENDS FOREVER

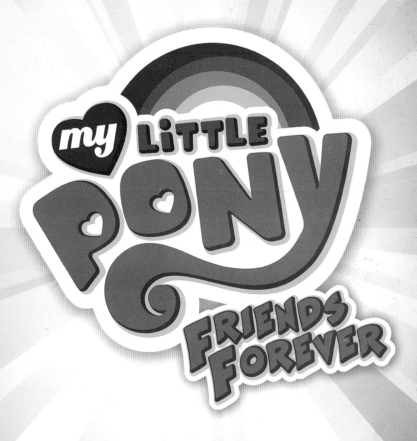

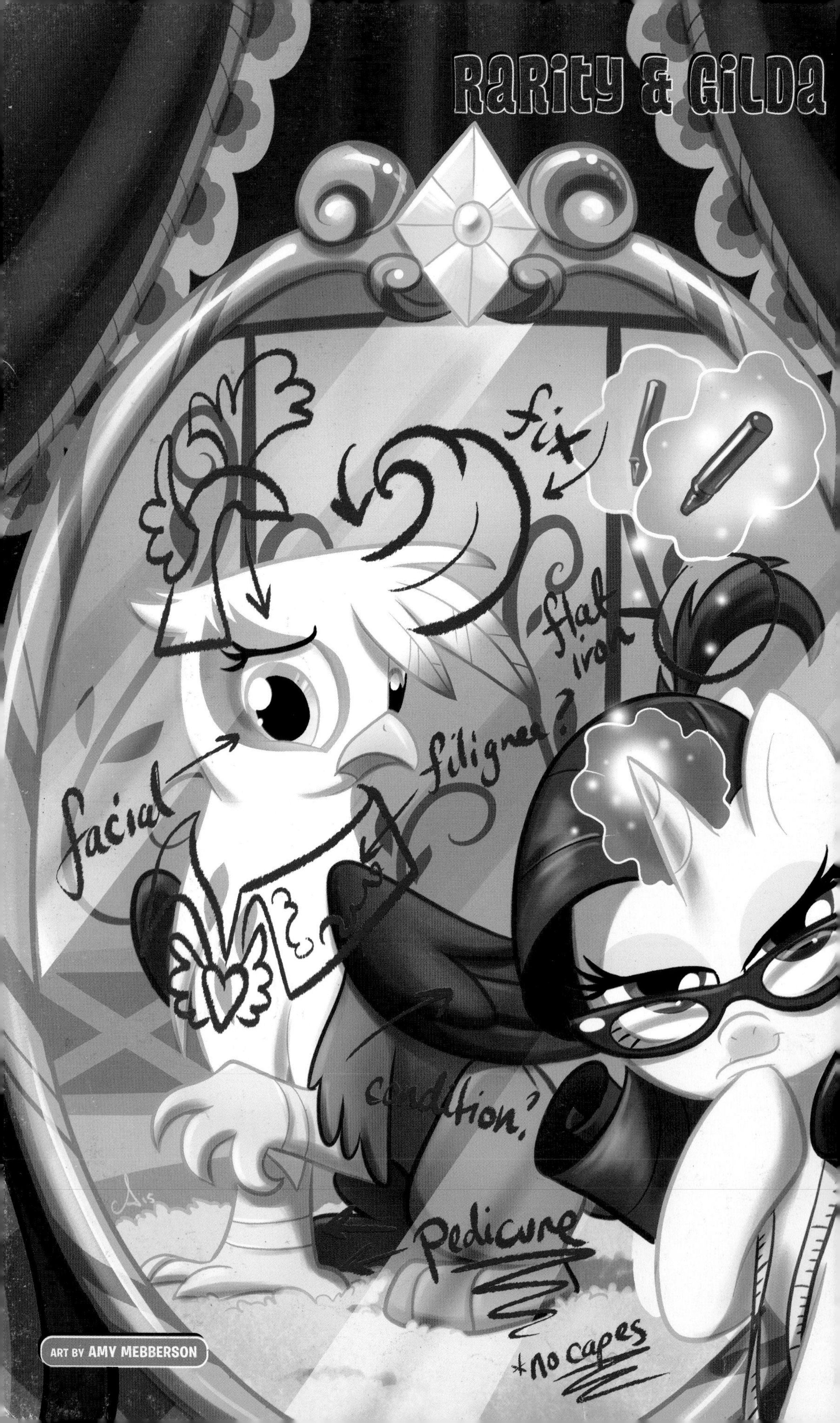

RARITY & GILDA
fix
flat iron
filigree?
facial
condition?
pedicure
*no capes
ART BY AMY MEBBERSON

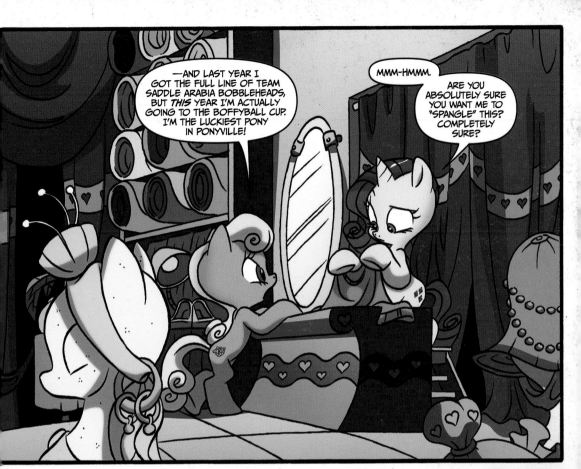

—AND LAST YEAR I GOT THE FULL LINE OF TEAM SADDLE ARABIA BOBBLEHEADS, BUT *THIS* YEAR I'M ACTUALLY GOING TO THE BOFFYBALL CUP. I'M THE LUCKIEST PONY IN PONYVILLE!

MMM-HMMM.

ARE YOU ABSOLUTELY SURE YOU WANT ME TO "SPANGLE" THIS? COMPLETELY SURE?

I COULD REPLICATE THIS IN A SHINY FABRIC THAT STILL HAS A LITTLE CLASS—I MEAN, "FLASH!"

BUT I NEED THE TEAM TO SEE ME FROM THE FIELD! AND I CAN'T BE SEEN IN ANYTHING LESS THAN AN OFFICIAL BOFFYBALL FEDERATION CUP TRADEMARKED JERSEY.

DON'T YOU RECOGNIZE A COVETED PIECE OF BOFFYBALL MERCHANDISE WHEN YOU SEE IT?!

I CAN'T SAY I FOLLOW THE SPORT MYSELF, LILAC LINKS. WE DON'T PLAY IT IN EQUESTRIA AND I'VE ALWAYS FOUND IT A TOUCH... UNCOUTH.

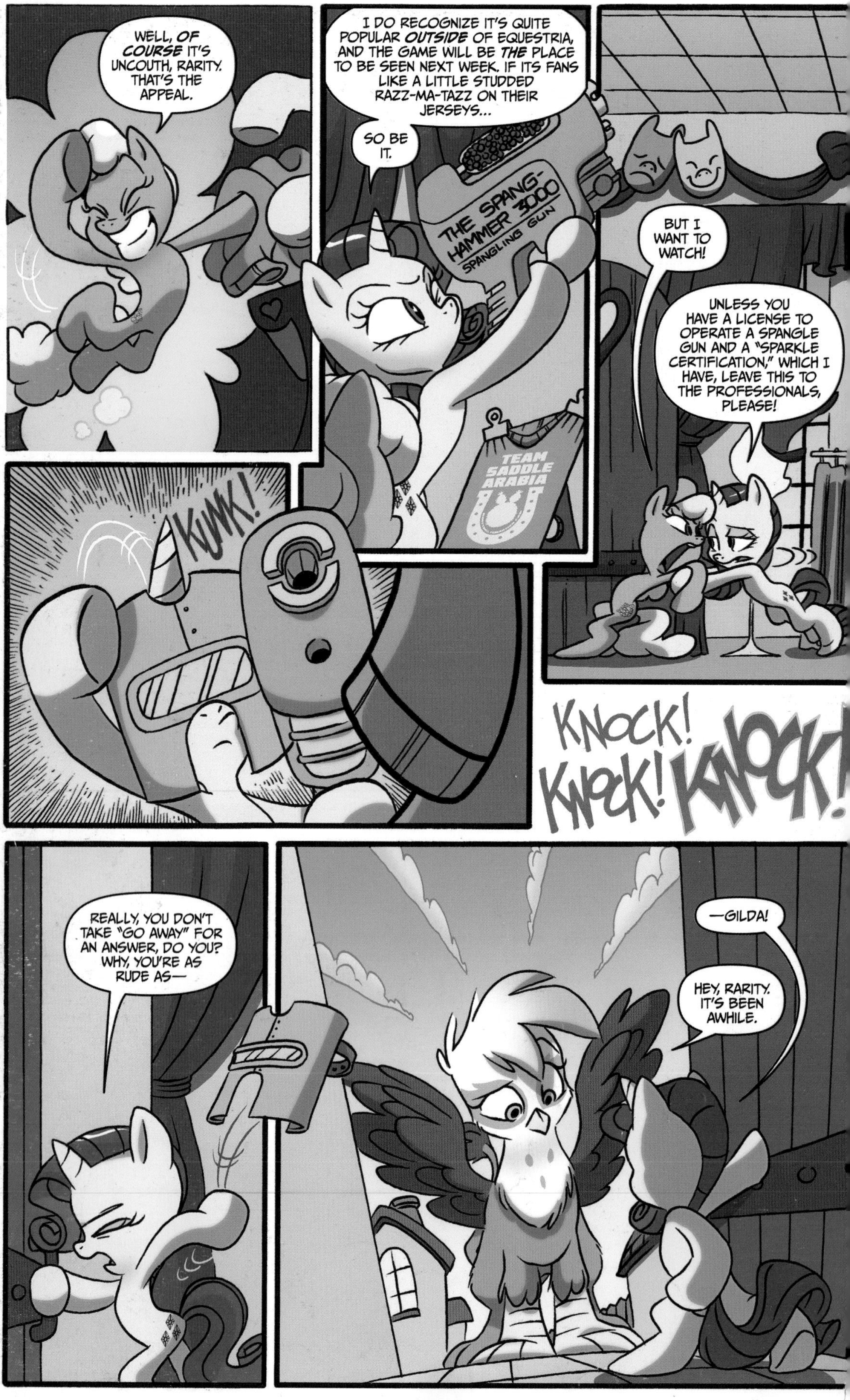
WELL, OF COURSE IT'S UNCOUTH, RARITY. THAT'S THE APPEAL.
I DO RECOGNIZE IT'S QUITE POPULAR OUTSIDE OF EQUESTRIA, AND THE GAME WILL BE THE PLACE TO BE SEEN NEXT WEEK. IF ITS FANS LIKE A LITTLE STUDDED RAZZ-MA-TAZZ ON THEIR JERSEYS...
SO BE IT.
THE SPANG-HAMMER 3000
SPANGLING GUN
TEAM SADDLE ARABIA
BUT I WANT TO WATCH!
UNLESS YOU HAVE A LICENSE TO OPERATE A SPANGLE GUN AND A "SPARKLE CERTIFICATION," WHICH I HAVE, LEAVE THIS TO THE PROFESSIONALS, PLEASE!
KUNK!
KNOCK! KNOCK! KNOCK!
REALLY, YOU DON'T TAKE "GO AWAY" FOR AN ANSWER, DO YOU? WHY, YOU'RE AS RUDE AS—
—GILDA!
HEY, RARITY. IT'S BEEN AWHILE.

SURPRISED TO SEE ME?

WELL... I DID HEAR THAT RAINBOW DASH AND PINKIE PIE RECONNECTED WITH YOU RECENTLY.

PERHAPS I AM A *LITTLE* SURPRISED TO SEE YOU IN A DRESS SHOP...

DON'T WORRY, I'M NOT HERE FOR ONE OF YOUR FRILLY LITTLE FROU-FROU DRESSY-POOS.

IS THIS... ECH... LACE?

I'M SURE YOU DIDN'T COME ALL THE WAY FROM GRIFFONSTONE TO CRITIQUE MY CHOICE OF TRIMMING.

MAYBE YOU FLEW BY TO WIN ME OVER WITH YOUR CHARMING NEW PERSONALITY?

ER, NO... ACTUALLY, I CAME TO ASK FOR SOMETHING.

I MEAN, TO ASK IF YOU'D LIKE TO *DO* SOMETHING... IF YOU'RE INTERESTED.

IT'S OK IF YOU'RE NOT. WHATEVER.

WELL! I CAN'T IMAGINE WHAT A GRIFFON MIGHT NEED FROM ME.

THE GRIFFIN KINGDOM IS NOT EXACTLY NOTED FOR THEIR DEVOTION TO FASHION...

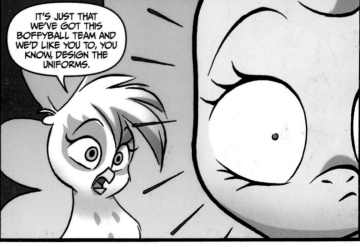

IT'S JUST THAT WE'VE GOT THIS BOFFYBALL TEAM AND WE'D LIKE YOU TO, YOU KNOW, DESIGN THE UNIFORMS.

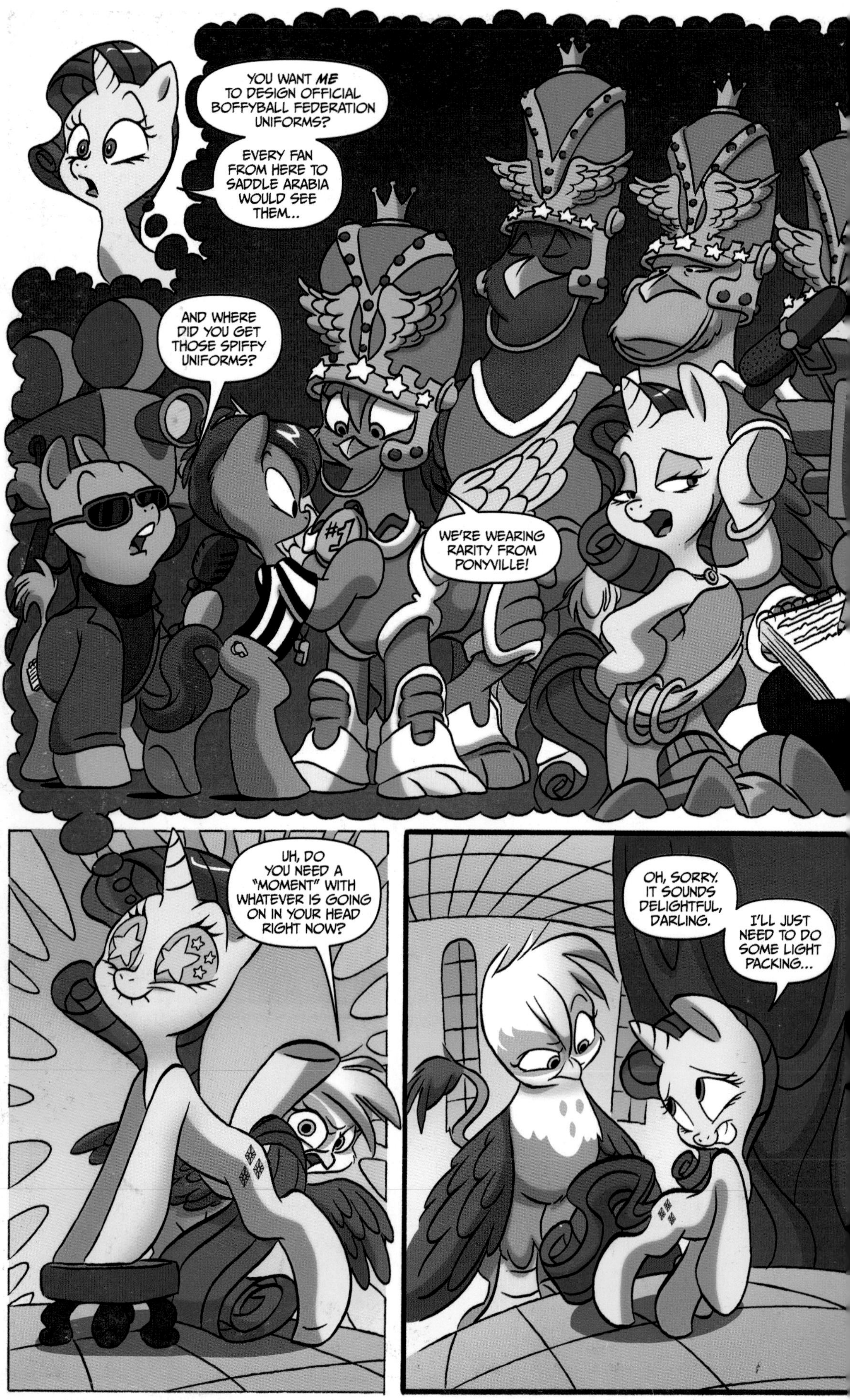

YOU WANT *ME* TO DESIGN OFFICIAL BOFFYBALL FEDERATION UNIFORMS?
EVERY FAN FROM HERE TO SADDLE ARABIA WOULD SEE THEM...
AND WHERE DID YOU GET THOSE SPIFFY UNIFORMS?
WE'RE WEARING RARITY FROM PONYVILLE!
UH, DO YOU NEED A "MOMENT" WITH WHATEVER IS GOING ON IN YOUR HEAD RIGHT NOW?
OH, SORRY. IT SOUNDS DELIGHTFUL, DARLING.
I'LL JUST NEED TO DO SOME LIGHT PACKING...

"BUT I'LL BE IN GRIFFONSTONE BY NOON TOMORROW."

GRIFFONSTONE TRAIN-STATION

YOU'RE KIND OF LATE?

NOT JUST LATE, DARLING. *FASHIONABLY* LATE. IT'S AN ART FORM.

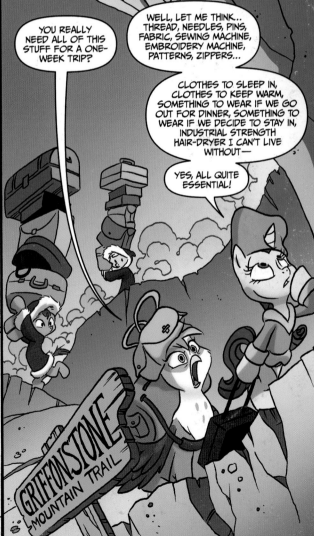

YOU REALLY NEED ALL OF THIS STUFF FOR A ONE-WEEK TRIP?

WELL, LET ME THINK... THREAD, NEEDLES, PINS, FABRIC, SEWING MACHINE, EMBROIDERY MACHINE, PATTERNS, ZIPPERS...

CLOTHES TO SLEEP IN, CLOTHES TO KEEP WARM, SOMETHING TO WEAR IF WE GO OUT FOR DINNER, SOMETHING TO WEAR IF WE DECIDE TO STAY IN, INDUSTRIAL STRENGTH HAIR-DRYER I CAN'T LIVE WITHOUT—

YES, ALL QUITE ESSENTIAL!

GRIFFONSTONE MOUNTAIN TRAIL

THE CONDUCTORS TOOK A LITTLE LONGER THAN EXPECTED TO LOAD ALL OF MY THINGS.

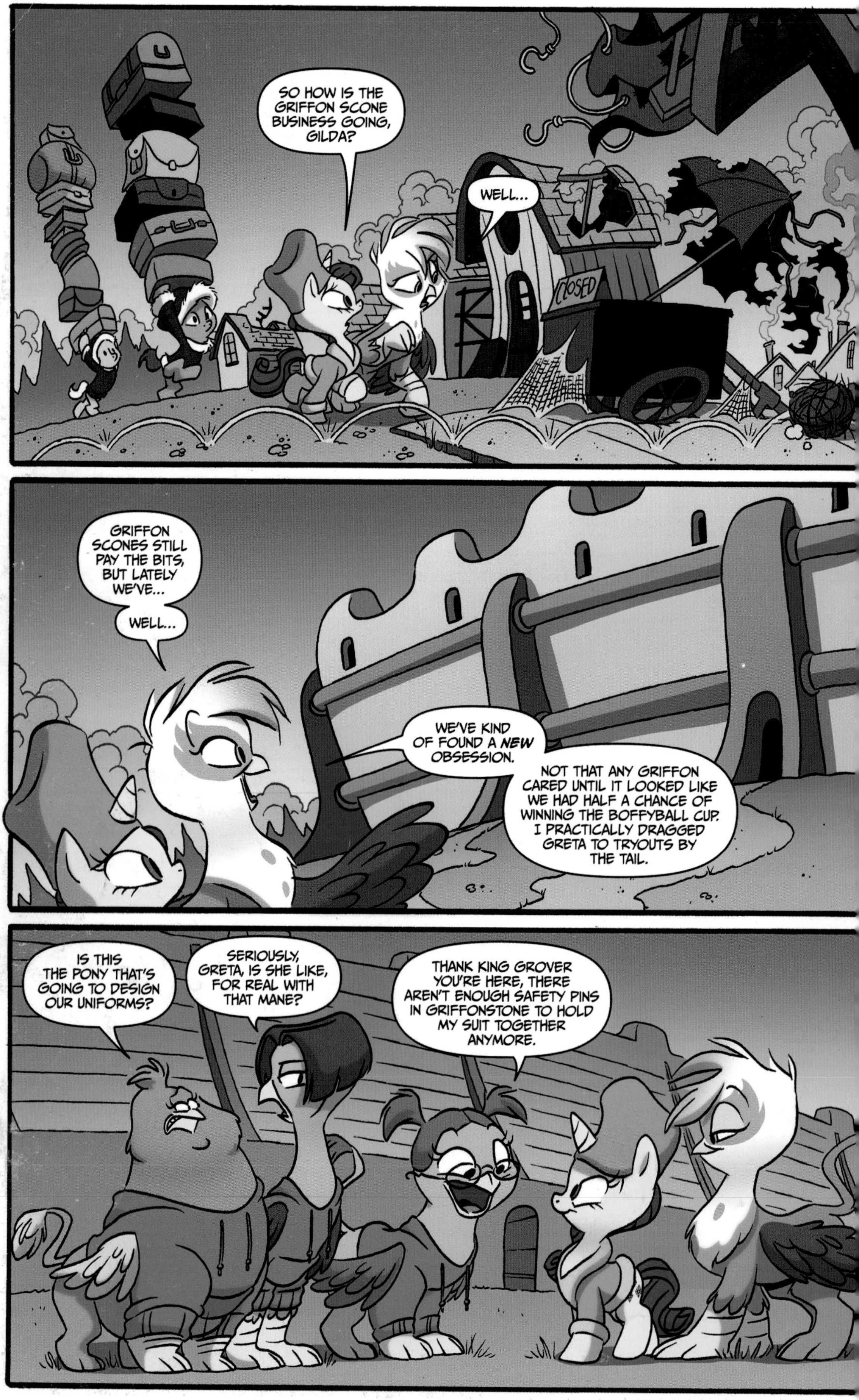
SO HOW IS THE GRIFFON SCONE BUSINESS GOING, GILDA?
WELL...
CLOSED
GRIFFON SCONES STILL PAY THE BITS, BUT LATELY WE'VE...
WELL...
WE'VE KIND OF FOUND A *NEW* OBSESSION.
NOT THAT ANY GRIFFON CARED UNTIL IT LOOKED LIKE WE HAD HALF A CHANCE OF WINNING THE BOFFYBALL CUP. I PRACTICALLY DRAGGED GRETA TO TRYOUTS BY THE TAIL.
IS THIS THE PONY THAT'S GOING TO DESIGN OUR UNIFORMS?
SERIOUSLY, GRETA, IS SHE LIKE, FOR REAL WITH THAT MANE?
THANK KING GROVER YOU'RE HERE, THERE AREN'T ENOUGH SAFETY PINS IN GRIFFONSTONE TO HOLD MY SUIT TOGETHER ANYMORE.

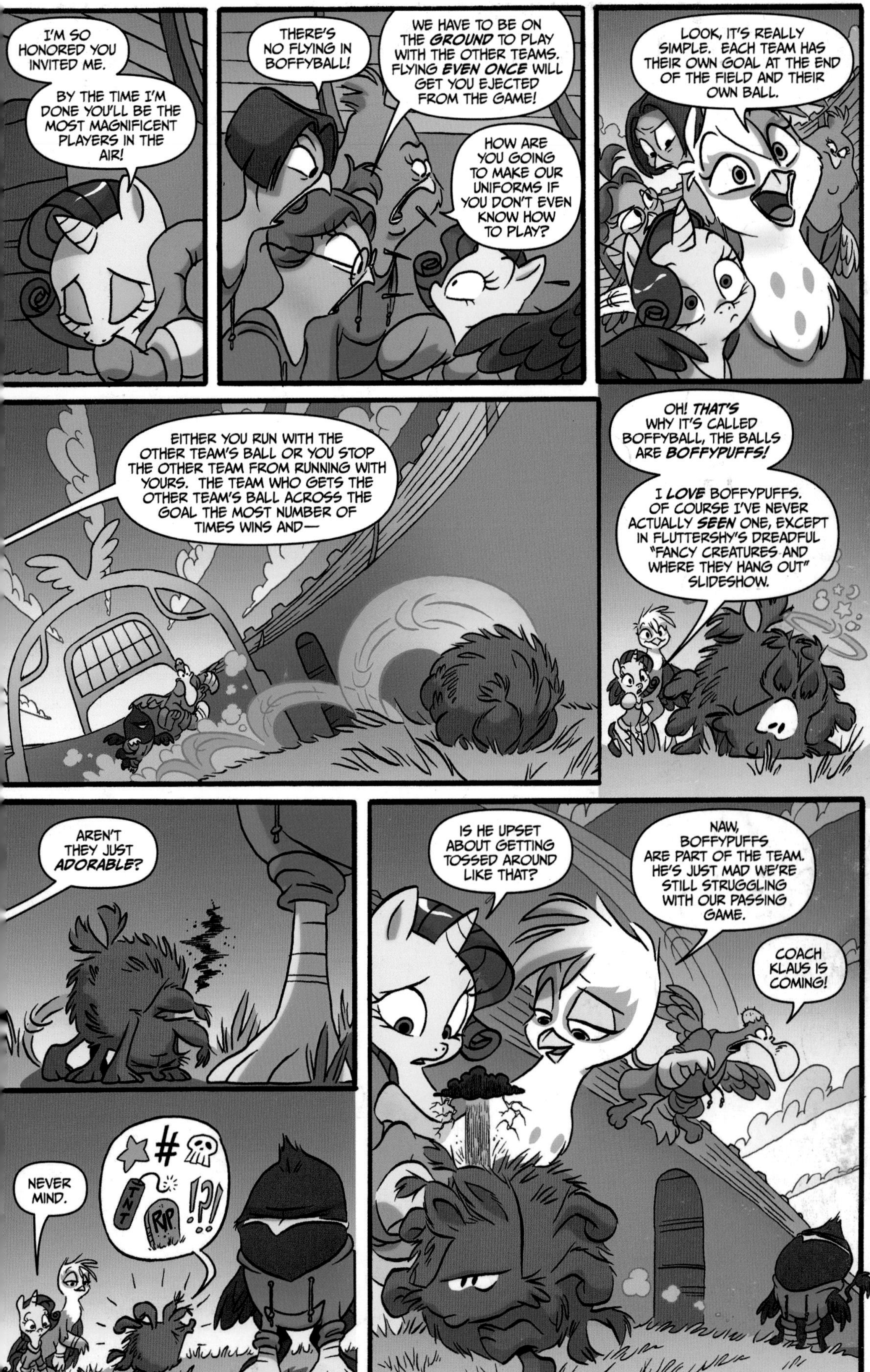
I'M SO HONORED YOU INVITED ME.
BY THE TIME I'M DONE YOU'LL BE THE MOST MAGNIFICENT PLAYERS IN THE AIR!
THERE'S NO FLYING IN BOFFYBALL!
WE HAVE TO BE ON THE GROUND TO PLAY WITH THE OTHER TEAMS. FLYING EVEN ONCE WILL GET YOU EJECTED FROM THE GAME!
HOW ARE YOU GOING TO MAKE OUR UNIFORMS IF YOU DON'T EVEN KNOW HOW TO PLAY?
LOOK, IT'S REALLY SIMPLE. EACH TEAM HAS THEIR OWN GOAL AT THE END OF THE FIELD AND THEIR OWN BALL.
EITHER YOU RUN WITH THE OTHER TEAM'S BALL OR YOU STOP THE OTHER TEAM FROM RUNNING WITH YOURS. THE TEAM WHO GETS THE OTHER TEAM'S BALL ACROSS THE GOAL THE MOST NUMBER OF TIMES WINS AND—
OH! THAT'S WHY IT'S CALLED BOFFYBALL, THE BALLS ARE BOFFYPUFFS!
I LOVE BOFFYPUFFS. OF COURSE I'VE NEVER ACTUALLY SEEN ONE, EXCEPT IN FLUTTERSHY'S DREADFUL "FANCY CREATURES AND WHERE THEY HANG OUT" SLIDESHOW.
AREN'T THEY JUST ADORABLE?
NEVER MIND.
!?!
RIP
TNT
IS HE UPSET ABOUT GETTING TOSSED AROUND LIKE THAT?
NAW, BOFFYPUFFS ARE PART OF THE TEAM. HE'S JUST MAD WE'RE STILL STRUGGLING WITH OUR PASSING GAME.
COACH KLAUS IS COMING!

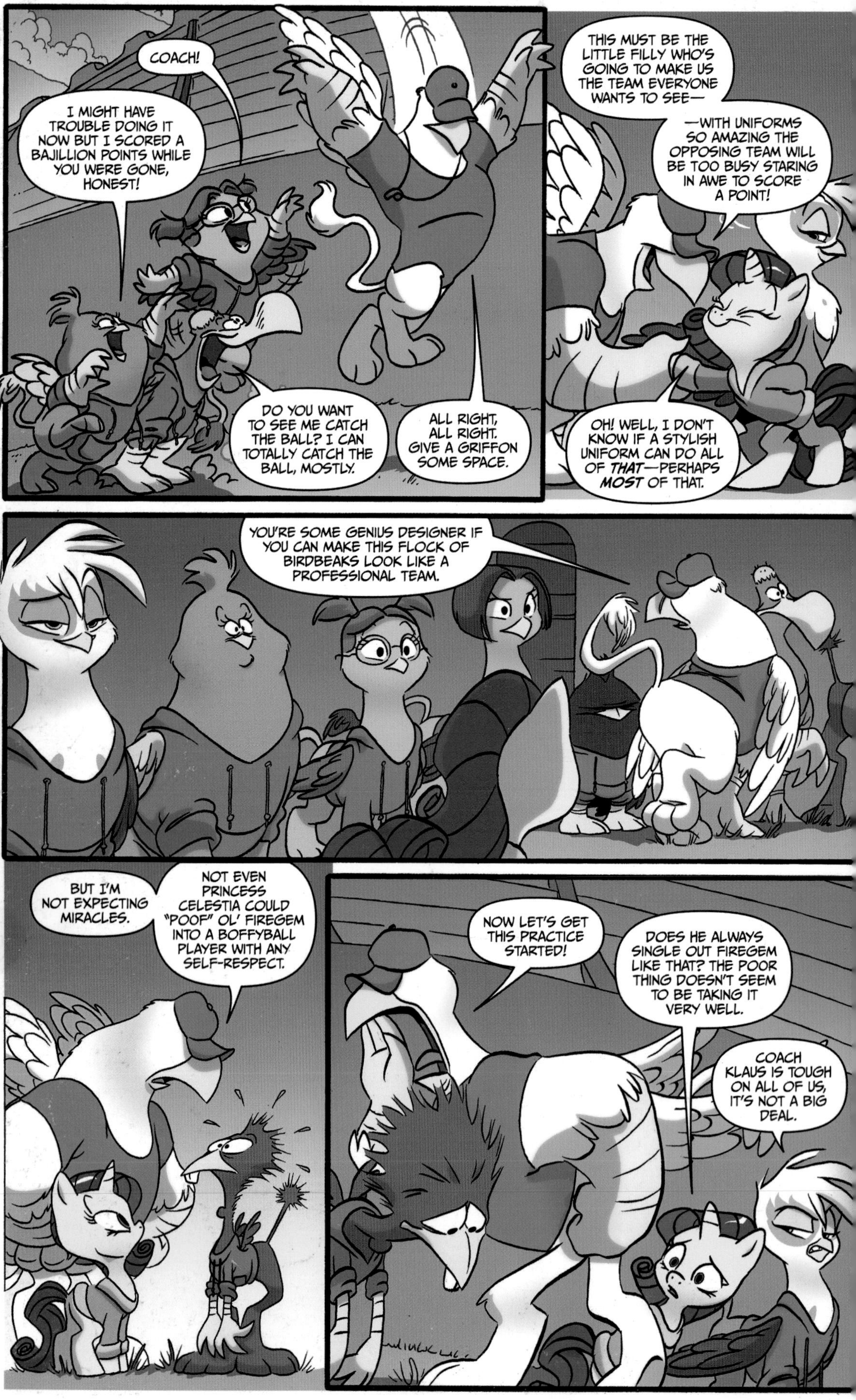
COACH!
I MIGHT HAVE TROUBLE DOING IT NOW BUT I SCORED A BAJILLION POINTS WHILE YOU WERE GONE, HONEST!
DO YOU WANT TO SEE ME CATCH THE BALL? I CAN TOTALLY CATCH THE BALL, MOSTLY.
ALL RIGHT, ALL RIGHT. GIVE A GRIFFON SOME SPACE.
THIS MUST BE THE LITTLE FILLY WHO'S GOING TO MAKE US THE TEAM EVERYONE WANTS TO SEE—
—WITH UNIFORMS SO AMAZING THE OPPOSING TEAM WILL BE TOO BUSY STARING IN AWE TO SCORE A POINT!
OH! WELL, I DON'T KNOW IF A STYLISH UNIFORM CAN DO ALL OF *THAT*—PERHAPS ***MOST*** OF THAT.
YOU'RE SOME GENIUS DESIGNER IF YOU CAN MAKE THIS FLOCK OF BIRDBEAKS LOOK LIKE A PROFESSIONAL TEAM.
BUT I'M NOT EXPECTING MIRACLES.
NOT EVEN PRINCESS CELESTIA COULD "POOF" OL' FIREGEM INTO A BOFFYBALL PLAYER WITH ANY SELF-RESPECT.
NOW LET'S GET THIS PRACTICE STARTED!
DOES HE ALWAYS SINGLE OUT FIREGEM LIKE THAT? THE POOR THING DOESN'T SEEM TO BE TAKING IT VERY WELL.
COACH KLAUS IS TOUGH ON ALL OF US, IT'S NOT A BIG DEAL.

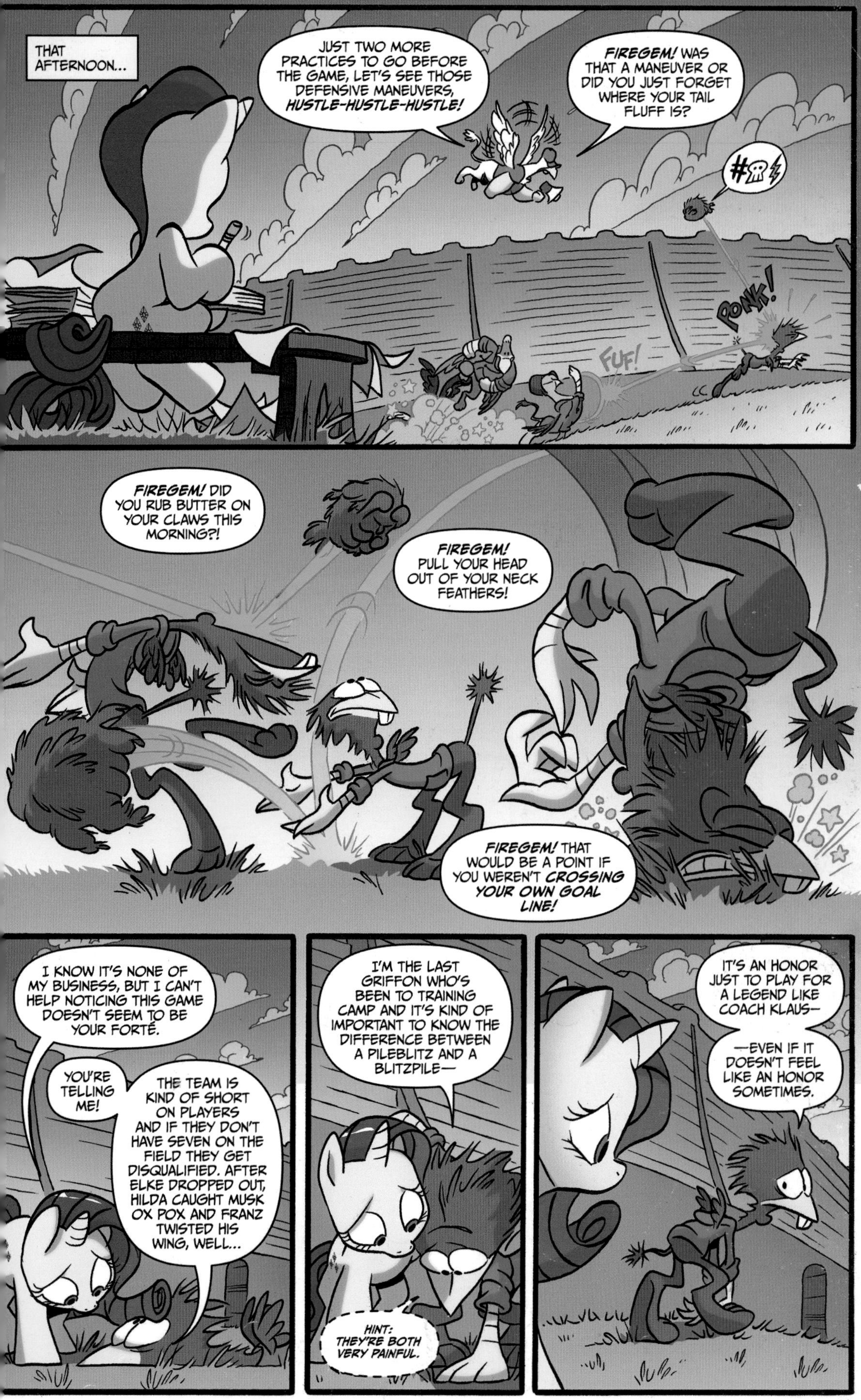
THAT AFTERNOON...
JUST TWO MORE PRACTICES TO GO BEFORE THE GAME, LET'S SEE THOSE DEFENSIVE MANEUVERS, HUSTLE-HUSTLE-HUSTLE!
FIREGEM! WAS THAT A MANEUVER OR DID YOU JUST FORGET WHERE YOUR TAIL FLUFF IS?
PONK!
FUF!
FIREGEM! DID YOU RUB BUTTER ON YOUR CLAWS THIS MORNING?!
FIREGEM! PULL YOUR HEAD OUT OF YOUR NECK FEATHERS!
FIREGEM! THAT WOULD BE A POINT IF YOU WEREN'T CROSSING YOUR OWN GOAL LINE!
I KNOW IT'S NONE OF MY BUSINESS, BUT I CAN'T HELP NOTICING THIS GAME DOESN'T SEEM TO BE YOUR FORTÉ.
YOU'RE TELLING ME!
THE TEAM IS KIND OF SHORT ON PLAYERS AND IF THEY DON'T HAVE SEVEN ON THE FIELD THEY GET DISQUALIFIED. AFTER ELKE DROPPED OUT, HILDA CAUGHT MUSK OX POX AND FRANZ TWISTED HIS WING, WELL...
I'M THE LAST GRIFFON WHO'S BEEN TO TRAINING CAMP AND IT'S KIND OF IMPORTANT TO KNOW THE DIFFERENCE BETWEEN A PILEBLITZ AND A BLITZPILE—
HINT: THEY'RE BOTH VERY PAINFUL.
IT'S AN HONOR JUST TO PLAY FOR A LEGEND LIKE COACH KLAUS—
—EVEN IF IT DOESN'T FEEL LIKE AN HONOR SOMETIMES.

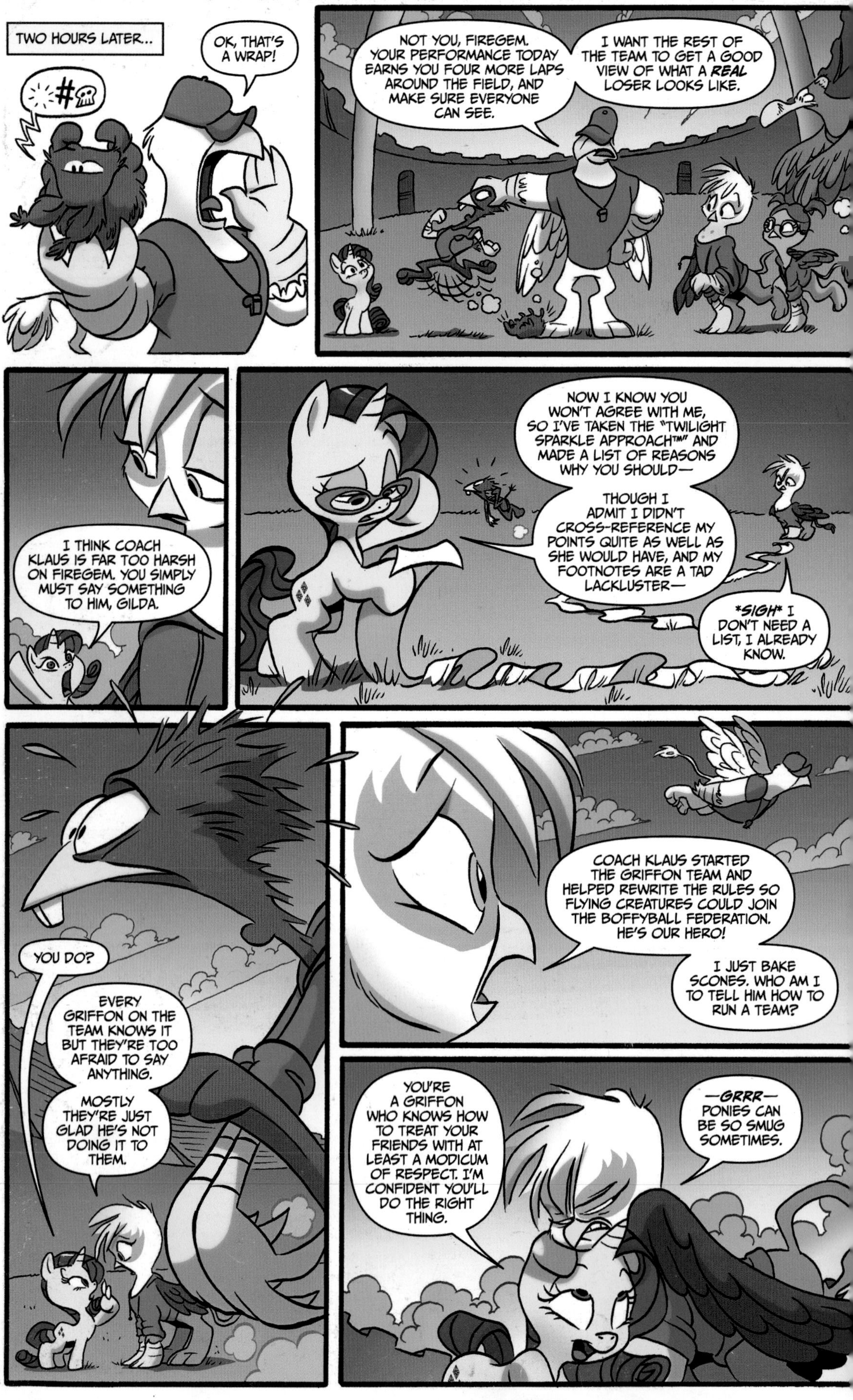
TWO HOURS LATER...
OK, THAT'S A WRAP!
#
NOT YOU, FIREGEM. YOUR PERFORMANCE TODAY EARNS YOU FOUR MORE LAPS AROUND THE FIELD, AND MAKE SURE EVERYONE CAN SEE.
I WANT THE REST OF THE TEAM TO GET A GOOD VIEW OF WHAT A REAL LOSER LOOKS LIKE.
I THINK COACH KLAUS IS FAR TOO HARSH ON FIREGEM. YOU SIMPLY MUST SAY SOMETHING TO HIM, GILDA.
NOW I KNOW YOU WON'T AGREE WITH ME, SO I'VE TAKEN THE "TWILIGHT SPARKLE APPROACH™" AND MADE A LIST OF REASONS WHY YOU SHOULD—
THOUGH I ADMIT I DIDN'T CROSS-REFERENCE MY POINTS QUITE AS WELL AS SHE WOULD HAVE, AND MY FOOTNOTES ARE A TAD LACKLUSTER—
SIGH I DON'T NEED A LIST, I ALREADY KNOW.
YOU DO?
EVERY GRIFFON ON THE TEAM KNOWS IT BUT THEY'RE TOO AFRAID TO SAY ANYTHING.
MOSTLY THEY'RE JUST GLAD HE'S NOT DOING IT TO THEM.
COACH KLAUS STARTED THE GRIFFON TEAM AND HELPED REWRITE THE RULES SO FLYING CREATURES COULD JOIN THE BOFFYBALL FEDERATION. HE'S OUR HERO!
I JUST BAKE SCONES. WHO AM I TO TELL HIM HOW TO RUN A TEAM?
YOU'RE A GRIFFON WHO KNOWS HOW TO TREAT YOUR FRIENDS WITH AT LEAST A MODICUM OF RESPECT. I'M CONFIDENT YOU'LL DO THE RIGHT THING.
—GRRR— PONIES CAN BE SO SMUG SOMETIMES.

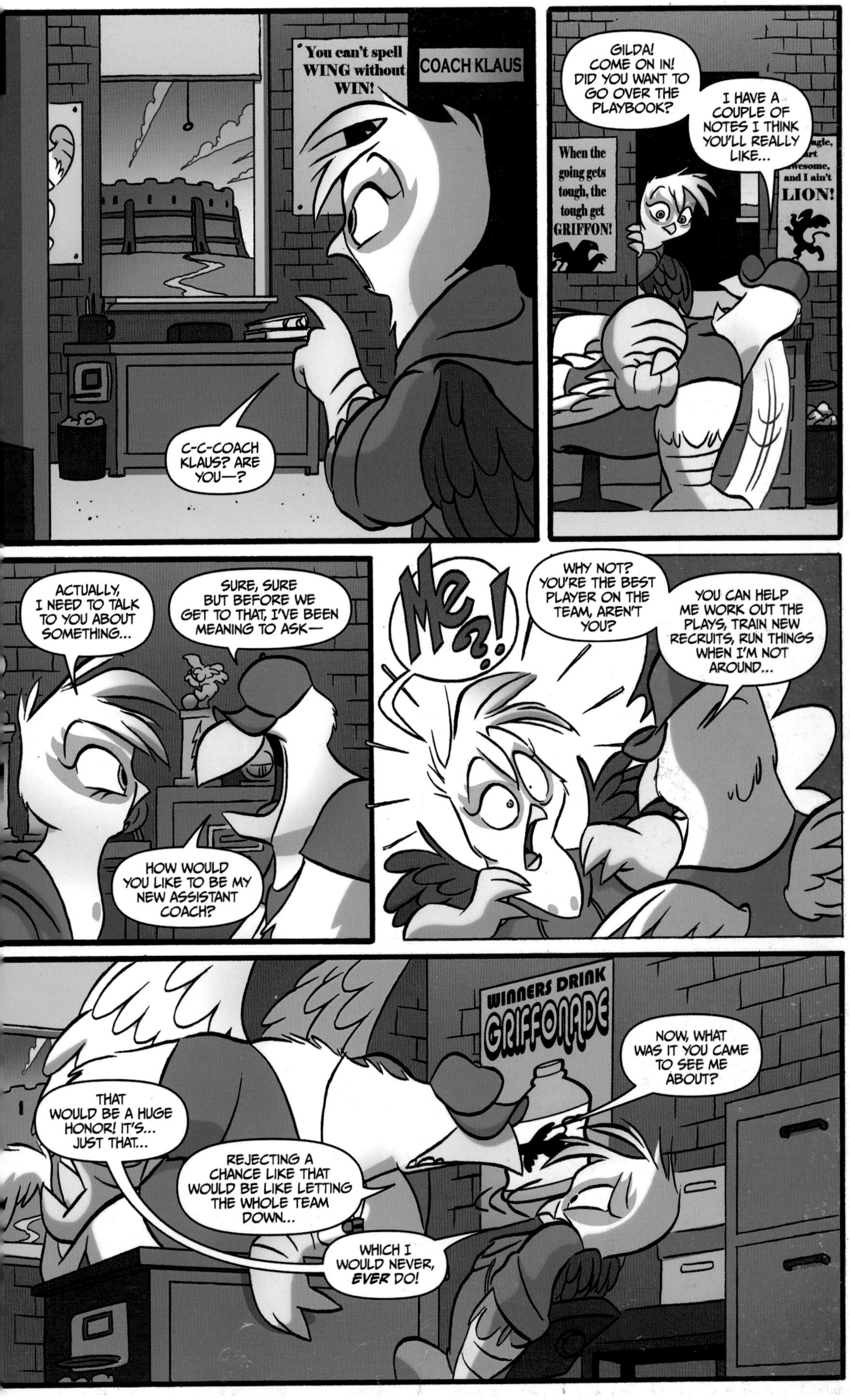

You can't spell WING without WIN!
COACH KLAUS
C-C-COACH KLAUS? ARE YOU—?
GILDA! COME ON IN! DID YOU WANT TO GO OVER THE PLAYBOOK?
I HAVE A COUPLE OF NOTES I THINK YOU'LL REALLY LIKE...
When the going gets tough, the tough get GRIFFON!
LION!
ACTUALLY, I NEED TO TALK TO YOU ABOUT SOMETHING...
SURE, SURE BUT BEFORE WE GET TO THAT, I'VE BEEN MEANING TO ASK—
HOW WOULD YOU LIKE TO BE MY NEW ASSISTANT COACH?
Me?!
WHY NOT? YOU'RE THE BEST PLAYER ON THE TEAM, AREN'T YOU?
YOU CAN HELP ME WORK OUT THE PLAYS, TRAIN NEW RECRUITS, RUN THINGS WHEN I'M NOT AROUND...
WINNERS DRINK GRIFFONADE
THAT WOULD BE A HUGE HONOR! IT'S... JUST THAT...
REJECTING A CHANCE LIKE THAT WOULD BE LIKE LETTING THE WHOLE TEAM DOWN...
WHICH I WOULD NEVER, *EVER* DO!
NOW, WHAT WAS IT YOU CAME TO SEE ME ABOUT?

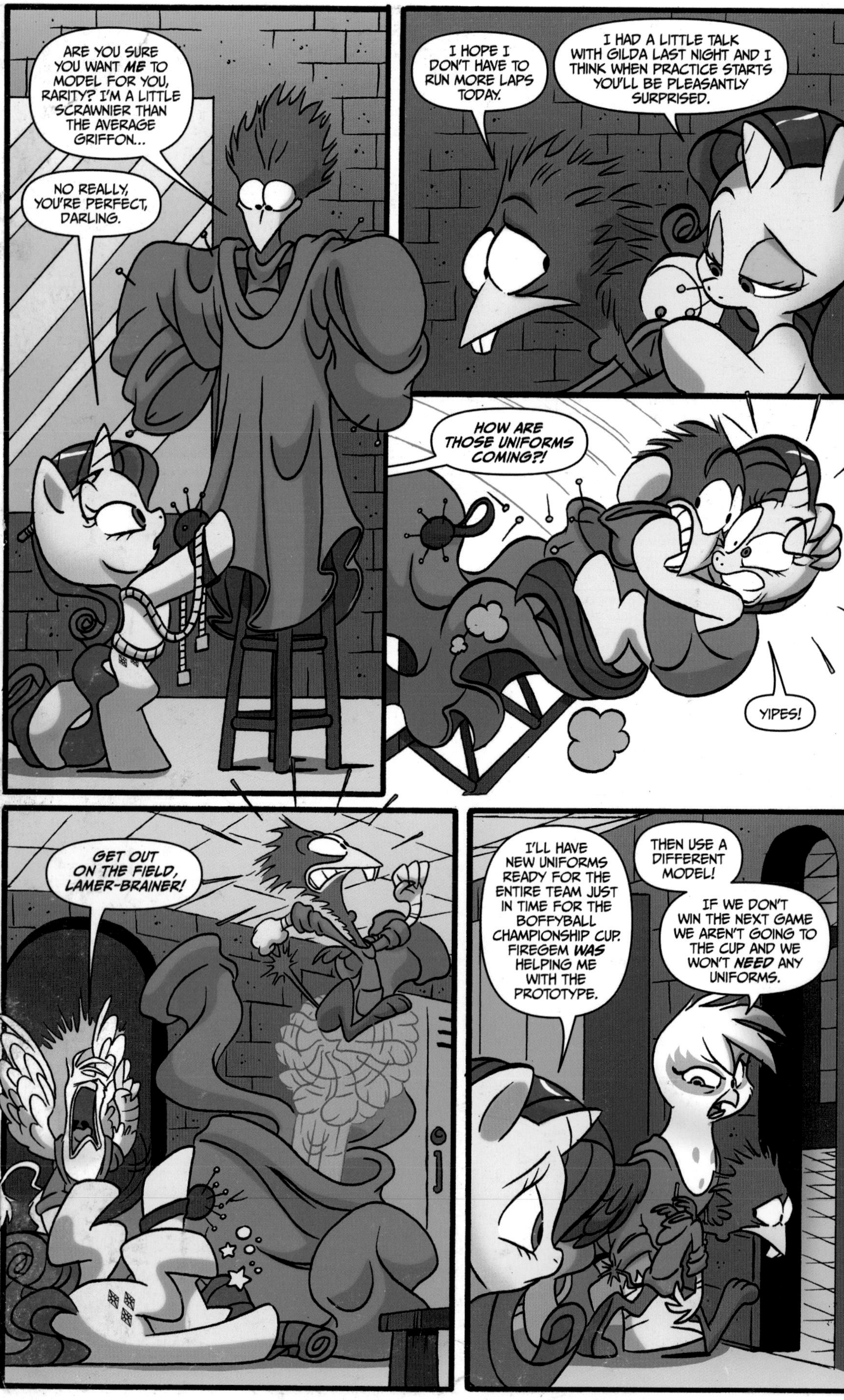
ARE YOU SURE YOU WANT *ME* TO MODEL FOR YOU, RARITY? I'M A LITTLE SCRAWNIER THAN THE AVERAGE GRIFFON...
NO REALLY, YOU'RE PERFECT, DARLING.
I HOPE I DON'T HAVE TO RUN MORE LAPS TODAY.
I HAD A LITTLE TALK WITH GILDA LAST NIGHT AND I THINK WHEN PRACTICE STARTS YOU'LL BE PLEASANTLY SURPRISED.
HOW ARE THOSE UNIFORMS COMING?!
YIPES!
GET OUT ON THE FIELD, LAMER-BRAINER!
I'LL HAVE NEW UNIFORMS READY FOR THE ENTIRE TEAM JUST IN TIME FOR THE BOFFYBALL CHAMPIONSHIP CUP. FIREGEM *WAS* HELPING ME WITH THE PROTOTYPE.
THEN USE A DIFFERENT MODEL!
IF WE DON'T WIN THE NEXT GAME WE AREN'T GOING TO THE CUP AND WE WON'T *NEED* ANY UNIFORMS.

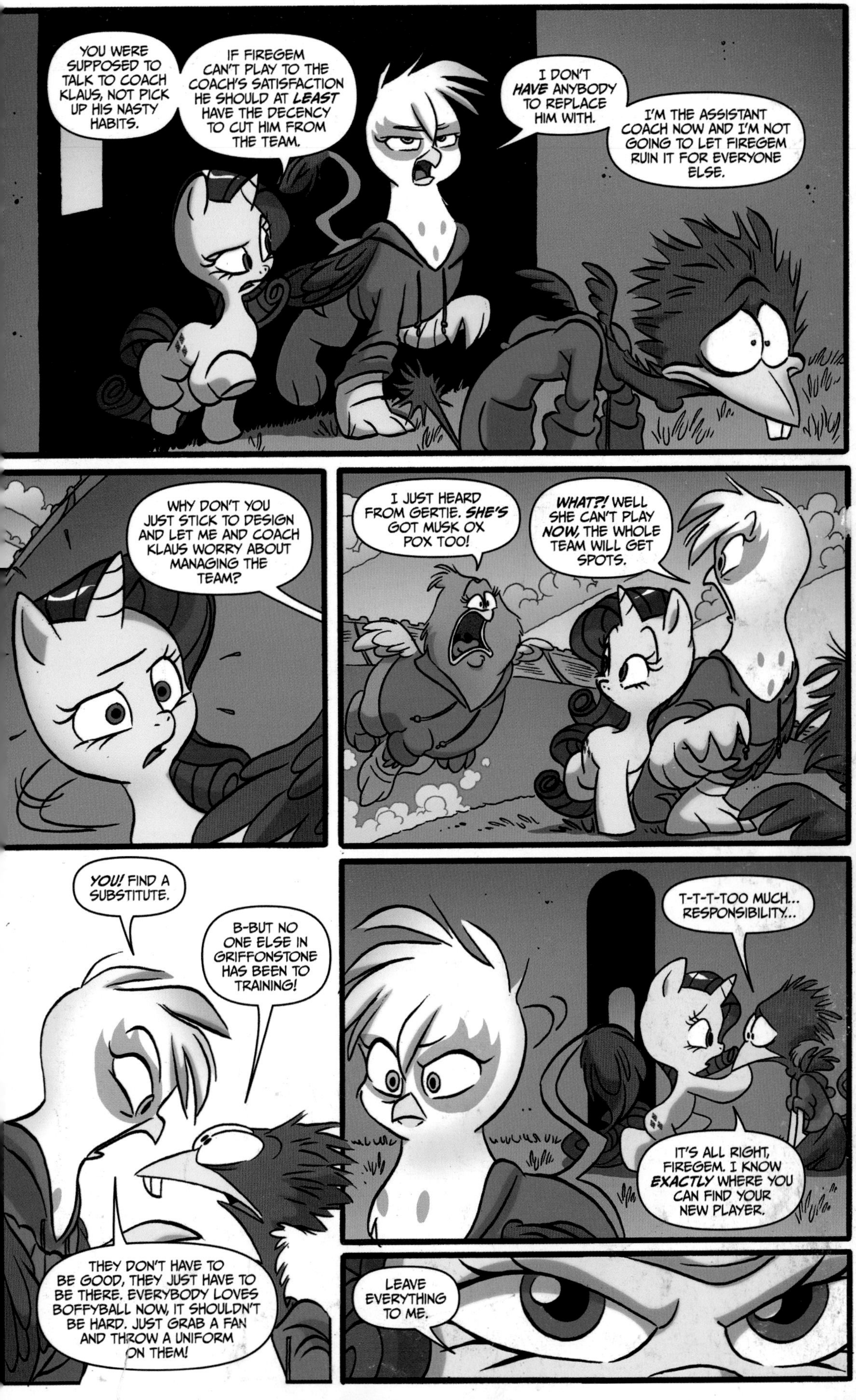
YOU WERE SUPPOSED TO TALK TO COACH KLAUS, NOT PICK UP HIS NASTY HABITS.
IF FIREGEM CAN'T PLAY TO THE COACH'S SATISFACTION HE SHOULD AT LEAST HAVE THE DECENCY TO CUT HIM FROM THE TEAM.
I DON'T HAVE ANYBODY TO REPLACE HIM WITH.
I'M THE ASSISTANT COACH NOW AND I'M NOT GOING TO LET FIREGEM RUIN IT FOR EVERYONE ELSE.
WHY DON'T YOU JUST STICK TO DESIGN AND LET ME AND COACH KLAUS WORRY ABOUT MANAGING THE TEAM?
I JUST HEARD FROM GERTIE. SHE'S GOT MUSK OX POX TOO!
WHAT?! WELL SHE CAN'T PLAY NOW, THE WHOLE TEAM WILL GET SPOTS.
YOU! FIND A SUBSTITUTE.
B-BUT NO ONE ELSE IN GRIFFONSTONE HAS BEEN TO TRAINING!
THEY DON'T HAVE TO BE GOOD, THEY JUST HAVE TO BE THERE. EVERYBODY LOVES BOFFYBALL NOW, IT SHOULDN'T BE HARD. JUST GRAB A FAN AND THROW A UNIFORM ON THEM!
T-T-T-TOO MUCH... RESPONSIBILITY...
IT'S ALL RIGHT, FIREGEM. I KNOW EXACTLY WHERE YOU CAN FIND YOUR NEW PLAYER.
LEAVE EVERYTHING TO ME.

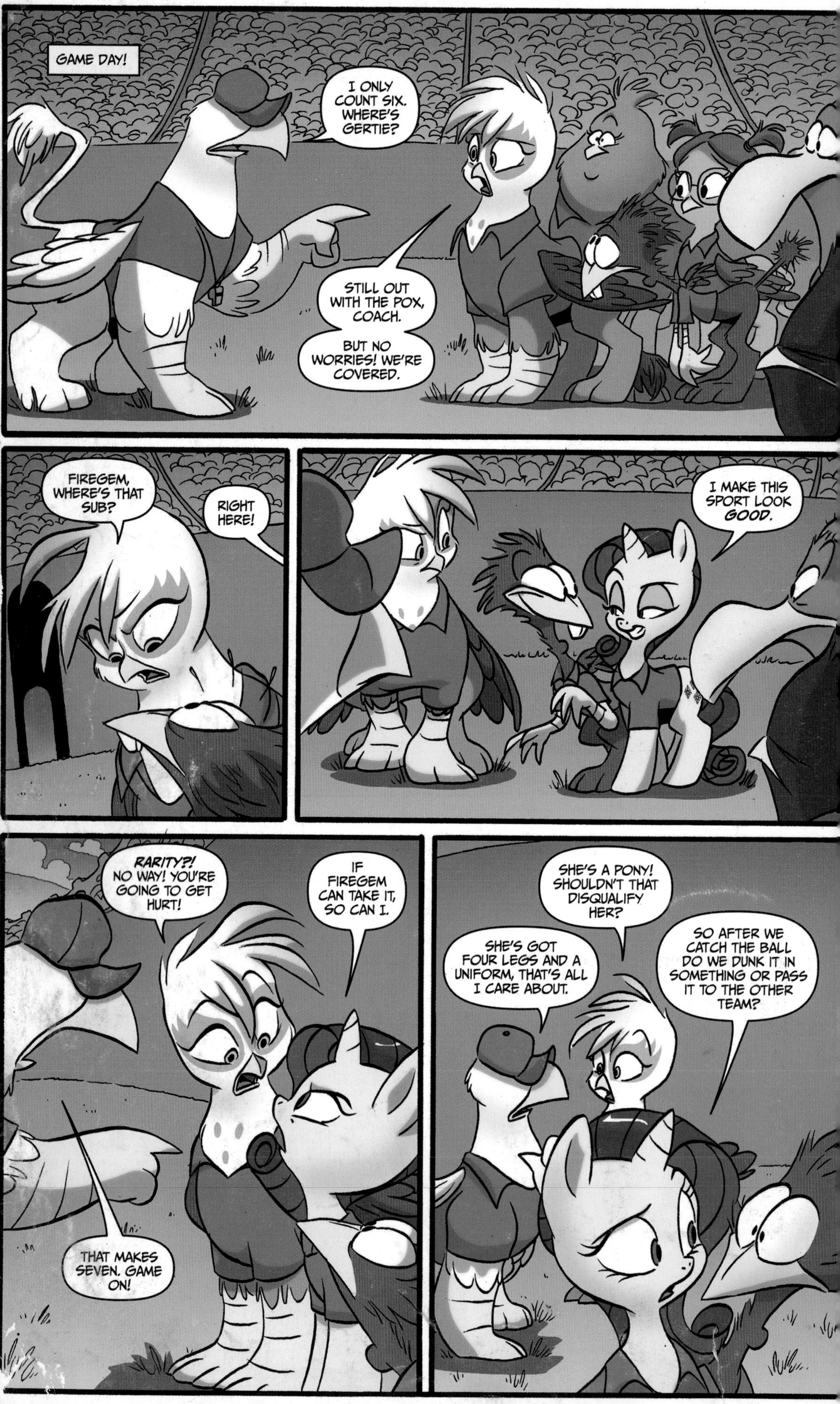
GAME DAY!
I ONLY COUNT SIX. WHERE'S GERTIE?
STILL OUT WITH THE POX, COACH.
BUT NO WORRIES! WE'RE COVERED.
FIREGEM, WHERE'S THAT SUB?
RIGHT HERE!
I MAKE THIS SPORT LOOK *GOOD*.
RARITY?! NO WAY! YOU'RE GOING TO GET HURT!
IF FIREGEM CAN TAKE IT, SO CAN I.
THAT MAKES SEVEN. GAME ON!
SHE'S A PONY! SHOULDN'T THAT DISQUALIFY HER?
SHE'S GOT FOUR LEGS AND A UNIFORM, THAT'S ALL I CARE ABOUT.
SO AFTER WE CATCH THE BALL DO WE DUNK IT IN SOMETHING OR PASS IT TO THE OTHER TEAM?

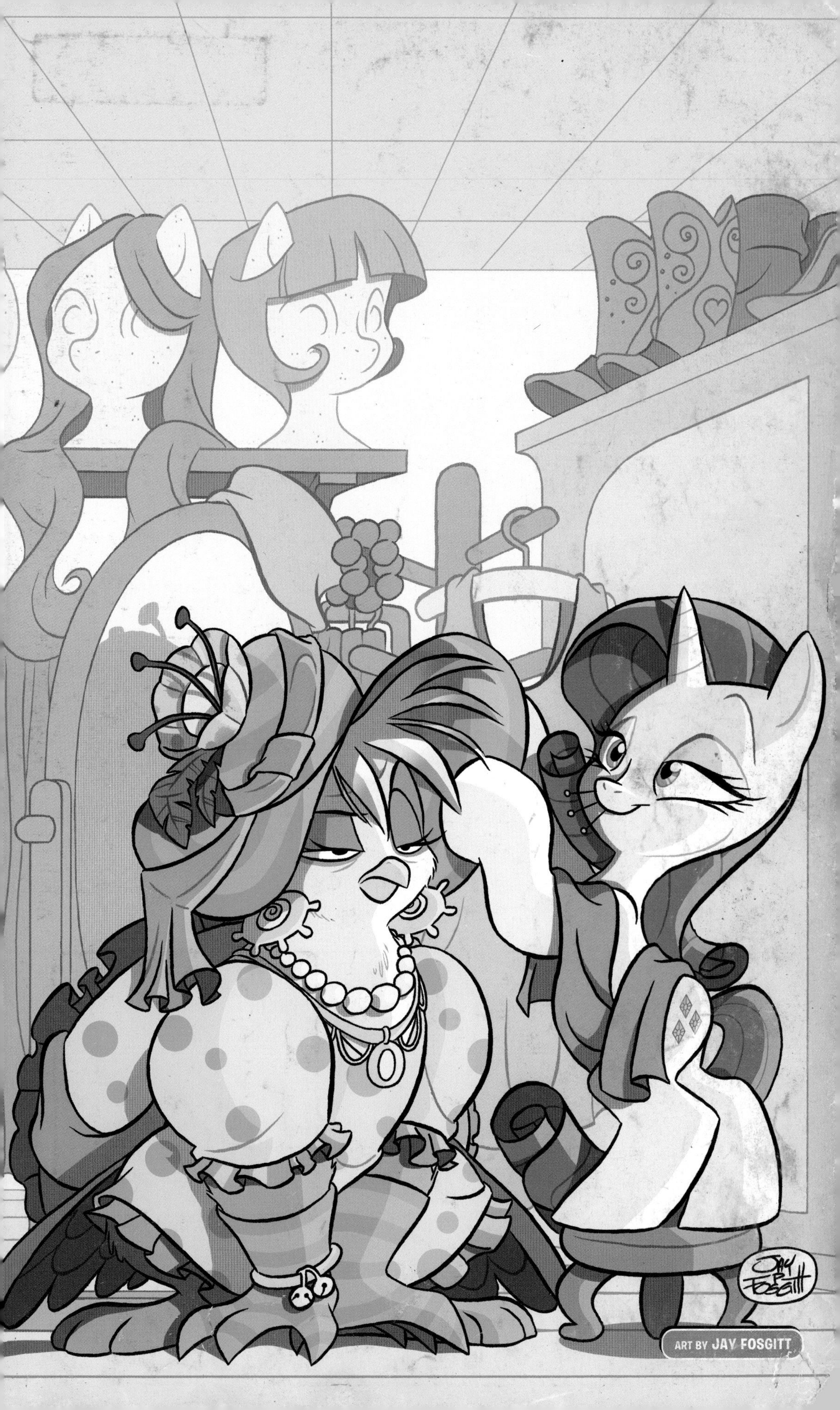
ART BY JAY FOSGITT

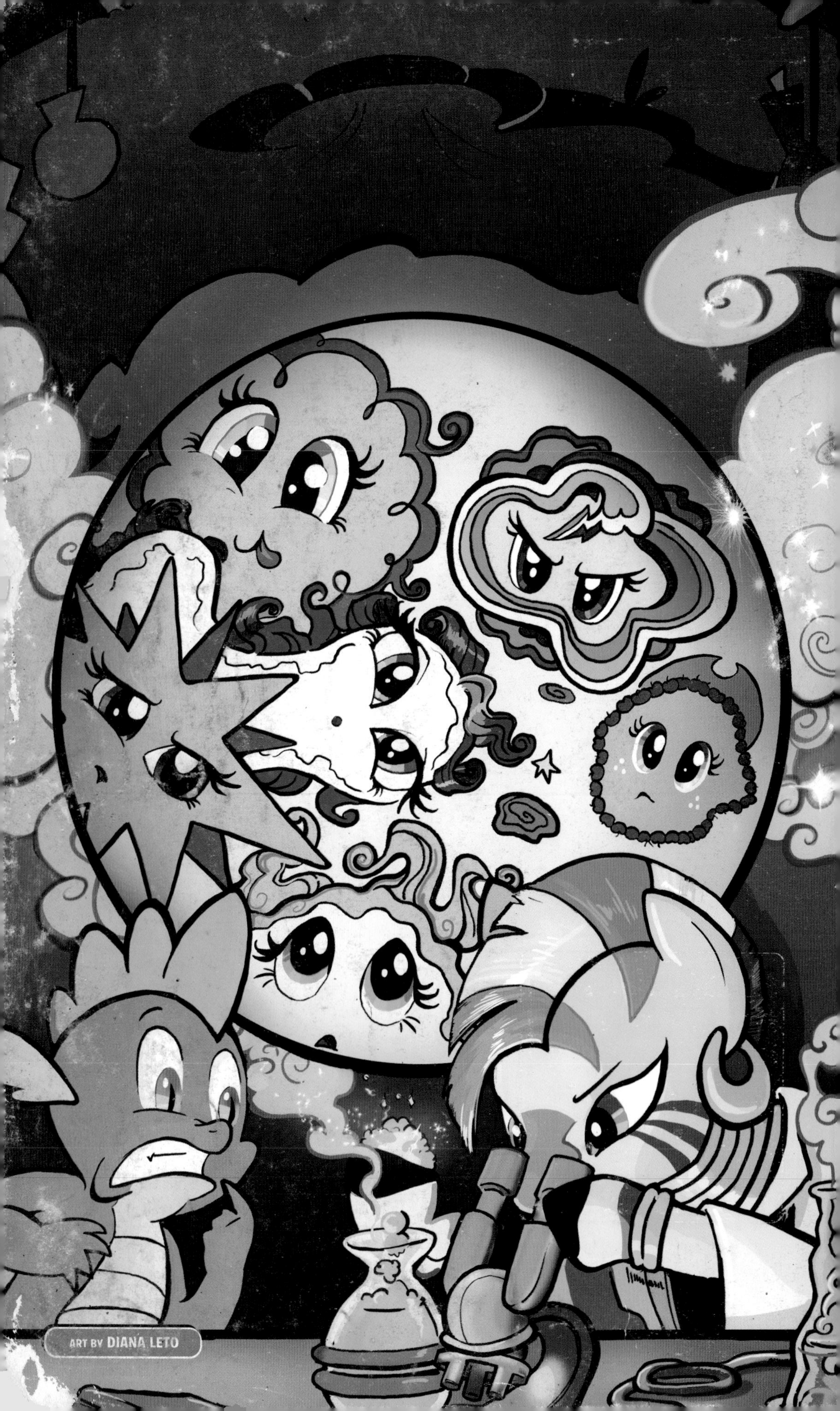
ART BY DIANA LETO